TARNISHED
HERO

James Mark Sullivan
and His Fight for Irish Freedom

To
Gary + Mary Sabin
Thanks for your support.
Now - another 600 copies and
I make a profit. Say— I can get
you a deal...
Hugs,
Dan

DR. DANIEL SCHULTZ

PAGE PUBLISHING, INC.
New York, NY

First originally published by Page Publishing, Inc. 2019

ISBN 978-1-64138-090-4 (Paperback)
ISBN 978-1-64138-091-1 (Digital)

Printed in the United States of America

P. 170   P. 231
P. 171
P. 177
P. 180
P. 228

CONTENTS

James Mark Sullivan
(1873 - 1935)
Lawyer, Diplomat, Irish Nationalist
Courtesy, Library of Congress*

ACKNOWLEDGMENTS

I owe a debt of gratitude to numerous individuals and institutions without whose assistance the completion of this manuscript would have been impossible. To Sharon Farrar, who accessed numerous materials through interlibrary loans and showed gracious patience with my overdue borrowings. I benefited from the assistance of Dr. MaryAnn Felter, professor of English at Cayuga Community College, who sparked my interest in Irish studies and with whom I coauthored several articles on James Mark Sullivan. I am extremely grateful to Mary Rose Callaghan, who so willingly shared documents and correspondence of her grandfather's family. A special thank you to Chris Warner, who patiently endured constant revisions of the manuscript. I am also grateful to former colleagues at Cayuga Community College for the Faculty Development Committee for funding presentations on Sullivan and other topics at numerous academic conferences. I am indebted to the archivists at the National Library of Ireland for giving me access to the Piaras Beasli papers. Other institutions that assisted me or kindly supplied me with documents and photocopies include Cornell University and the University of California–Berkeley. A special thank you to Oliver Juengel from the German embassy in Port-au-Prince, Haiti, and Gerhard Keiper, archivist of the German Foreign Ministry, for supplying me records of Sullivan's communications during his final months as ambassador to

Santo Domingo. Because the correspondence was in German, the efforts of Rahel Elmer-Reger in translating the documents were especially helpful.

I benefited also from the patience and support of my wife, Mildred, through the entire writing process.

Daniel F. Schultz
Auburn, New York
August 2015

ABSTRACT

The manuscript is the biography of a man whose life is known only in bits and pieces, often associated with scandal. The author placed him in his social/political context, looking at various aspects of his life to obtain a full understanding of the man, his work, his times. James Mark Sullivan lived during a significant period of United States history—its emergence as a world power, its growing ethnic diversity, its urban political machines, and its involvement in the Great War. Ireland too was undergoing change, its population restive under British control. All had an influence on him, but the focus of his life was to have his native Ireland become free of British rule. The topic is timely, given the centennial of the Easter Rebellion, the current observance of World War I and the formation of Sullivan's most important contribution to Irish freedom—the creation of the Film Company of Ireland. In an effort to portray the total man, the author employed previously unused or underutilized primary sources—e-mails from current family members, government documents, contemporary newspapers, letters, and government investigations of activities in which he was involved. The result sheds new light on a man little understood or appreciated for his efforts to achieve material success in his adopted country and to obtain independence for Ireland. He graduated from prestigious Yale University Law School yet associated with urban lowlifes, gamblers and murderers and Tammany politicians. Ironically, this leveraged him to prominence and a patronage appointment as ambassador to Santo Domingo. Pursued by scandal, he resigned and reinvented himself in his native land as a movie producer.

The manuscript sheds light in his role as propagandist for the Irish cause in the moving pictures produced by the Film Company of Ireland. And while he did live to see the independence of his native land, it was not without personal struggle, privation, and tragedy.

CHAPTER I

History's Mystery
The Early Life and Celtic
Connections of James M. Sullivan

The Social Context of
Postfamine Ireland

The Ireland that James Mark Sullivan emigrated from in the late nineteenth century was restive with discontent. The famine years devastated Ireland, especially the West. Killarney, County Kerry, in the extreme southwest of Ireland, is the ancestral home of James M. Sullivan.[1]

Kerry was particularly hard-hit during the famine years. In the Dingle Peninsula alone, over 5,000 people died and were interred in its pauper's burial ground.[2] The population of County Kerry decreased from 293,880 in 1841 to 201,039 four decades later.[3] The intense suffering further distanced the Irish from their British overlords. It found expression in two ways. On the one hand, there was an increased stream of immigration to Canada, Australia, and America. And the Irish of the diaspora gave aid and comfort to those at home involved in the movement for Irish independence.

When Gladstone took power in 1868, he stated his mission was to "pacify" Ireland. He had good cause for alarm. The Fenian Brotherhood in America established a skirmish fund in 1875 to overthrow the British. Shane Kenna suggests it was they who initiated a policy of general terror. Aimed not only at elites but at the general public, it was a policy supported by many Irish-American politicians, such as Illinois congressman John Finerty. In fact, American Fenians established a dynamite school in Brooklyn supported by O'Donovan Rossa. Its goal was to train terrorists and have them return to Ireland and wreak havoc.[4] One of its graduates was Tom Clarke, later martyred in the Easter Rebellion.[5] Due to their activities, several Irish leaders were arrested. Incidents of violence increased, including a failed rising in 1867. Gladstone's measures disestablishing the Irish church and freeing Irish Catholics from economically supporting it and moves toward granting land rights to Irish tenants did not allay Irish agitation. The British government responded by increasing its powers of repression.

By 1871, the agitation resulted in Ireland being divided into four military districts, eight military sub-districts with a total militia of 31,000 officers.[6] The Fenians in Ireland and the Clan na Gael in the United States were two offshoots of Irish efforts at liberation.

The potato blight returned in 1879, bringing with it the threat of renewed starvation and further evictions. Only this time, the Irish were more organized.

While the famine of 1879 was not as severe as the Great Famine of the 1840s, it caused widespread suffering, but not the mass deaths that typified the earlier privation. Improvements in transportation, transfer payments from relatives abroad, an immediate response from the British government, and the growth of an Irish land-owning class mitigated its impact.

However, it did focus on the West. The memories of the Great Famine caused panic among residents. Many left, immigrating to urban areas or overseas. The impact of this latest famine, aside from population loss, was its link to the larger struggle going on in Ireland being waged by Michael Davitt, the Land League, and Charles Stewart Parnell. Their organized agitation for reform was referred to as the Land War of 1879–1882. Boycotts and violence were not uncommon as resistance to forced evictions increased. These efforts culminated in

Gladstone's Land Reform Act of 1881, which guaranteed fair rents and made it possible for Irish tenants to buy the land they farmed.[7]

The famine of 1879 received widespread publicity in the United States. It was featured in a series of articles in *Harper's Weekly*, which highlighted the misery of the Irish tenants in several cartoons during the winter and spring of 1880. The famine was also the focus of a series of reports in the *New York Tribune* by journalist, abolitionist, lecturer, and reformer James Redpath, who endorsed the Irish cause in his Talks about Ireland in 1881.[8] Relief efforts in America were coordinated by the *New York Herald*, which collected over $200,000 for famine victims. By spring 1880, the United States Navy dispatched a ship with food and clothing for the suffering.[9]

Additional coverage was provided in *The Irish World*, the most popular Irish-American paper. Established by Patrick Ford in 1870, an Irish immigrant from the first famine. It soon became the voice of radical ideas and causes, providing an outlet for Irish nationalists in America, such as John Devoy and the Clan na Gael—and in Ireland—Charles S. Parnell and Michael Davitt.[10] So by the time Sullivan's family immigrated to America, both Ireland and Irish America had become hotbeds of agitation for an independent Ireland.

Despite attempts at improving the lot of the Irish peasant, the situation for them in the 1880s was dire at best. Statistics reveal the peak of postfamine Irish immigration were the years 1881–1885, when 62,736 went to the United States with much smaller contingents immigrating to Canada, Australia, New Zealand, and Great Britain.[11] In 1881, County Kerry's population was slightly over 200,000 with one in fifty-five receiving relief under the poor law system.[12]

In the peak years of the famine, Kerry lost 30 percent of its population due to death and immigration, although most outmigration occurred in the later decades of the nineteenth century. Of the ten counties in Ireland with the highest rates of immigration, Kerry was at the top of the list. About two-thirds of postfamine immigrants went directly to the United States, many coming from counties with large agricultural populations, the least urbanized, with the poorest farmland. On the positive side, many of these same displaced Irish tended to be more literate.[13] According to Halton and Williamson, the vast majority of immigrants chose the more expensive passage to America rather than Britain. Apparently, the image of "impoverished Irish becoming birds of passage" was a myth.[14] Hence, the postfamine Irish were described by Kerby Miller not as exiles but as ambitious souls seeking to improve their material well-being.[15] The family of James M. Sullivan was part of this second great wave of Irish immigration.

Sullivan's Early Life: Journalist, Gambler, Lawyer

James Mark Sullivan was born to James and Mary Coakley Sullivan in 1870 (or 1873).[16] His father chose to immigrate to America in 1884, a time when the British government under William Gladstone was attempting to settle the land question through a series of Irish land acts that effectively created a large class of Irish property owners, undermining the power of the Anglo-Irish. Rather than dissipating the antipathy to Britain, it encouraged the movement toward Home Rule.

By the time Sullivan was born, Ireland was experiencing a nationalist cultural rebirth.

Julia H. Wright expanded these categories to include romantic, civic, diasporic, antiquarian, and cultural nationalism. The first ties people to the land in an organic sense—its hills, rivers, and fields. Civic nationalism demands the participation of free individuals in affairs of the state. Diasporic nationalism reflects the migration of ethnic peoples, the result of their loss of physical attachment to the land. Antiquarian nationalism is defined as remembrance of historic sites and "archaeological residue of the past." Cultural nationalism is a fondness for its material culture—art, music, and poetry, for example. These nationalisms are complementary, building over time to coalesce into political nationalism. All elements are implicitly anti-imperialistic and came together in Ireland at the end of the nineteenth century.[17] Coming from the devastated West of Ireland, these events must have had an impact on the young James M. Sullivan. Collectively these movements led to the Easter Rebellion and to the origins of a Free Irish State.

Under Charles Stewart Parnell, the Home Rule Party had become a potent political force by the time Sullivan's family immigrated to America in 1882, at the height of violence against Britain. Parnell had been imprisoned for encouraging Irish to intimidate tenants taking advantage of Gladstone's land program, being released from Kilmainham Jail only after agreeing to cooperate with The Liberal government. The 1882 murder of the British secretary and undersecretary for Ireland in broad daylight by Fenians in Dublin emphasized the increasing resentment to British rule. England's reaction was to impose repressive measures, circumventing civil rights. The Irish response was extreme, resulting in the dynamite campaign against public buildings in England. Largely the result of his changing circumstances, Sullivan never abandoned his Irish heritage, and over time, it may have increased in fervor, as witnessed by his involvement in activities and organizations that helped win support for Irish independence.

To a young man from rural County Kerry, Ireland, moving to the urban sprawl of industrializing America must have been something of a culture shock. A largely rural people, the Irish settled in urban America—Boston, New York City, Philadelphia, and Baltimore. New England, like much of the northeast at the time, had become a center of textiles, hardware, machinery, and manufacturing. Along with many others, Sullivan's family contributed to the growing Irish population of Connecticut, making it the second-largest immigrant group in the state during the last decades of the nineteenth century. Hartford, another Connecticut city where Sullivan began his journalist career, still retains a strong concentration of Irish.[18]

James M. Sullivan initially lived in Connecticut after graduation from Yale Law School in 1902. Five years later, he moved to New York City, where he began to build his legal career. Attached to Tammany Hall, he achieved notoriety in the Becker-Rosenthal murder case, which resulted in his patronage appointment as ambassador to Santo Domingo.

At the time he began his legal career, American cities, big and small, were a teeming multicultural mix of races, cultures, and religions. Life was made even more complex as a result of issues associated with contemporary urban America: slums; the need for efficient sanitation, public utilities, and transportation; the crime and corruption associated with city life. The Irish came seeking material improvement, but with limited skills in an urban, industrial America, they faced an uncertain future. Novelist Mary Rose Callaghan describes her grandfather's probable experience at Ellis Island: "The hungry Irish, having to face doctors, [were] afraid of being sent back to starvation and certain death. But the sweatshops of New York and Boston were as bad a fate. Worse."[19] Brown is more scathing in his assessment of the reality of the initial Irish experience in the New World: "[T]he tenements of Boston's Fort Hill, New York's Five Points and Chicago's Bridgeport were as unhealthy as the wretched huts of Ireland's West and Southwest."[20]

In coming to the New World, the Irish sought out their own kind, a process called chain migration. Irish from certain regions of the mother country tended to cluster together; Boston received many from the west of Ireland, whereas Philadelphia and New York City received a majority from the north.[21] By 1900, New York and Philadelphia obtained 35 percent of all Irish immigrants.[22]

The problems new immigrants faced were overwhelming. With limited political experience, they were often at the mercy of urban political bosses. Many bosses were Irish, the first large-scale urban-based immigrants to arrive. City machines maintained themselves in power by rendering services to their constituents, finding jobs, distributing food, arranging picnics, and providing aid during family crises. The provision of such services allowed many first-generation immigrants to adapt to their new surroundings. But the price of this was their unquestioned political support. Despite their thievery of the public purse through bribes, corruption, and kickbacks, many bosses were popular among their voters. In the face of corruption, vice, and inefficiency, the cities grew in size, establishing hospitals, museums, sewage, water works, and transit systems. Often these projects provided patronage jobs for the urban bosses; hence they opposed urban political reform movements. For example, the State Tenement House Act of 1901, the first piece of housing legislation in the nation, was an anathema to Tammany Hall. "Human misery," according to Connable and Silberfarb, "was the stuff of Tammany victories."[23]

Possibly the best example of an urban political boss was Big Tim Sullivan, a second-generation Irish ward politician who rose to prominence during Richard Croker's dominance of Tammany. His background was similar to James M. Sullivan, to whom he is not related. Both had fathers who abandoned the family, leaving the sons to help support their siblings. Big Tim became leader of a youth gang in the Five Points, the Whyos, engaging in street brawls with rivals. The gang often hired out to Tammany Hall to ensure voters made the correct choice in municipal balloting.[24] To keep the gang members loyal, Tammany employed them as bouncers, runners, and enforcers at local gambling houses. Beginning in 1886, Big Tim began a career in the state legislature. Sullivan was known best for the Sullivan law, which made illegal the carrying of concealed weapons and for his espousal of women's rights, allegedly due to his mother's influence on him, and for making Columbus Day a legal holiday, a recognition of the increasing multicultural composition of his electoral district in the wake of the new emigration from Southern and Eastern Europe. He made sure that many of his new recruits were representatives of these emergent ethnic groups. His personal fortune derived from control of illegal prizefights, brothels, gambling, saloons, including the shakedown of pushcart operators, was estimated at $2–3 million but was dissipated by his largess. He reportedly gave away shoes and sponsored dinners and outings for his constituents. These efforts provided entertainment and welfare by taking a personal interest in the people of his district.[25] The reality was closer to Sante's assessment:

> [W]hat helped Tammany succeed over so many years was that its operators did not stand on ceremony, did not make class distinctions with anyone willing to play the game, and, above all, had a realistic understanding of weakness and vice. Tammany, in its many guises was a confidence game, an often foolish embezzlement ring, an oligarchy of wise guys, and it cost the city incalculable millions in various boondoggles, swindles and white elephants, but is provided the people with bread and circuses, and with no lectures to spoil enjoyment of the latter.[26]

McCaffrey noted how journalists and novelists exaggerated the positive side of Irish politics and its power broker significance.[27] Even Callaghan had her narrator state the following: "The historians say we changed American history by the parish mentality of our representatives, who made sure of votes with buckets of coal and bags of groceries . . . The bad result then was Tammany."[28]

"Big Tim" Sullivan (1862-1913)
Timothy D. Sullivan: Memorial Address delivered in the House
of Representatives of the United States Sixty-Third Congress
21 June 1914*

Often this part of Irish-American history has been ignored, glossed over or romanticized. Callaghan reinforces Sante's comments: "How many Irish-Americans knew their ancestors had staked out territory in the city? You thought of them as rosary-muttering Catholics, but many were thugs."[29]

James M. Sullivan quickly accommodated himself to this new urban American milieu. He took advantage of opportunities emanating from the enormous expansion of America's cities. Nonetheless, as late as 1900, the Irish were still 92 percent of the nation's poor.[30] However, they were gradually assimilating into the better classes as a result of the rise of trade unions, public services, increased access to education, and the concomitant growth of managerial and white-collar occupations. Still, they were often excluded from the big investment houses on Wall Street until the middle of the twentieth century. "[T]he old stock Protestant investment bankers thought little of the Irish."[31]

One vehicle that made upward mobility possible for many Irish were the social networks provided by the Clan na Gael, the Ancient Order of Hibernians, the Society of the Friendly Sons of St. Patrick, the Knights of Columbus, and urban political machines. They provided, in Miller's phrase, the "system of intracommunal patronage [and] the ubiquitous nepotism essential for what had been a discontented and marginalized group in urban America."[32] Their collective sense of anomie encouraged a nostalgic view of the old country, which blamed its ills on the "perfidious Albion," Great Britain. These experiences resulted in wrapping their own role in American history in myth and legend in what Thomas Brown referred to as "apologia," or "works of justification." Examples of apologia include the idea the New World was discovered by St. Brendan, that Columbus was rowed ashore by an Irish navigator; the "fighting Irish" won the American Revolution, the Civil War, the Spanish-American

War, and without Irish labor, America's material progress would have been impossible.[33]

These two streams of consciousness were effectively used by spokesmen and organizations agitating for Irish independence. Thus could the Celtic myth provide for the Irish-American pride in the past, nurturance for their imagined dispossession, with its accompanying attitude for vengeance, and which supported nationalism in Ireland.

Some of the biographical facts about James M. Sullivan are cloudy, even including the date of his birth. Family lore suggests he was born in 1863 or 1870, a date he used when he went to Yale Law School so as not to appear older than his classmates.[34] As noted, his family was part of a large postfamine Irish immigration to America. Allegedly, his family was middle class. According to his granddaughter, Irish novelist Mary Rose Callaghan, Sullivan's father was a mathematics teacher. His father apparently lost his job because he was critical of British policy in Ireland. His family immigrated to America with two servants in 1884.[35] Given the privations of the second famine, the violence in Ireland at that time, and his father's alleged mistreatment, James M. Sullivan's anti-British attitude was understandable.

Sullivan's father may have been promised work as a school-teacher in Brooklyn, but the job did not materialize. His old world skills useless, his father may have succumbed to drink. Their few fiscal resources quickly evaporated. His father failed at factory work, and he later deserted the family, leaving his mother to support the family as a scrubwoman and a domestic.[36]

An obituary in the *Hartford Courant* says Sullivan was educated in the cotton factory villages of Thorndike and Waterbury, Massachusetts. But again the facts are ambiguous.[37] Family lore suggests he had to quit school to work to support the family when his father left.[38] James M. Sullivan was compelled to hold a variety of jobs—newsboy, carpenter, boxer, baseball player—in order to supplement his mother's meager earnings as a laundress and housekeeper.[39] He was a voracious reader and became a stump speaker for the Democratic Party.[40] Education gave him entree to a journalist's career at the *Waterbury American* in Connecticut and later at the *New Haven Register*, the *New Haven Union*, and the *Hartford Courant*.[41] He quite possibly associated with a prominent local journalist, Henry C. O'Sullivan, "a cultured news writer of the *Register*" whose stories covered the state legislative sessions of the period.[42] Then again, he may have simply sold subscriptions, possibly getting subscribers to cancel theirs and sign up again with him.[43] According to Mary Rose Callaghan, her grandfather was referred to as Legs because he would go anywhere to get a story.[44] Apparently, he also covered other news items. Callaghan has him interviewing William J. Bryan in 1896 on the controversial silver issue. The story gave Sullivan some prominence as a journalist and a connection to Bryan, who would be pivotal in appointing him ambassador to Santo Domingo in the wake of Wilson's election as President in 1912.

According to Sedgwick, with Sullivan's experience as a sportswriter, he learned the franchise for a local Waterbury baseball team was on the market. According to his obituary, he secured the team "and soon was a baseball magnate."[45] Then again, he may have been a short-time partner with gamblers Bald Jack Rose and/or and Herman Rosenthal with the Danbury team in the Connecticut State League.[46]

Bald Jack Rose was prizefight promoter, gambler, and underworld figure. It was this connection, Sedgwick alleges, "that [. . .] prove[d] a life force and lever to metropolitan, even national prominence. They formed a friendship which gave Sullivan a springboard to leap within a decade into New York life as a lawyer."[47] It would also taint his reputation and give

Rose leverage in obtaining Sullivan's assistance in an effort to exonerate him for his role in the Becker-Rosenthal murder case of 1912.

Allegedly, Sullivan's experience in baseball encouraged him to pursue a law degree, entering Yale Law School in 1899. An alternative story, according to the *National Cyclopedia*, is that he worked his way through college, working as a night clerk in New Haven. Then again, Andy Logan is convinced Sullivan attended Yale, financed by his "well-fixed cousin" Tim Sullivan.[48] Knight, on the other hand, suggests the money he made on baseball and gambling allowed him to attend Yale.[49]

Supposedly, the capture of the Townsend Prize for oratory at Yale in 1902 led to his being considered a candidate for a clerkship in the Massachusetts state legislature. This effort failed because the chamber was Republican dominated. He was a resident of Connecticut, and the spokesperson bungled the presentation.[50]

Following graduation from Yale in 1902, Sullivan was briefly associated with New Haven attorney Edward J. Maher.[51] Or he may have worked as a lawyer representing the poor in Connecticut. At this juncture, Sullivan allegedly became acquainted with James Michael Curley. Curley, a rising star in Boston politics at the turn of the century, was himself the son of impoverished Irish immigrants. He established an organization to rival one which he felt cheated him. Called the Tammany Club, it was named to honor the "decent side" of the similarly named New York City machine. Essentially, it meant helping the poor and dispensing patronage. According to Callaghan, Curley gave Sullivan numerous clients.[52]

Within five years, Sullivan moved to New York City, where he continued his legal career, but again, opinions vary. Sedgwick proclaims he "flourished" due to his connections to Tammany Hall, whereas the Phelan Report suggests he maintained a "struggling practice,"[53] largely based on his connections to gambling and the underworld.[54] The latter source might be the more accurate. Logan, for example, refers to Sullivan as a "Tammany ambulance chaser."[55] Possibly, Sullivan was an associate counsel to Daniel O'Reilly in the scandalous Harry Thaw / Sanford White murder case, but this too is open to speculation.[56] His modest success may have been possible by his association with his cousin Little Tim Sullivan, a member of the New York City Board of Aldermen and possible source of funding for his Yale education.[57] It could also have been a function of his connection to Tammany politics. According to his *New York Times* obituary, Sullivan had an active role in Wigwam affairs.[58]

Sullivan's Irish Nationalist Credentials

The other side of Sullivan's political life centered on Irish independence. Through family connections, Sullivan had strong Irish nationalist credentials. Two relatives, Timothy Daniel Sullivan (1827–1914) and Alexander Martin Sullivan (1830–1884) were active in the Young Ireland movement, editing its official organ, *The Nation* (1842–'92). Timothy was lord mayor of London, associated with the Land League, and later served as a member of Parliament. Timothy was allied with Parnell in the Irish Parliamentary Party, breaking with him after the O'Shea scandal became public. He was a historian, poet, and author of "God Save Ireland" in 1867, which was the official Irish national hymn. Alexander was also a writer of Irish history. As a lawyer, he defended a nationalist who murdered a British informant. Like his brother Timothy, he too was imprisoned for his nationalist activities. Alexander's son, also a lawyer, unsuccessfully defended Roger Casement in 1916.[59] In addition, according to Sedgwick,[60] Sullivan was an active member of the Ancient Order of Hibernians, an organization described as intent on avenging the wrongs Ireland had suffered at the hands of Great Britain. If accurate, it reinforces Sullivan's nationalist ties insofar as other sources indict the AOH as the "great unknown power behind the Irish Nationalist Party."[61] Ashtown, *The Catholic Encyclopedia*, and Feeley connect the AOH to earlier terrorist groups such as the White Boys and the Defenders of the late eighteenth century and the Ribbonmen of the nineteenth century. All were secret societies designed to defend Catholic tenants against the land-lords, often using violence to achieve their goals.[62]

According to Sedgwick, James M. Sullivan organized classes in the study of "Native Irish and Irish literature and he advocated its being taught in the New England schools." He also gives credence to the rumor Sullivan invited William B. Yeats to lecture in New Haven.[63] If true, this connects James Sullivan to the emerging Gaelic Renaissance of the period.

In the United States, the Gaelic Renaissance was an example of diasporic nationalism. In part, it was broad-based effort to create a respectable culture by revising the nega-tive stereotype of the Stage Irishman, the gorilla image, dirty clothes, short-stemmed pipe, shillelagh, and alleged fondness for strong drink.[64] Sullivan's ally, James K. McGuire, was also outspoken in his condemnation.[65] On the downside, the Gaelic Renaissance nourished a hatred of all things British. It was encouraged by such expatriate journalists as John Devoy and his *Gaelic American*, John Boyle O'Reilly's *Boston Pilot*, and Patrick Ford's *Irish World*. Irish-American scorn was such that even innocuous events were perceived as a conspiracy by Britain to influence American foreign policy. When the Brooklyn Bridge was opened on what happened to be Queen Victoria's birthday, for example, Irish Americans mobilized mass meet-ings and threatened to destroy it.[66] On a local level, Sullivan associate James K. McGuire used his paper, *The Catholic Sun*, to condemn the trip of the Syracuse militia to Canada to celebrate the queen's birthday. McGuire reiterated the sins of Britain's long occupation of Ireland, condemning the queen, who did little to alleviate their suffering.[67] At her death, McGuire, then mayor of Syracuse, New York, refused to lower the flag at city hall in tribute.[68] The Society of the Friendly Sons of Saint Patrick also refused to pay tribute to Victoria. Its President, James O'Gorman, stated, "The Irish could take no part in the manifestations of grief and sorrow following her death without the grossest betrayal of their nationality.[69]

Sullivan too played his part endorsing the cause of National liberation by his impassioned speeches "which brought audiences to their feet in outbursts of applause at banquets honoring Irish patriots." At Yale, he won the Townsend Prize for oratory in 1902 on the topic of Home Rule,[70] again revealing an interest in Irish independence.

Sullivan was also tied to Irish Nationalism through his wife's family. His marriage to Ellen O'Mara in 1910 linked him to another prominent family with strong ties to the Irish cause. Ellen was the granddaughter of Stephen O'Mara, a member of the Land League. During World War I, Stephen O'Mara became active in Sinn Fein. Two of his sons, James and Stephen, were involved in fighting during the Easter Rising. James, Nell's father, while serving as a member of Parliament, successfully introduced legislation making St. Patrick's Day a national holiday.[71] He later joined the nascent Sinn Fein, rising to director of finance and trustee of Dail Eirann funds. In that capacity, he traveled with DeValera to America in 1920 in a fund-raising drive. Like his father and brother-in-law, James M. O'Mara, James M. Sullivan was protreaty and briefly served as Irish Republic's ambassador to the United States. Stephen O'Mara, also active in Sinn Fein, served as mayor of Limerick during the Irish War for Independence and was allegedly on the hit list of the Black and Tans.[72] He supplanted his brother James as DeValera's director of finance. As a staunch supporter of DeValera, he was interned by the free state government. When James M. Sullivan was jailed during the rising, his wife's niece, Eithne O'Mara, stayed with her. Eithne later married Dick Humphrys, an Irish nationalist educated for a time at St. Enda's. As a member of the Irish Volunteers, Humphrys fought at the General Post Office in the Easter Rebellion, where his uncle, the O'Railey, was killed. O'Railey was educated with Paddy O'Mara, brother of James and Stephen, and was a good friend of James Sullivan. In the wake of the rising, both Dick Humphrys and James M. Sullivan were interned at Kilmainham Jail together.[73]

Subsequent to his marriage to Nell O'Mara, Sullivan delivered a speech on Republicanism at the grave of Wolfe Tone in 1911. It was organized by Arthur Griffith and the IRB to minimize Irish nationalist agitation during the state visit by George V.[74] At that time, this was no small thing. National independence appeared to be a distant dream. Yet under the calm surface, a current of resentment was stirring. There was labor union unrest under the leadership of Jim Larkin. There was a resurgent nationalist culture, and a growing Unionist threat of partition under Sir Edward Carson. Nonetheless, Nationalist demonstrations against the visit of King George V in June 1911 were overshadowed by the thousands lining the street to view his procession.[75] The sentiment of the crowd would turn against the crown in the wake of its bloody suppression of the Easter Rising.

According to his granddaughter, Sullivan was always intensely Irish, often traveling between New York and Ireland.[76] Because his wife "hated living in New York," all their children were born in Ireland. His marriage to a notable family solidified his Irish political and social contacts. James McGuire, a former mayor of Syracuse, New York, at the time with close ties to the Wilson administration, was prominent in urging Sullivan's appointment to the position of ambassador to Santo Domingo, praising his Irish origins, his Yale law degree, and his importance in the Irish nationalist movement.

As noted previously, Sullivan's Irish nationalist sentiment was also revealed during the Gaelic Renaissance in America. One of its major efforts was an attempt to revise the negative

SULLIVAN'S IRISH NATIONALIST CREDENTIALS

stereotype of Irish culture and history. Just as earlier in Ireland, one of the vehicles for projecting this new image was resuscitating Irish sports and the Gaelic language. Sullivan, given his strong Nationalist credentials, was part of these efforts. For example, along with other prominent Irish Americans, Sullivan protested the 1912 production of *Playboy of the Western World*, proclaiming it an insult to Irish womanhood.[77] In addition, prior to his departure to Santo Domingo as the new United States ambassador, he shared the dais at Celtic Park with local Irish priests, reviewing regiments of Irish volunteers who later played Gaelic football[78] seizing on the symbol, if not the substance, of Irish cultural revival. These activities and individuals whom he associated connect Sullivan to the militant, pro-German Irish nationalist movement in America. Subsequent events reveal President Woodrow Wilson, both before and after the election of 1916, would have his revenge in full measure against those who opposed his policies. One of his victims was James M. Sullivan. His appointment as ambassador to Santo Domingo was an intriguing mix of Democratic Party patronage, Tammany politics, and business interests, which sought to capitalize on various projects in the Republic and also his connections to Irish nationalism. It also suggests Sullivan seized opportunities for his own advancement. It reveals Sullivan as quite possibly a situational nationalist, cognizant of how his Irish connections could advance his own personal agenda as well. Quite possibly Sullivan was playing the ethnic card to his own advantage rather than revealing a true commitment to the cause of Irish freedom. The vehicle that brought him to the attention of these various elements—Irish nationalism, Tammany politics, international intrigue—was the controversial Becker-Rosenthal case of 1912.

End Notes

1. http://goireland.com/geneaology, Retrieved 12 January 2012.

2. "6000 Years of History on the Dingle Peninsula," http://www.celticnature.com/history.html, Retrieved 12 January 2012.

3. "A Description of County Kerry from Guy's Postal Directory of Munster 1886," http://homepage.eircom.net/~dinglemaps/genoki/KER/Guy1886.htm. Retrieved 12 January 2012.

4. Shane Kenna, "The Fenian Dynamite Campaign and the Irish-American Impetus for Dynamite Terror, 1881-85." *Inquiries Journal* 3, no. 12 (2011): 1.

5. Tobias O'Coisdealhi, "Thomas James Clarke, 1852–1916," "Fenian Graves," http://www.Irishfreedom.net/Fenian graves/ T.J. Clarke/T.J.Clarke.htm.

6. "Ireland: King, Church, Dublin, Time and Called," http://www.libraryindex.com/encyclopedia/pages/cpxlgeny2b/ireland, Retrieved 8 February 2012,

7. "On This Day: February 28, 1880," http://www.nytimes.com/learning/general/onthisday/harp/0228.html.

8. "James Redpath," http://americanabolitionistliberalarts.iupui.edu/redpath.htm, Retrieved 8 February 2012.

9. "On This Day," op. cit.

10. "Though Not an Irishman: Henry George and the American-Irish-Special Issue: Commemorating the Hundredth

Anniversary of the Death of Henry George," http://findarticles.com/mi_n0254/is_n4_v56ai_20381866, Retrieved 8 February 2012.

[11] Timothy Halton and Jeffrey Williamson, "After the Famine: Emigration from Ireland, 1851–1913," *Journal of Economic History* 53, no. 3 (September 1993): 575–600. Table 1, 577.

[12] "A Description of County Kerry," op. cit.

[13] "Ireland-Irish, King, Church, Dublin, Time and Called," op. cit.

[14] Halton and Williamson, op. cit., 590.

[15] Kerby Miller, *Emigrants and Exiles: Ireland and the Irish Exodus to North America* (New York: Oxford University Press, 1985), 412.

[16] Maryanne Felter and Daniel Schultz, "The Making of an Irish Nationalist: James Mark Sullivan and the Film Company of Ireland in America," in "Screening the Past," http://screeningthe past.com/2012/02/the-making-of-an-irish-nationalist," Spring 2012. The Humphry's Family Tree States Sullivan was born 6 January 1873.

[17] Julia N. Wright, *Representing The National Landscape In Irish Romanticism* (Syracuse: Syracuse University Press, 2014), xviii–xxix.

[18] "The History and People of Connecticut," http://kindredtrails.com/Connecticut-History-2.html, Retrieved 12 January 2012.

[19] Mary Rose Callaghan, *Emigrant Dreams* (Dublin: Poolbeg Press, 1966), 10.

[20] Thomas Brown, *Irish-American Nationalism, 1870–1890* (New York: Lippincott, 1966), 18.

[21] Vincent Parillo, *Strangers to These Shores*, 4th edition (Boston: Allyn and Bacon, 1995), 155.

[22] Miller, op. cit., 496.

23   Alfred Connable and Edward Silberfarb, *Tigers of Tammany: Nine Men Who Ran New York* (New York: Holt, Rhinehart, Winston, 1967), 181.

24   Morris Robert Werner, *Tammany Hall* (New York: Doubleday, Doran and Company, 1928), 493.

25   Lawrence J. McCaffrey, *Forging Forward and Looking Back in* Bayor, Ronald H. and Timothy Meagher, eds. *The New York Irish (Baltimore*: Johns Hopkins University Press, 1996), 227; Herbert Asbury, *The Gangs of New York* (New York: Thunder's Mouth Press, 1927), 262; Andy Logan, *Against the Evidence: The Becker-Rosenthal Affair* (New York: McCall Publishing, 1970), 56–58.

26   Luc Sante, *Low Life: Lures and Snares of Old New York* (New York: Random House, 1992), 277.

27   McCaffrey, op. cit., 228.

28   Callaghan, op. cit., 176.

29   Ibid.

30   Miller, op. cit., 493, 499, 500.

31   Chris McNickle, "When New York Was Irish and After," In Bayor and Meagher, eds., op. cit., 337–357.

32   Miller, op. cit., 525.

33   Brown, op. cit., 25–31.

34   "James M. Sullivan, Ex-Diplomat, Dead," *New York Times*, 24 August 1920. The *New York Times* erroneously reported his death as 1920.

35   Maryanne Felter and Daniel Schultz, op. cit; Mary Rose Callaghan, op. cit., 234. Felter e-mail to author 7 February 2011.

36   Callaghan, op. cit., 235.

37   Hulbert Sedgwick, "Sullivan Had Rapid Rise to Success," *Hartford Courant*, 18 August 1935, 2.

38 "Sullivan, James Mark." *National Cyclopedia of American Biography*, vol. xxix (New York: James T. White and Company, 1941), 362–363; Callaghan, op. cit., 237.

39 Sullivan's granddaughter, Irish novelist Mary Rose Callaghan, relates details of James M. Sullivan's life in her novel *Emigrant Dreams* (Dublin: Poolbeg Press), 1996, Ch. 19, 233–250. A brief biography of Sullivan can be found in various publications as noted in the citations. See also Maryanne Felter, *Crossing Borders: A Critical Introduction to the Works of Mary Rose Callaghan* (Newark: University of Delaware Press, 2010), fn. 2, 136–138.

40 Callaghan, op. cit., 236; "Minister Sullivan Oniverous [sic] Reader," *New York Times*, 28 January 1915.

41 Sedgwick, op. cit.; Andy Logan, op. cit., 16.

42 Sedgwick, op. cit.

43 Melvin Knight, *Americans in Santo Domingo* (New York: Vanguard, 1928), 53; James Duval Phelan, *Santo Domingo Investigations: Copy of Report of Findings and Opinions* (Washington: Gibson Bros, 1915), 6.

44 Callaghan, op. cit., 237; Callaghan e-mail to author, 10 September 2002.

45 Sedgwick, op. cit.

46 Callaghan, op. cit., 48; 237. However, before that "great leap forward" occurred, James M. Sullivan was involved in prizefight promotion with Bald Jack Rose, the outcome of which, although denied publicly, were always fixed. Allegedly, it was this that Rose used as leverage to get Sullivan, then a lawyer in New York City, to defend him by implicating an innocent man, Charles Becker. If it became public, fixing prizefights could have led to Sullivan's disbarment. Callaghan, op. cit., 240.

47 Sedgwick, op. cit.

48 Andy Logan, op. cit., 76. This cousin was a New York City alderman and associate of the more prominent Big Tim Sullivan of the Bowery.

49 Knight, op. cit., 56. Phelan Report, op. cit., 5.

50 Sedgwick, op. cit.

51 "Sullivan, James Mark," *National Cyclopedia*, op. cit.

52 Callaghan, op. cit., 238. Curley later went on to serve in the Massachusetts State Legislature as congressman, as mayor of Boston, and as governor of Massachusetts. His various activities also brought him three prison terms, none of which seriously hampered his popular appeal, but it may have prevented him from obtaining a desired ambassadorial appointment under Franklin D. Roosevelt. For details, see Beatty, Jack. *The Rascal King: The Life and Times of James Michael Curley* (1874–1958). (New York: MacMillan, 1992).

53 Sedgwick, op. cit.; Phelan Report, op. cit., 6.

54 Andy Logan, op. cit.; Arthur Link, *Woodrow Wilson and the Progressive Era, 1910–1917*. (New York: Harper, 1954), 107.

55 Andy Logan, op. cit, 281–282.

56 *Phelan Report*, op. cit., 6; Callaghan, op. cit., 238.

57 Gustavus Myers, *History of Tammany Hall* (New York: 1917), 311.

58 "James M. Sullivan, Ex-Diplomat, Dead," op. cit.

59 "Timothy Daniel Sullivan: Biography," www.farmpeople.com/cat-timothy-daniel-sullivan. Retrieved 26 November 2014; "Alexander Martin Sullivan (1830–1884)," world-heritage.org/articles/Alexander_Martin_Sullivan (Irish Politician). Retrieved 26 November 2014.

60 ibid.

61 Sedgwick, op. cit.

62 Ashtown, op. cit., 60; "Ancient Order of Hibernians," *Catholic Encyclopedia*, http://www.newadvent.org/cathen/07320a.htm. Retrieved 13 September 2011; Pat Feeley, *"Whiteboys and Ribbonmen: Early Agrarian Secret Societies,"* City of Limerick Public Library, n. d., 23–27.

63 Sedgwick, op. cit.

64 Bhromheil, Una Ni, "The Creation of Irish Culture in the United States: The Gaelic Movement, 1870–1915," *New Hibernia Review* 5, no. 3 (Autumn 2001): 87–100.

65 "Celt as Athlete Leader of the World," *Catholic Sun* (1900): 1; "The Gaelic Movement," *Catholic Sun* (17 March 1911): 1; "Movement for Suppression of the Stage Irishman," *Catholic Sun* (16 May 1902): 1, 5.

66 Florence Gibbon, *The Attitude of the New York Irish Towards State And National Affairs, 1848–1902* (New York: 1951), 375–377.

67 "Queen's Birthday," *Catholic Sun* (21 April 1899): 1; "In Empire Hall," *Catholic Sun* (26 November 1897): 1; "Shame on Such Irishmen," *Catholic Sun* (18 November 1898): 7.

68 "Would Not Lower Flag," *New York Times* (25 January 1901): 2; "Why Flag Wasn't Lowered," *Syracuse Herald-Journal* (9 February 1901).

69 Richard Murphy and Lawrence Marmion, *History of the Society of the Friendly Sons of St. Patrick in the City of New York, 1784–1955.* (New York: 1962), 397. James K. McGuire and his brother, Edward, were active members of the SOFSOSP.

70 "James M. Sullivan Ex-Diplomat, Dead," *New York Times* (24 August 1920). The date of his death was premature. Sedgwick, op. cit.

71 Mark Humphrys, PhD, "Humphrey Family Tree," http://humphrysfamilytree.com. Retrieved 5 June 2011.

72 "Death of Prominent Limerick Citizen," *Limerick Leader*, n.d.; "Stephen M. O'Mara," http://en.wikipedia.ord/wiki/StephenM0%27Mara (1 June 2011).

73 Mark Humphrys, PhD, op.cit,: "Irish Blood on the Streets: The Easter Rising of 1916," http://www.suite101.com/content/irishbloodonthestreets. Retrieved 31 January 2011.

74 Maryanne Felter and Daniel Schultz, "James Mark Sullivan and the Film Company of Ireland," *New Hibernia Review* 8, no. 2 (Summer 2004): 27.

75 "What Was Dublin Like in 1911?" http://www.census.nationalarchieves.ie/exhibition/dubliln/main.html.

76 For example, the *New York Times* reported Sullivan's sailing to Liverpool en route to Ireland on the Cunard liner *Etruria* in January 1907 ("Ocean Travelers," *New York Times*, 12 January 1907); Callaghan e-mail to author, 27 June 2002.

77 Callaghan e-mail to author, 9 October 2002.

78 "Irish Regiments Meet," *New York Times* (11 August 1912), 7. Retrieved 5 June 2011. "Gaelic" football was a creation of the Gaelic League in the late nineteenth century to assert a culture of manliness among the Irish. See Kiberd, Declan, *Inventing Ireland: the Literature of the Modern Nation* (London: Random House, 1996), 25, 151, 152, 154, 201, 207.

CHAPTER II

A Most Shameful Deed
Sullivan and the Becker-Rosenthal
Case of 1912

A most Shameful Deed
Sullivan and the Becker-Rosenthal
Case of 1912

I n her novel *Emigrant Dreams*, Mary Rose Callaghan has the fictionalized version of her grandfather, James M. Sullivan, refer to his involvement in the Becker-Rosenthal case as his "most shameful deed." It may very well have been. Sullivan suborned perjury and aided and abetted District Attorney Charles Whitman in prosecutorial misconduct in the arrest, conviction, and execution of an innocent man.[1] As in many aspects of Sullivan's life, the details often conflict, but the net result was it helped launch his short-lived career as a diplomat.

Sullivan's record as to direct involvement in Irish freedom is relatively sparse until his establishment of the Film Company of Ireland. Some of his Celtic connections were noted previously. Perhaps he was too concerned with earning a living, hanging on the fringes of Tammany society and the urban underworld of New York City.

His wife hated New York—its climate, its hectic pace of life, the crime-ridden neighborhood in which they lived. Apparently, he was trying to maintain a lifestyle on a par with his wealthy O'Mara in-laws. Frequent visits to Ireland were commonplace. According to Callaghan, an attempt to maintain the lifestyle of his wife and her affection led to his involvement in the Becker-Rosenthal case.[2]

Yet his ties to the murder case reveal associations with some leaders of the Irish nationalist community, such as John Goff, John

C. McIntyre, and James K. McGuire. Sullivan used his Yale-learned oratorical skills as a speaker for the Democratic Party from 1896 to 1912, during the heyday of William Jennings Bryan, the three-time Democratic candidate for president. Sullivan was known as the man with the golden voice, focusing his efforts among Irish Americans in the northeast, working under the tutelage of James K. McGuire, three-time Democratic mayor of Syracuse, New York.[3] The nickname may have confused Sullivan with Bryan, the latter known as the Boy Orator of the Platte.[4] Further, the confusion may have stemmed from Sullivan's longtime association with James K. McGuire, whose eloquence won for him the title the Silver-Tongued Orator of Onondaga.[5] Meanwhile, Sullivan's law practice in New York may have brought him some prominence, but again, accounts differ. Sullivan's granddaughter, author Mary Rose Callaghan, says her mother, Sheila Sullivan Callaghan, told her that Sullivan had worked on the Harry K. Thaw case, perhaps as a junior lawyer under Daniel O'Reilly. The Phelan Report reinforces that claim, stating Sullivan came to New York specifically to work with Daniel O'Reilly on the Thaw murder case. But the *New York Times* reports of the Harry Thaw / Stanford White murder case of 1907 mention O'Reilly only once, and then only to say that he was the first lawyer to counsel Thaw. Other attorneys joined O'Reilly for Thaw's defense. Sullivan's name is not mentioned at all. Callaghan gives Sullivan a more prominent role in the murder case, but if he was involved, it was only tangentially and for a short time. According to the Phelan Report, "Mr. Sullivan found that O'Reilly's practice was highly sensational and unpleasant, but it appears that he divided some fees with him and remained associated with him for nearly two years." Subsequently O'Reilly was disbarred and imprisoned. He reportedly had an affair with his client, Harry Thaw's wife, the famous Evelyn Nesbitt Thaw.[6] Nonetheless, apparently Sullivan made good. Logan attributes his "thriving practice" to his close ties to the Murphy wing of Tammany Hall.[7]

Charles Becker (1870-1915)
Becker in uniform circa 1912
Library of Congress[*]

Sullivan's Role in the
Becker-Rosenthal Case

The year 1912 was a turning point in Sullivan's career. Not only did he campaign successfully for Woodrow Wilson, but as noted previously, he achieved some notoriety as a result of his role in the Becker-Rosenthal case. Sullivan's connection with the case provided him with the contacts he needed to obtain a patronage post with the Wilson administration. The case also reveals the nature and extent of Tammany Hall in police corruption, bribery, and graft. Some leaders in the cause of Irish nationalism—W. Bourke Cockrane, Daniel Cohalan, Judge John Goff, John C. McIntyre, and James K. McGuire, a former mayor of Syracuse, New York—were intimately tied to Tammany politics. The most penetrating analysis of the case has been told elsewhere, but a brief overview is necessary to understand how Sullivan, Tammany, Santo Domingo, and Irish Nationalism are linked.

Policemen Charles Becker was the product of a corrupt system that included individual police officers, entire police departments, lawyers, judges, prostitutes, informers, dope addicts, saloon keepers, bordello operators, politicians, and "legitimate" businessman, as the asphalt and other trust scandals of the period have shown. Appointments to the force were purchased, as were promotions. Once rookies learned merit was irrelevant, they went into debt to finance their careers. To do so, they were drawn into a system of graft, becoming ever more greedy and brutal. Becker was connected to the Tammany machine through Big Tim Sullivan, a state senator whose fortune was made in prostitution, gambling, extortion, and prizefighting, who is often incorrectly believed related to James M. Sullivan. Becker was thus able to play both sides of the law to his own advantage. In his role as head of one of the Strong Arm Squads, police units that focused on closing down illegal gambling parlors, Becker was initially praised for his efforts. Big Tim Sullivan, Becker and Herman Rosenthal allegedly were partners in a gaming house, the Hesper Club. As Big Tim Sullivan was suffering from increasing bouts of insanity, Becker sought to supplant him. Becker assessed Rosenthal a $500 contribution for a colleague's legal fees.[8] Rosenthal refused to pay and threatened to expose the whole scheme of police corruption to crusading District Attorney Charles S. Whitman. To prevent exposure, Becker allegedly got Bald Jack Rose to hire some hit men to eliminate Rosenthal. Rose had been an acquaintance of James M. Sullivan when they were both associated with sports, gambling houses, prizefights, and vaudeville shows in Connecticut, ostensibly when Sullivan was working as a journalist. The relationship continued sporadically after both moved to New York City. According to Andy Logan, by then Sullivan had a "thriving practice" due to his ties to Tammany Hall. After Rosenthal was murdered, Rose sought Sullivan's advice, and the two conferred. As noted previously, Rose and Sullivan, as partners in sports promotion, often fixed fights, a point acknowledged by Callaghan. Sullivan had no option but to assist his former colleague. If discovered, his fight-fixing schemes could have led to his disbarment. According to Callaghan, Sullivan was motivated by more than obligation to a former associate. He saw it as a vehicle for career advancement. "Whitman's career would rise on the issue, and mine with it."[9] Sullivan told Rose to turn himself in. He then allegedly reported these developments to Tammany boss Charles Murphy. After Rose was booked, Sullivan held another conference with his client, claiming the police were at the bottom of the murder.[10] The fact that two Murphy-men lawyers—James M. Sullivan and Aaron Levy (attorney for the alleged driver of the murder car)—were present so quickly after the murder supports the contention Becker was being framed for the crime, and the Tammany machine was working hard to keep one of its key figures, Big Tim Sullivan, out of the picture.

Not only was the Wigwam trying to protect one of its own by keeping a low profile, it was avoiding negative publicity involved in Murphy's open rift with Governor William Sulzer, whose efforts to remain free of Tammany control led to his impeachment. These actions resulted in a wave of anti-Tammany resentment and a loss of its political influence for several years.

But Tammany was not united in its condemnation of Becker. John C. Fitzgerald, former state senator and current member of the state assembly, was a political ally of Big Tim Sullivan. He stood firmly behind Becker. It was rumored that Big Tim did as well. Fitzgerald was not alone in his opinion. Callaghan suggests Mayor William Gaynor, Police Commissioner Rhinelander Waldo, and former frontiersman turned sportswriter Bat Masterson supported Becker as well.[11] There may be some truth to this. Gaynor was a prominent jurist and anti-Tammany reform mayor who denied it patronage positions.[12] Waldo was a well-intentioned but naive blueblood. A West Point graduate and veteran of the Philippine Insurrection, he was New York City's fire commissioner, resigning in the wake of the Triangle Fire of 1911 to become police commissioner. He instituted the Strong Arm Squads to intimidate the underworld into submission. Instead it established a gang of thugs. At their discretion, they would raid and destroy gaming establishments or not, depending on whether they paid bribes. Charles Becker was the leader of one such group whose efforts were supported by Waldo.[13] Waldo was naive in that two of his trusted associates, Winfield R. Sheehan and Cornelius Hayes, were notorious grafters.[14] Bat Masterson, by then a prominent reporter for the *New York Morning Telegraph,* was Becker's friend who stood by him throughout his ordeal.[15] Masterson was also a friend of fellow sports enthusiast and Progressive Party presidential candidate Theodore Roosevelt, who as president appointed him a deputy marshal in New York City. Roosevelt as police commissioner had commended Becker's work and was hostile to Whitman for trying to abort his Progressive Presidential bid. In addition, Bourke Cochran, who was attorney for Becker in his second trial, despite his Tammany connections, openly supported Roosevelt in 1912.[16]

So Becker was not without strong support, but it was all to no avail as a crusading district attorney and an embattled political machine forged an alliance to railroad a crooked, but in this case, innocent cop. Most members of the Big Tim Sullivan clan were with Murphy in having Becker take full blame for the murder of Rosenthal. However, Fitzgerald paid politically for his stand. Despite being Big Tim's designated heir, he was ousted within a year by Sullivan's brother, Patrick, and his half-brother, Larry Mulligan.[17] That Big Tim Sullivan backed Becker came out in a deposition Becker wrote to Governor Charles Whitman in a desperate effort to save himself from electrocution. He alleged Big Tim feared Rosenthal's blabbing to the press and to then district attorney Charles Whitman would create undue negative publicity of Big Tim Sullivan's gambling operations. Supposedly, Rosenthal was offered a sizeable sum of money to leave town. Bald Jack Rose was the alleged courier. It was for this payoff that Rosenthal was waiting. Instead, Bald Jack Rose decided to murder Rosenthal, pay the killers $1,000, and keep the rest of the $15,000 cash. Becker was made aware of the cash transfer by Big Tim himself but had sworn to keep silent about it. There were also phone calls from Big Tim to Whitman's assistants, urging them to assist Becker. Whitman was unmoved by Becker's plea. Bourke Cockran's appeal to the State Supreme Court for a new trial was equally fruitless.[18]

Sammy Schepps (? - 1936)[*]
Gangster, Informer in Becker-Rosenthal case

---

[*] Bain Collection, ggbain 12129. Courtesy/Library of Congress

"Baldy Jack" Rose (1876 - 1947)*
Rose c. 1915
Mobster, Gambler, Sullivan Associate,
Informer in Becker-Rosenthal Case

*   courtesy, Library of Congress ggbain 15864

Another Boss Murphy lawyer, Max Steuer, also condemned Becker. His involvement reinforces the conviction that Tammany was anxious to have Becker take the blame and have the Wigwam avoid any taint of scandal. But as with other aspects of Sullivan's life, his role in the case is suspect. For example, Richard F. Welch, in his biography of Big Tim Sullivan, *King of the Bowery*, makes no mention of Sullivan's involvement in the case, instead giving credit to Max Steuer. Because of his legal expertise, he was encouraged to become involved to protect Big Tim Sullivan. Steuer would be a logical choice since he was "considered . . . by some as the greatest criminal lawyer of his time."[19] Andy Logan has Steuer as attorney for Bridgey Webber, one of the murderers of Herman Rosenthal, with James M. Sullivan acting as intermediary for Rose in discussions with Steuer and District Attorney Whitman. Callaghan says Rose admitted his guilt in the murder plot to Sullivan. The latter owed Rose. The financial rewards of fixing fights may have made possible Sullivan's Yale education. However, Rose's story needed corroboration, which was provided by Sammy Schepps, a gambler and coconspirator with Rose and others in Rosenthal's murder. Rose, Schepps, and Becker supposedly had a meeting to arrange the murder. This was the so-called Harlem Conference. The meeting never took place. Schepps, along with Rose, disappeared the day after the murder. Schepps had been identified as one of the passengers in the car used in the killing. James M. Sullivan initially encouraged Schepps to leave town in the wake of the investigation. He was later found in Hot Springs, Arkansas, subpoenaed and returned to New York City. Schepps immediately signed an immunity agreement similar to that of the other conspirators, implicating Becker as the person responsible for the murder of Rosenthal.[20] Sullivan coached Schepps, "who would swear Becker had ordered the murder." At the trial, Schepps' testimony was apparently effective, although

Callaghan had James M. Sullivan warn him his insolence was making a bad impression on the jury. During an intermission, he cautioned Schepps to behave appropriately, intimating that he could be in Becker's place if he did not change his demeanor.[21] Apparently it worked. "Schepps' performance was cool, shrewd and smart-alecky."[22] It provided additional independent corroboration of Becker's guilt. Callaghan alleges Sullivan was fearful of the wrath of crusading District Attorney Charles Whitman then pursuing indictments against his friend James K. McGuire and others in the Asphalt Trust investigation. Apparently a plea bargain was struck for Rose and others involved in the murder. In return for their testimony against Becker, they would have no charges leveled against them. Steuer was Big Tim Sullivan's lawyer, hence his focus on keeping Big Tim's name out of the proceedings.

The politically ambitious district attorney, Charles S. Whitman, was willing to use Becker to advance his own career, as was Sullivan. The Tammany/Irish nationalist connections were reinforced when Tammany had its pliant governor, John Dix, select John Goff as presiding judge at Becker's trial at Whitman's request.

John William Goff (1848–1924) was an Irish immigrant who overcame poverty by hard work, attending night school and apprenticing as a lawyer. He was admitted to the bar in 1876. An ardent member of the Irish Land League in 1874, he organized, with John Boyle O'Reilly, an expedition to free his companions imprisoned in Australia. Given his ties to Fenian organizations, many of his compatriots were also his clients. Goff maintained his ties to Irish nationalist organizations throughout his life, becoming involved in the Clan na Gael, the Friends of Irish Freedom and later, the American Association for Recognition of the Irish Republic. He was made an assistant district attorney in 1888 for New York City. His attempt to be elected district attorney was a failure as a result of electoral fraud. Goff was chief counsel to the Lexow Committee investigating police corruption, earning him a reputation as a crusading attorney. In 1906, he was elected to a fourteen-year term as justice to the New York Supreme Court. The *National Cyclopedia of American Biography* noted Goff's selection by Governor Dix as a "special judge in the Rosenthal murder case." It conceded a jurist better fitted for this particular task could not have been selected. It charitably states that "one of Goff's chief characteristics is a disposition to disregard minor technicalities in the admission of testimony when a strict adherence to the letter of the law of evidence would defeat the ends of justice." The *Dictionary of American Biography* more accurately notes, "Goff was not profoundly learned in the law, and after his admission to the bar his professional and other interests precluded any extended study."[23] Hence, Goff probably was not the best choice of judge in this matter, nor any other case. Apparently, it wouldn't have mattered. Logan asserts both Whitman and Goff met regularly to discuss issues.[24] Callaghan had Sullivan's coached witnesses, Rose and Schepps, following his instructions, which apparently had a strong impact at the first trial. Becker was convicted, largely on circumstantial evidence. Sullivan left the case, hoping Becker would be cleared. On appeal, the verdict was overturned. Judge Frank H. Hiscock condemned Whitman's "prejudicial statements" and Goff's "erroneous rulings" and awarded Becker a second trial.[25]

Judge John Goff (1848-1924)*
Lawyer, Judge, Irish Nationalist, Judge in Beckers First Trial

---

*   public domain

The lawyer who got Becker off in his first trial was John C. McIntyre. He was chosen as Becker's attorney by Tom Foley, former sheriff of Manhattan and a close associate of Big Tim Sullivan. McIntyre's grandfather had been exiled to America in 1878 because he was involved in extremist Irish politics. McIntyre himself was a member of the Clan na Gael. In 1896, he won acquittal for a Fenian accused in a plot to bomb Parliament. McIntyre was allegedly paid $13,000 from a Tammany account with the understanding to keep Big Tim Sullivan's name out of the proceedings. Citing procedural errors and Goff's obvious antipolice bias, McIntyre won Becker a second trial, after which, he, like James M. Sullivan, retired from the case. Both men believed Becker was innocent of the crime, but their roles could not have been more different. McIntyre later went on to become a New York State court justice.[26] Sullivan went to Santo Domingo. Both jobs were political payoffs.

Logan gave Sullivan a prominent role in the proceedings preliminary to the first trial of Becker. She had Sullivan acting as attorney for Louis Krause, a waiter who allegedly had been present at the murder.

According to Logan, Louis Krause had initially stated that he could not identify any of the gunmen, that he had been too far away to see them. But believing there could be a financial reward for reassessing his recollection of events, he discussed it with his lawyer, James M. Sullivan. Sullivan encouraged Krause's presence at the police station, which led to the arrest of Jacob Reich as a material witness for the prosecution. Reich (AKA Jack Sullivan) was identified as a passenger in a car with Becker near the scene immediately prior to the murder. When asked the reason for his presence at the station, he said he was urged to do so by his lawyer, James M. Sullivan.[27] It was the revised testimony of Reich in Becker's second trial, which essentially sealed the defendant's fate. Reich had apparently been promised immunity for supporting the testimony of the other witnesses. Hence, Logan put Sullivan's involvement in the case as critical to the prosecution. According to Logan, Sullivan was responsible for getting Rose to turn himself in, having Krause place Reich at the murder scene, and getting Sammy Schepps out of town. Krause later identified three of the murderers. At Becker's second trial, a clerk in the court was forcibly removed after remarking aloud that Krause had been well-drilled in his testimony and the case was a frame-up from the start. It was later discovered Krause's living expenses for nineteen months were paid by Whitman, and he had been put on salary as an investigator for Reverend Parkhurst's Society for the Prevention of Crime.[28] Sullivan suborned perjury, but he was aided and abetted by Whitman. Whitman's debt to Sullivan was repaid by the district attorney's glowing recommendation for him at hearings for his appointment as ambassador to Santo Domingo. Callaghan reinforces the point, having Sullivan state: "[T]he witnesses were all bought and paid for . . . The Rosenthal Case was rigged to gain political popularity for Charles Whitman."[29]

After Becker's first conviction was overturned on appeal, his second trial was handled by W. Bourke Cockran. Like Goff and Sullivan, Cockran was born in Ireland. He immigrated to America and studied law at night. Initially opposed to Tammany, he joined the Wigwam at the urging of Boss Honest John Kelly. His allegiance to Tammany was solidified when he forced the Democratic State convention to place its controversial upstate rival, David B. Hill, as the party's nominee for governor, a move that destroyed Hill's political career and solidified Tammany's power upstate. As congressman, he was a Progressive Democrat, a position which put him occasionally at odds with Tammany boss Charles F. Murphy.[30] Cockran was always close to Big Tim Sullivan. Welch suggests that in his strong efforts to win a reprieve for Becker, he was acting in this regard. Logan asserted

Big Tim made numerous phone calls to Whitman's assistants, asking them to help Becker.[31] If true, it supports Callaghan's contention that Sullivan knew Becker was innocent.[32] Cockran, initially skeptical, was later convinced of Becker's innocence. However, prosecuting District Attorney Charles G. Whitman and State Supreme Court Justice Samuel Seabury refused to take Cockran's arguments seriously. Seabury's reputation as an anti-Tammany reformer was the reason for his selection as judge in the second Becker trial. With his eyes on the prize of an appointment to the Appellate Division of the Supreme Court, Seabury was willing to work in tandem with Whitman to assure Becker's conviction.[33] Cockran's efforts to obtain a change of venue due to the prejudiced atmosphere of the court created by Whitman fell on deaf ears. Cockran, in a rage, said, "This is not a trial but an assassination," leaving his assistant, Martin Manton, to handle the case.[34] Seabury's instructions to the jury were prejudicial to the defense. Despite Manton's objections, after deliberating only four hours, a second guilty verdict was delivered. Governor William Sulzer, also a protégé of Big Tim Sullivan, was allegedly going to pardon Becker, believing him innocent. By the time the court of appeals reversed the decision in the Becker's first trial, Sulzer had been impeached by Tammany Boss Charles Murphy. The impeachment was due in part, to Sulzer's efforts to remain independent of Boss Murphy. But the fact he was sympathetic to Becker's plight suggests Murphy had an additional reason for sabotaging the career of Governor Sulzer. This assertion is more than speculation. Boss Murphy loyalists, Al Smith and Robert Wagner, led the assembly and the Senate in their efforts to oust Sulzer. They were aided and abetted by Tammany lawyer and assemblyman Aaron Levy, attorney for the owners of the getaway car in the Rosenthal murder.[35] Levy was instrumental in getting immunity for his client in exchange for stating his passengers were nowhere near the murder scene.

Lt. Governor Martin Glynn replaced Sulzer, becoming the first Catholic Governor of New York. Initially embraced by Tammany, Glynn committed the same egregious error of his predecessor. He tried to put distance between himself and Boss Murphy. In alliance with fellow reform Democrat Franklin Delano Roosevelt, he was able to secure many appointments to civil service posts. The public had turned against the Tammany machine in the wake of the Sulzer debacle, electing a majority of anti-Tammany candidates to the legislature. One of these was Thomas Mott Osborne, who was made warden of Sing Sing Prison. Osborne, an upstate reform Democrat, had unorthodox ideas about the treatment of prisoners. Sing Sing was where Becker was confined. Osborne became sympathetic to Becker's position. Martin Glynn had replaced the disgraced Sulzer as governor, but Glynn was not reelected in 1914. Instead, he was replaced by the crusading Republican district attorney Charles S. Whitman. The new governor was not about to reverse himself nor show mercy.

Charles Whitman, now governor, visited Sing Sing allegedly to review the reform conditions put in place by Osborne. Within six months, Osborne was indicted on several felonies, one alleging incidents of sodomy with inmates, basically silencing him during Becker's appeal. Osborne spent $75,000 defending himself and was eventually reinstated. It was Osborne who presided at the electrocution of Charles Becker. He sent a bouquet of remembrance to Becker's widow suggesting his compassion for a miscarriage of justice. Osborne later resigned his position as warden to campaign against Whitman's reelection in 1916.[36] Big Tim Sullivan, who may have had doubts about Becker's guilt, may have been suffering from paresis, a degeneration of the brain caused by syphilis, and confined to an asylum.[37]

By the time Martin Manton, Becker's lawyer, delivered his 540-page brief to the court of appeals, Seabury had been appointed to the high court. Although he took no part in the deliberations, the fact of his recent appointment to a fourteen-year term undoubtedly had an impact. Logan suggested the other justices would be loathe to overturn a decision based on their new colleague's alleged judicial misconduct.[38] In 1916, Seabury resigned his seat to run as Democratic candidate for governor, believing he had Progressive Party support. The Progressives, led by Theodore Roosevelt, abandoned him for Republican incumbent Charles Whitman.[39]

Bourke Cochran reentered the case in July 1915, urging before the United States Court that Whitman's dual role as prosecutor and new governor deprived Becker of his constitutional right to an impartial review, that Whitman had inflamed the media against his client, that the real perpetrators had been granted immunity and perjured themselves to win a guilty verdict for Whitman. The court rejected his argument, stating no federal questions were at issue.[40] Whitman, who had been touted as a possible Republican presidential candidate, was not reelected to a third term as governor, the voters instead choosing Tammany favorite, Al Smith. Nor was he chosen as candidate for president, the Republicans instead opting for Charles Evans Hughes. Although the circumstantial evidence suggests otherwise, Charles Murphy denied any ties to the Becker-Rosenthal case, an advocate proclaiming, "No one can just say that there has been any connection between the police and Tammany in the division of such sordid spoils while Murphy is the mortal enemy of the grafting cop, and you have heard little of red lights since he has been at the head of the organization."[41]

Charles Whitman was also the district attorney investigating the Asphalt Trust scandals in New York. At that time, he was also pursuing evidence in the Becker-Rosenthal murder case. His efforts brought to light Tammany corruption of bid-rigging in paving contracts, kickbacks, and illegal contributions to the Democratic Party. One of the major coconspirators was James K. McGuire, longtime associate of James M. Sullivan. Both were eloquent and active speakers on behalf of Democratic candidates. McGuire supported Sullivan's appointment as ambassador to Santo Domingo. McGuire, an agent of the Asphalt Trust, was in Santo Domingo, living with Sullivan at the United States legation, pursuing paving construction contracts. Under indictment for his involvement in corruption, McGuire was later forced to return to New York to answer charges.

As to the Becker case, Whitman was furious at the loss of his chief witness, Rosenthal. He was determined to get Becker. James M. Sullivan, with his ties to Tammany Hall, was a willing coconspirator. He got Rose to confess Becker was the mastermind behind the Rosenthal murder. He also was instrumental in obtaining confessions from the perpetrators who were granted immunity for their perjured testimony. There were some who were close to Big Tim Sullivan who alleged he was murdered in 1913 because, despite his increasing bouts of insanity, he had lucid moments, and it was feared he would testify and clear Becker. By 1914, his death gave Becker the excuse to appeal to Governor Whitman, disclosing Big Tim's role in the Rosenthal case. Whitman was deaf to his appeal for clemency.[42] There is a final touch of irony. The Becker-Rosenthal case undoubtedly launched James M. Sullivan's career as diplomat. It lasted about as long as Becker's two trials and appeals. Becker's execution occurred three weeks after Sullivan was forced to resign his ambassadorial post on July 8, 1915.

Sullivan had essentially sold out. Not only were some ethical issues skirted by Sullivan in the hope of advancing his career, it reveals the nexus of Irish nationalism, Tammany patronage, the naiveté of Wilsonian Caribbean diplomacy, and political corruption. All would come together in Sullivan's appointment and brief tenure as ambassador to Santo Domingo.

Many associated with the Becker-Rosenthal case were tarnished with scandal. There was Boss Charles Murphy, for his role encouraging his henchmen—Max Steuer, Aaron Levy, and James M. Sullivan—protect the name of Big Tim Sullivan, and hence Tammany from any taint of corruption. It failed when his role in the impeachment of Governor William Sulzer became public. The net result was a short-lived decline in Tammany power. John Goff was exposed as a judicial incompetent. Samuel Seabury was equally willing to cozy up to Charles Whitman in Becker's second trial, only this time around, few were paying attention to prosecutorial malfeasance. Whitman became governor and a Republican presidential hopeful. His mediocre record as governor and a fondness for the bottle destroyed his political career. Seabury would have revenge in his commission hearings of the 1930s, exposing Tammany corruption. Goff, like James M. Sullivan, would focus his efforts on Irish nationalism, joining the Friends of Irish Freedom and later its rival, the American Association for Recognition of the Irish Republic. James M. Sullivan would reinvent himself, entering a more active phase as Irish nationalist by forming the Film Company of Ireland in 1916. This is perhaps his most enduring legacy, extending beyond the scandals that marked his life between 1912 and 1915.

End Notes

1   Mary Rose Callaghan, *Emigrant Dreams* (Dublin: Poolbeg Press, 1996), 239.

2   Ibid.

3   "Phelan Reported Sullivan Unfit," *New York Times* (27 July 1915): 5; "Sullivan, James Mark," *National Cyclopedia,* 362; Phelan Report, 6–7; Link, <u>Neutrality</u>, 107; Callaghan, op. cit., 250.

4   Callaghan e-mail to author, 9 October 2002.

5   "McGuire, James K," *National Cyclopedia of American Biography* (1897), 19. Syracuse is in Onondaga County, New York.

6   Phelan Report, 6; Callaghan, op. cit., 238–239, 250; "Murder's Row Gets Harry Thaw," *New York Times* (27 June 1906); "Thaw Mistrial: Jury 7 to 5," *New York Times* (13 April 1907).

7   Andy Logan, *Against the Evidence: The Becker-Rosenthal Affair* (New York: McCall Publishing, 1970), 76.

8   "Work of Strong Arm Squad," *New York Times* (2 September 1911). He was Charles Plitt, a man used by Becker as a press agent. During a raid on a gambling parlor at which Becker was not present, a janitor was killed. Plitt was identified as the murderer. Becker allegedly felt obligated to assist his associate and assessed Rosenthal a $500 fee. Rosenthal refused to pay, and Becker raided Rosenthal's casino, destroying much of the gambler's property. At Becker's first

trial and its immediate aftermath, Plitt supported Becker. He later testified against Becker, receiving financial assistance from District Attorney Charles Whitman. Plitt later reneged his testimony after Becker's second trial; Andy Logan op. cit., 45, 263–64, 300; "State to Call Becker's Aids," *New York Times* (18 May 1914); "Seeks Terms for Becker," *New York Times* (13 July 1914).

9   Callaghan, op. cit., 238–240. Callaghan has her grandfather deny the allegation of the fights being fixed. Ibid, 53.

10 Andy Logan, op.cit.75–77. "May Be Samuel Schepps," *New York Times* (22 July 1912), 99, 123, 125; Callaghan, op. cit., 240.

11 Callaghan, op. cit.,185.

12 Logan, op. cit. 164–165; William Bryk, "Mayor William J. Gaynor, Primitive American," http://nypress.com/mayor-william-j-gaynor-primitve-amercian. Retrieved 30 November 2014.

13 "Commissioner Rhinelander Waldo/Joe Bruno on the Mob," http://wordpress.com/tag/police commissioner-rhinelander-waldo. Retrieved 30 November 2014.

14 Bryk, op. cit. "Commissioner Rhinelander Waldo" op. cit; Sheehan, Artist Direct.com/nad/store/movies/principal/0,,1988 484co.html. Retrieved 30 November 2014.

15 Logan, op. cit., 46 and 160.

16 "Bat Masterson," http://www.history net.com/bat-masterson.html. Retrieved 30 November 2014; Logan, op. cit., 110, 220, 253.

17 "Fitzgerald Getting Well," *New York Times* (16 September 1913); "Fitzgerald Out as Leader," *New York Times* (14 April 1914).

18 Logan, op. cit., 305–306; 308; 308.

19 Richard F. Welch, *King of the Bowery* (Albany: State University Press, 2008), 170–186.

[20] Logan, op. cit., 71, 93, 128, 155.

[21] Callaghan, op. cit. 240; 241; 243.

[22] Logan, op. cit., 197.

[23] "Goff, John William," in Johnson, Allen, and Malone, Dumas, (eds). *Dictionary of American Biography*, Vol. IV (New York: Charles Scribner's and Sons, 1932), 359–360; "Goff, John William,". National Cyclopedia of American Biography. Vol. XV (Ann Arbor: University Microfilms, 1967), 254; Callaghan, op. cit., 241–242, Logan, op. cit., 158.

[24] Logan, op. cit., 159.

[25] Callaghan, op. cit., 242–3, 244, 245; Logan, op. cit., 239, 245.

[26] Logan, op. cit., 99, 128.

[27] Ibid., 269.

[28] Ibid., 180, 251, 260.

[29] Callaghan, op. cit., 242, 244.

[30] "Cockran, William Bourke," (1884–1923) in Johnson and Malone, eds., *Dictionary of American Biography*, vol. 4, op. cit. 1930, 256–257.

[31] Logan, op. cit., 307.

[32] Callaghan, op. cit., 241, 243.

[33] Logan, op. cit., 259–9. Their coziness was replaced with bitter animosity in 1916. Seabury, believing he had Theodore Roosevelt's support, resigned from the bench to run as Democratic candidate for governor. The Republicans and the rump Progressives endorsed Whitman. The campaign degenerated into vicious acrimony on both sides. Whitman won. Seabury would later revenge himself on Tammany by heading an investigation of its activities during the 1930s under the governorship of Franklin D. Roosevelt (Logan, op. cit., 334). The findings forced the resignation of New York City's colorful Tammany mayor,

Jimmy Walker, launched FDR on the path to the presidency, during which FDR forced Tammany candidate Al Smith to the sidelines.

34 Ibid., 86, 307, 154–157, 256–258; Alfred Connable and Edward Silberfarb, *Tigers of Tammany: Nine Men Who Ruled New York* (New York: Holt, Rhinehart, Winston, 1967), 250–252. Manton apparently learned the economic value of judicial corruption. He went on to become a judge of the Federal District Court, and later to the United States Court of Appeals. He was a possible contender for an appointment to the Supreme Court. Unfortunately, Manton was indicted in 1939 for corrupting his judicial office and obstruction of justice. He served two years in federal prison; Logan, op. cit., 332.

35 Ibid., 72, 76, 80; "Summon Levy to Court," *New York Times* (4 November 1913); "Honor Levy at Dinner," *New York Times* (4 December 1913); "Shapiro Clears Up a Point," *New York Times* (7 August 191); William Shapiro was the driver of the murder car.

36 Logan, op. cit., 206, 298, 299, 301, 325, 334.

37 Welch, op. cit., 176–180; Sullivan's mental decline became worse as his financial woes increased. The passing of his estranged wife in 1912 exacerbated his condition, despite efforts by his family to find a cure. No medical report attributes his mental decline to syphilis. Officially his illness was attributed to depression, paranoia, and schizophrenia.

38 Logan, op. cit., 289.

39 "Some Seabury Bias," *New York Times* (7 May 1958).

40 Logan, op. cit., 298.

41 Alex Warn, "Charles Francis Murphy: Human Being," *New York Times* (22 February 1914).

42 Logan, op. cit., 17, 233, 305–307.

CHAPTER III

Envoy Extraordinaire and Minister Plenipotentiary: Sullivan's Sojourn in Santo Domingo

James Mark Sullivan as diplomat, 1873 - 1935
Official Portrait as Minister
to Santo Domingo, 1913 - 1915[*]

[*]   Courtesy of Library of Congress, 1913. catalogue 924.223

The Circumstances Surrounding Sullivan's Diplomatic Appointment

Because of William Jennings Bryans's support for his candidacy at the hotly contested Democratic convention of 1912, following his election, Woodrow Wilson appointed him Secretary of State.

Both men initially worked well together, although Link thought them ignorant, naïve, or uninterested in foreign policy. Both had an obsession with missionary diplomacy, believing it was America's destiny to bring the blessing of peace, prosperity, Christianity, and democracy to its less advantaged neighbors. They worked to reform the State Department and the Foreign Service, "determined to break the custom of rewarding rich contributors" and "worn out politicians" to diplomatic posts abroad.[1] It was a frustrating effort for two reasons: American diplomats were underpaid relative to their foreign counterparts, and they had to maintain a lavish lifestyle on their meager salaries. Obviously, ambassadors had to subsidize their salaries with their own resources. Often the problem was insurmountable. Some appointments continued to be made on the basis of patronage and/or wealth. For example, James Gerard, a Tammany judge appointed to the New York Supreme Court by Boss Charles Murphy, married into a wealthy Irish American family. He contributed $120,000 to the Wilson campaign, which was not officially reported. He was subsequently appointed ambassador to Germany with the backing of Senator James A. O'Gorman, who also endorsed James M. Sullivan for the diplomatic post in Santo Domingo. Gerard was appointed when Wilson's first choice, Henry Fine, a colleague of Wilson's at Princeton, refused for financial reasons.[2]

Bryan sought to purge the Foreign Service, which had begun being "professionalized" under Presidents McKinley and Taft. In part, it was due to his being a spoilsman, but also because he believed the diplomatic corps consisted of either incompetent Republicans and/or a professional elite that was becoming an aristocracy. Wilson shared his views.[3]

Wilson delegated the duties of awarding patronage to his personal secretary, Joseph Tumulty, an Irish Catholic political ally from his days as governor of New Jersey. Frequently, "exigencies of the situation" forced them to overlook the intrinsic merits of the candidate in order to strengthen Wilson forces."[4]

In Santo Domingo, Democratic patronage produced a pattern of inefficiency and corruption that repudiated Wilsonian idealism, resulting in yet another version of dollar diplomacy and military intervention. Tammany wanted Champ Clark as the party standard-bearer and lost; Wilson lost New York State in the election of 1912, and it was possibly thought politically expedient to throw the party regulars some patronage. The first one was not James M. Sullivan but Walker Vick, the man who would reveal Sullivan's "importunities" to Wilson's intimates. When stonewalled, he later went public with his accusations.

Under pressure from both Tumulty and O'Gorman, Bryan dismissed William W. Russell, minister to the Dominican Republic and a Foreign Service veteran since 1895.[5] His replacement was Walker W. Vick, a New Jersey Democrat and assistant to William McCombs, head of the Democratic National Committee during

William Jennings Bryan (1860-1925)
Secretary of State 1913-1915[*]

[*] Courtesy, Library of Congress (LC 2016864425)

the Wilson campaign. He had not only McCombs's support but that of Colonel Edward M. House, a Texas Democrat, Wilson's chief deputy and most intimate advisor; Dan Fellows Platt, an archaeologist, mayor of Englewood, New Jersey, and delegate to the 1912 Democrat convention;[6] Joseph E. Davies, a Wisconsin Democrat and head of Wilson's western campaign;[7] and Homer Cummings, coordinator of the Democratic Speakers Bureau in the election of 1912. Joseph Tumulty was adamant in supporting Vick's appointment as receiver of customs in Santo Domingo. Vick had thought he would get Tumulty's job, and he needed to be rewarded. Vick's memos, outlining problems in Santo Domingo, were later made public. They would haunt the Wilson administration in the wake of the exposure of policies pursued by yet another patronage diplomatic appointee, James M. Sullivan.

The Phelan Report states that soon after the election of 1912, James M. Sullivan sought public office. "Under the direction and leadership of James K. McGuire, Mr. Sullivan was on guard to prevent Mr. Wilson from losing any Irish-American votes through misrepresentation." Sullivan first sought to be a United States district attorney in New York, but influenced by men who wanted a minister to Santo Domingo friendly to their interests, he applied for the position in May 1913, was appointed in July, confirmed in August, and arrived at his post in September 1913.[8] Some choices for ministers and ambassadors were no better or worse than in previous administrations, but the choice of James M. Sullivan would prove an embarrassment. According to the Phelan Report, Sullivan admitted his lack of diplomatic experience could be problematic given the dynamics of the country's politics. The Report also noted his inability to speak Spanish. Sullivan's stated purpose in obtaining the position: "I was anxious to secure this post for the purpose of getting even by means of the good salary that goes with the place."[9] Sullivan became a key agent importing the Tammany model of malfeasance onto an already corrupt Dominican political system. His words and actions reveal he was obviously using this position for self-promotion. Nonetheless, "the exigencies of the situation" won him the appointment.

Sullivan had powerful friends on his side. For example, Republican district attorney Charles Whitman endorsed him as a reward for his assistance in the Becker-Rosenthal case, calling Sullivan "honorable, upright and reliable," a man whose behavior was "professional and commendable."[10] So too did Judge Gray of Delaware, who believed Sullivan's efforts among Catholic voters should be rewarded. Gray was also attorney for the Banco Nacional, a point relevant insofar as Sullivan's activities on its behalf in Santo Domingo are concerned. Gray was also reportedly a good friend of Secretary of State Bryan.[11]

Other Yale alumni rushed to support one of their own. They included New York senator and Tammany loyalist James A. O'Gorman,[12] and Simeon Baldwin, professor at Yale Law School, founder and president of the American Bar Association, and a presiding Connecticut Supreme Court Justice.[13] There was also Homer Cummings, coordinator of the Democratic Speakers Bureau for the election of 1912. Undoubtedly, it was in that context Cummings[14] knew of Sullivan's efforts on behalf of Democrats.

President Wilson's personal secretary, Joseph Tumulty, was initially reluctant to endorse Sullivan because of the sordid aspects of the Becker-Rosenthal case, but he too fell in line after being pressured by New Jersey congressman James Hamill.[15] Hamill and Tumulty had both attended St. Peter's College in Jersey City, and the two worked together to promote Woodrow Wilson as governor after he resigned the presidency of Princeton. Link states Tumulty too was a friend of Sullivan.[16]

Even Secretary of State Bryan had reservations about Sullivan's appointment, but pressure by Tumulty forced his hand.[17]

According to Blum, Tumulty used a "fine clean-cut Irishman, who stood high in the ranks of the Clan na Gael to enlist Irish support for the Wilson campaign."[18] While unnamed, the description fits James K. McGuire, who, at that time, was a prominent member of the Democratic Party and a key figure in the Clan. McGuire was also a prolific speaker for the Democratic Party, had been member of a commission, along with James G. McAdoo and James A. O'Gorman, which encouraged Irish Catholic support for Wilson's election. Letters on file in the Bancroft Library from McGuire to James D. Phelan one month prior to the election of 1912 requested names of fifty Catholic citizens willing to become involved in the Wilson campaign. Phelan apparently responded, for which he received a note thanking him for his efforts on behalf of the Democratic victory.[19] McGuire also sent out thousands of letters to Irish organizations endorsing Wilson. He put forward suggestions for various cabinet positions, praising Wilson's selections of Joseph Tumulty as his personal secretary and Joseph Burke as United States treasurer.[20] Hence, it is no wonder his counsel was listened to when he endorsed Sullivan as ambassador to Santo Domingo.

There were some critics who referred to Sullivan's "unsuitability" and shady background as reason for his exclusion. One was J. H. McBride, managing editor of the *New York Daily News*, who openly questioned Sullivan's qualifications.

> Can we have endorsement [sic] of Irish-Americans? Will he have support of the Catholic Church? It is hard for me to understand the slight recognition of 15 million Catholics received from the Administration, but to appoint a man like Sullivan's is adding insult to injury.[21]

In addition, Sutton notes the opposition of Wilson's treasury secretary and later son-in-law, William Gibbs McAdoo. McAdoo had been vice chairman of the Democratic National Committee and may have been privy to some of the rumors associated with Sullivan's character. With all the innuendo flying about relative to Sullivan's qualifications, it was obviously imperative to have positive letters of endorsement for his candidacy in order to obtain vital Congressional support. James McGuiness, former assistant superintendent of Railway Mail Services, initially lined up to support Sullivan but later refused given the persistent rumors as to Sullivan's character.

McGuiness may have had another agenda. He had prior acquaintance with William C. Beer, one of the major supporters of Sullivan's nomination for ambassador to Santo Domingo. Beer had allegedly made promises of lucrative jobs to McGuiness, which never came to fruition. According to the Phelan Report, Sullivan had been an acquaintance of Beer since 1904, had received some legal business from him, and had several conversations with Beer prior to his appointment. Sullivan admitted as much in his application for the position. Supposedly Beer, McGuiness, and Sullivan encouraged Theodore Roosevelt's postmaster general, George Cortelyou, to push for the Republican nomination for vice president with William Howard Taft in the election of 1908. The boomlet was short-lived. Cortelyou angered the Republican establishment, and he was ousted after Taft was elected. The incident is relevant insofar as it ties Sullivan to Beer five years prior to his seeking the diplomatic post in 1913. In the first place, it suggests that Sullivan's Democratic Party identification was opportunistic, especially in light of the fact Sullivan knew William J. Bryan, the Democratic nominee, when he first ran for president in 1896. This may be why Bryan was initially suspicious of Sullivan. According to Sutton, Sullivan was actively involved in campaigning for William Howard Taft, the Republican candidate in 1908. Failing that, he turned to the Democrats and worked to secure Irish votes in 1912.[22] It was in this context that Sullivan became acquainted with James K. McGuire. McGuiness reported back that Sullivan had been seen drunk in Buffalo and in Washington, DC, had pawned a friend's watch, and had forged a check. According to McGuiness, it was these allegations of criminality against Sullivan that made the forces endorsing him line up and swear to his good character.[23] If accurate, these allegations did not augur well for Sullivan's diplomatic career.

Sumner Welles, Harvard graduate and a career diplomat, was a specialist in Latin American affairs, was fluent in Spanish, who served as special commissioner to the Dominican Republic, 1923–1926. His insight into James M. Sullivan's stay in the Caribbean nation is relevant, although written in hindsight.

> It was, however, in the selection of the new minister the Dominican Republic, in the person of James Mark Sullivan, that a far greater error had been committed by Secretary Bryan, and one of deplorable consequences both to the Dominican Republic and to the United States. With the exception of Mexico, there is no other post in Latin America where there is more urgently needed at that moment, an American diplomatic representative capacitated by experience, appreciation of the manner in which the interest of the Dominican People might be identified with the interest of the American people . . . The President required . . . at least, a representative capable of understanding that policy . . .

Mr. Sullivan, whose previous career had been limited to various activities in ward politics possessed not one of those qualifications.[24]

George Harvey also condemned numerous appointees made by Bryan, referring to the lot as "aged party hacks. A clearer case of partisan political debauchery cannot be imagined."[25] According to Blum, Vick, Tumulty, and Sullivan initially cooperated to make Santo Domingo "a repository of New Jersey worthies recommended by Senator William Hughes, an Irish-born, Spanish-American War veteran, Democratic lawyer, judge and New Jersey Congressman."[26] Another Jersey congressman, Scottish-born journalist and Spanish-American War veteran Robert Bremner, was part of that inner circle,[27] along with James Hamill and Chancellor Edwin Robert Walker, chief justice of the New Jersey Supreme Court.[28]

The critic's efforts came to naught. Sullivan was appointed. Upon his confirmation, he hastened to Syracuse, New York, to thank former mayor, Democratic colleague, and fellow Irish nationalist James K. McGuire for his support, the mayor taking time away from a family vacation at his in-laws home for the occasion.[29] Given what was to be exposed in a subsequent investigation, since they visited for a "few hours," it might be justifiably assumed more than compliments were exchanged.

A key figure behind the scenes to obtain the appointment of James M. Sullivan was William C. Beer, a lawyer and lobbyist for Samuel M. Jarvis. Beer had known Sullivan since 1904 and had sent him several clients. Jarvis was an Illinois-born lawyer and banker who moved to New York City in 1893, where he formed the North American Trust Company, a bank specializing in real estate and capital development projects. During the Spanish-American War, he realized the investment potential of the Caribbean. Under the McKinley administration, his bank was the repository for funds of the Cuban and United States governments. Hence, he was well positioned to take advantage of opportunities as they arose in Santo Domingo. From the outset, Jarvis's goal was to obtain control of Dominican customs revenues in order to finance millions of dollars in capital improvements. Had Jarvis been awarded the contracts, Sullivan was allegedly to receive $100,000.[30]

Jarvis may have been influenced by his contemporary Roger Farnham, a vice president of the National City Bank, whose maneuvers in the neighboring country of Haiti were known in the banking community. Given that American diplomats with limited experience were appointed to sensitive posts in the Caribbean, the State Department often had to rely on a variety of sources for information when trying to formulate a coherent policy for the countries involved. Farnham, with numerous business interests in Haiti, was one such individual. Farnham was also politically connected.

One of his contacts was Boas W. Long, the new chief of the Latin American Affairs Division, whose foreign policy mind-set was pragmatic and protective of American capitalism.[31] Long was, as were other diplomatic appointees, one of Bryan's "deserving Democrats." According to the Phelan Report, Long was also a friend of James M. Sullivan.[32] Long's only qualifications for the job were that his business had a branch office on Mexico City and that he had intimate connections with Wall Street.[33] It was Long who, in collusion with Roger Farnham, encouraged American intervention in Haiti. It is interesting to note in light of what happened to James M. Sullivan that Long later became minister to El Salvador, where his close ties to the United Fruit Company were the subject of an investigation by the Senate Foreign Relations Committee in 1914.[34] Farnham was partner with William R. Grace, the Irish-born shipping magnate, who had numerous business interests in

Latin America. Grace essentially controlled the finances of Peru by securing a loan to finance the country's debt in return for obtaining business concessions from the government. Nicknamed the Pirate of Peru, Grace expanded his operations into other Latin American countries.[35] In order to put Haitian finances in order, Farnham got John A. McIlheny appointed as economic adviser to the Haitian government. McIlheny was a Louisiana-born businessman, veteran, and a Democratic member of the Louisiana legislature. He was also heir to a tabasco sauce fortune.[36] None of this, however, fitted him for the office as financial advisor to the Haitian government. By withholding salaries of key government officials, he put pressure on them to give City Bank a virtual monopoly on the financial affairs of the country. Ultimately, Farnham had the United States intervene in Haiti, obtain its currency reserves, and have them placed in the vaults of National City Bank in New York. This was allegedly[37] because the government of Haiti posed threats to American interests there. Thus precedents had been set in Haiti for both political and financial intervention. James M. Sullivan's role was similarly pivotal for causing American intervention in Santo Domingo.

Sullivan and Scandals in Santo Domingo

B oth Wilson and Bryan were largely ignorant of events in the small Caribbean countries whose location near the Panama Canal made them assume a strategic importance in American foreign policy, especially as the nation drifted toward war. According to Link, Bryan initially believed Sullivan had integrity and considered his Catholic faith a plus for this strategic Caribbean country. Bryan later admitted he had been "deceived as to the interests supporting Mr. Sullivan's candidacy."[38] Wilson and Bryan reversed the policies of Republican predecessors Mckinley and Taft, who sought to professionalize the Foreign Service. Bryan dismissed many who had earned their posts by merit and training, replacing them with candidates whose only virtue had been loyalty to the Democratic Party. This was especially true in the case of Santo Domingo. Under pressure from Tumulty and O'Gorman, Bryan dismissed veteran Walter W. Russell, a Republican, a former naval officer, engineer, and career diplomat since the 1890s.[39] His replacement was James M. Sullivan. The agent put in charge of Dominican customs revenues was Walker W. Vick, a New Jersey Democrat and former assistant to William Mccombs, head of the Democratic National Committee. Vick thought he would be appointed secretary to the president, but Tumulty got the job.[40] It was to Vick that Secretary Bryan wrote the infamous memo requesting information as to the number of subordinate positions available to the receiver of customs in Santo Domingo:

> Can you let me know what positions you have at your disposal with which to reward deserving Democrats? . . . You have had enough experience in politics to know how valuable workers are when the campaign is on and how difficult it is to find suitable rewards for all the deserving.[41]

The note would come back to haunt Wilson when the scandals surrounding Sullivan became public. When it was translated into Spanish in the Dominican Republic, it caused a furor.[42] Thus had an experienced diplomat been sacrificed on the altar of political expediency. If ever a diplomatic post needed an experienced, professional appointment, it was Santo Domingo.

The country had a long, chaotic history marked by the dramatic failure of self-government and democracy. For example, there were nineteen constitutions promulgated between 1844 and 1918. Of forty-three presidents, only three completed their terms; the others were either killed, deposed, or resigned. There had been twenty-three revolutions in the territory since 1844. Its leaders' plans for development meant borrowing large sums from foreign investors. Continued chaos meant debt payments were often in arrears. The loans were secured by payments from customs duties. In the past, failure to pay debts had been an excuse for foreign creditor nations to seize control of the debtor country. John Bassett Moore, lawyer, scholar, and assistant secretary of state under McKinley, noted the precedent was set by Britain when it took over Egypt and the strategic Suez Canal.[43] According to the *Dictionary of American Biography*, it was Judge Gray of Delaware who encouraged Moore to enter the diplomatic service. This was the same Judge Gray who was lawyer for Banco Nacional, a major player in the Democratic Party, and a key spokesperson for the appointment of James M. Sullivan as ambassador to Santo Domingo.

Given its political instability, the Dominican Republic fell behind in its payments. President Theodore Roosevelt was concerned that a rival European country would use this as a pretext for intervention in Santo Domingo. He was also anxious to defend the access routes to the Panama Canal, then under construction. Hence the Roosevelt Corollary to the Monroe Doctrine. The result was that 55 percent of Dominican customs receipts were placed in a New York bank.[44] Numerous American businessmen had also pressured Roosevelt to intervene since the continued chaos threatened their extensive property holdings. Relative stability prevailed in Santo Domingo from 1905 to 1911 under the leadership of General Ramon Caceres, who undertook a series of internal improvements. His land reform program, however, allowed foreign sugar companies to obtain large landholdings.[45] Caceres's assassination in 1911 plunged the country once again into political and fiscal chaos. Suppressing rebellions destroyed the government surplus, incurring a debt of $1,500,000. In the name of peace and stability, the United States dispatched a contingent of marines, forcing the provisional president to resign by threatening to withhold customs revenues unless he accepted a government selected by the United States.[46] In the interim, the Dominican Congress elected General Jose Bordas Valdez as provisional president for a one-year term.

With its history of constant rebellion, political turmoil, and increased indebtedness, Wilson and Bryan placed a naive and unprepared patronage appointee in an extremely difficult position. Subsequent events would tarnish Bryan, Wilson, and Sullivan, embroiling his administration in a diplomatic and political scandal that played itself out in the media. Almost from the beginning, there were rumors of Sullivan's unfitness for the job. The first scandal involved Jarvis's Banco Nacional Santo Domingo. According to Schonreich, the bank was incorporated by Americans in 1909 with a working capital of $500,000. It opened formally in 1912 during a four-way campaign for president, during which the Irish vote was considered critical. According to Knight, the bank's goal from the start was to obtain the lucrative customs receivership from Santiago Michelena.[47] Recall that many of Sullivan's supporters were confidantes and agents of Jarvis's Banco Nacional. Jarvis's concern for obtaining a "friendly" ambassador predate Sullivan's appointment and had been a subject of diplomatic correspondence in Foreign Relations for at least a year. There were two banks contesting for control of Dominican customs revenues—Jarvis's Banco Nacional and Santiago Michelena, an agent for the National City Bank, who had transmitted customs revenues to the United States since the negotiation of the Roosevelt Corollary in 1905.[48]

Mitchell apparently regarded Michelena as a foreign interloper and believed the financial incentives belonged to American banks. Unfortunately, his logic was incorrect. As a result of the Spanish-American War, nationals of Puerto Rico were now American citizens, and Michelena, as such, was entitled to protection under the United States Constitution.[49] The dispatches questioned which bank was to be the sole repository. Initially the contract was awarded to Michelana and National City Bank. Payments on a $1.5 million loan would be $30,000 per month from the country's customs receipts, an amount equal to deducting 20 percent of the Dominican government's operating expenses. According to Knight, the negotiated loan lacked about $450,000 to cover the government's existing deficit.[50] The contract stipulated the interest on the loan was 7 percent. Jarvis contended National City Bank would be paid more than the contract amount, and it was therefore illegal. An investigation by the State Department found both banks had submitted proposals within the stipulated requirements, but the rates submitted by National City Bank were more favorable, and since the Dominican government had chosen National City Bank, it saw no reason to interfere in the matter.[51]

In addition, William Beer, Jarvis's agent for Banco Nacional, charged that William T. S. Doyle, a member of the Taft Commission, sent with a detachment of the U.S. Marines to resolve the factional warfare in the wake of the assassination of President Caceres, was in the pay of the National City Bank.[52] In fact, the real villain may have been George R. Colton, former head of the Dominican Customs Service, a previous governor of Puerto Rico, and after 1913, a "key member of the Foreign Trade Department of National City Bank."[53] Hence, Jarvis had valid reasons to the suspect machinations of the money trust in Santo Domingo. These suspicions were shared by Secretary of State Bryan,[54] who dismissed Doyle and for a time came under the influence of Jarvis and the Banco Nacional.

Apparently, Jarvis had not given up in his efforts to secure control of Dominican customs revenues, especially in light of events in Haiti noted previously. He saw his chance with a new-elected Democratic administration, especially in its purging of the veteran diplomatic corps in favor of patronage appointees. Hence, Jarvis agent William Beer's enthusiastic marshaling of support for the appointment of his acquaintance James Mark Sullivan as ambassador to Santo Domingo. Allegedly, Banco Nacional President, Frank Mitchell, boasted he knew Sullivan would be appointed minister, and there would be a general house-cleaning in Santo Domingo as a result.[55] Following Sullivan's appointment as ambassador, both he and Mitchell were frequent visitors. Apparently, the meetings bore fruit. By November 1913, the accounts were transferred to Banco Nacional.[56]

José Bordas Valdez
(1874-1965)*
Provisional President of Santo Domingo, 1913-1914

* (public domain) http://www.agn.gov/do/

Sullivan was apparently complicit in the Banco Nacional scandal. As a subsequent investigation unfolded, the *New York Times* reported he was to receive $100,000 when Jarvis's bank was awarded the contract. In addition, the Banco Nacional was to use the revenues from the customs receipts to finance $100 million in contracts for infrastructure improvement. These two issues are integral to understanding Sullivan's commitment to the Banco Nacional, his political cronies whom he encouraged to submit bids for internal improvements, and his close ties to the Bordas Valdes government and its successor under Juan Isidro Jimenez. Collectively, these issues played no small role in the demise of his diplomatic career.

Sullivan did not speak Spanish. He often used the Jarvis bank for his downtown office and its personnel as his interpreters. A Jarvis crony was made the bank's purchasing agent in New York. The Dominican minister of Foreign Relations, Eliseo Grullon, was uncle to Henry Niese, cofounder with Jarvis of the Banco Nacional.[57] Judge George Gray, prominent Delaware Democrat, close friend of Secretary Bryan, was also attorney for Banco Nacional.

What is certain is that as of February 18, 1913, the agent of the National City Bank, Santiago Michelena, was unwilling to extend credit to the Dominican government until the financial situation was clarified,[58] despite the Dominican government's acceptance of the contract provisions. An interesting addition to the contract stated such cash disbursements had to be countersigned by the minister or secretary of the legation in the Dominican Republic and by a person designated by the receiver of customs.[59] Thus the stage was set for two new patronage appointees of the incoming Wilson administration to be at odds with each other regarding the dispersal of cash to the chaotic Dominican government.

One of the major problems facing Sullivan in his new position was the payment of back salaries to Dominican officials. Apparently, there was a request by Santo Domingo for a loan of $356,000 for that purpose. The United States State Department questioned whether those sums were diverted to pay off the costs of uprisings in September and October 1913. Sullivan urged a quick payment so as to maintain political stability. An advance of $20,000 was authorized, the funds to come from customs revenues.[60] To obtain an additional loan from a foreign bank, the Dominican government agreed to give greater powers of financial oversight to the "minister of the United States."[61] Grullon, remember, was the Dominican minister of Foreign Relations and uncle to Henry Niese, a cofounder of the Banco Nacional. Hence Link's assertion that Sullivan entered into some kind of alliance with then president Bordas Valdes's government.[62] Secretary of State Bryan indicated a temporary loan of $20,000 was to be secured from Banco Nacional.[63] A hint of concern on the part of Bryan as to Sullivan's actions was noted in a communication of January 18, 1914, which stated, in part, "Whenever in doubt consult Department before taking action. Keep us informed as to all issues raised between parties."[64] Banco Nacional had apparently wanted greater control over customs revenues. Sullivan encouraged the State Department to allow this so as to prevent further chaos in Santo Domingo, pleading its necessity so as to stabilize Bordas Valdes's government.[65]

Obviously, the American minister was working in tandem with the current Dominican government and the Banco Nacional. The problem for Sullivan was that he had tied himself and the United States to a sinking ship of state. Bordas Valdes's increased efforts to maintain himself in power beyond his mandate as provisional president made him increasingly unpopular at home, aroused discontent in the Dominican Congress, and once again raised the specter of revolution.

Desiderio Arias
(1872-1931)[*]
Dominican soldier, Caudillo

_____

[*]   (public domain) www.wikipedia.org.Q5804174

Government Investigations I: The Election Commissioners

D espite opposition from many in the Dominican Congress, Sullivan supported the interim incumbent, Jose Bordas Valdes, who in turn attacked and persecuted his rivals, especially Desiderio Arias, an outspoken opponent of American intervention.[66] This, despite American insistence on free, fair elections. Sullivan's suggestion to have agents in place to assure democratic procedures was approved by Secretary of State Bryan, a proposal that met with hostility from the Dominican government.[67] A flurry of diplomatic correspondence followed between Sullivan, Bryan, and representatives of the Dominican government. The net result of this pressure was the submission under protest of the Dominican government to America's demands.[68] Sullivan communicated the elections, for the most part, were held in an "orderly manner." Special elections were held in provinces where the results were in dispute. Evidence of the fairness of the results was the fact that, despite some harassment by Dominican government officials, a majority of opposition members were elected.[69] Despite evidence of plots and rumors of revolutionary discontent, Sullivan continued to claim the political climate in Santo Domingo was tranquil.[70] The report of the election commissioners endorsed Sullivan's efforts in peacefully resolving the elections of December 1913. Sullivan apparently still had solid support from the administration.

The American Commissioners' warm support of Sullivan's efforts may not have accurately reflected the true state of affairs. According to their own statements, they were briefed by Sullivan before dispersing observers to their various posts. They were also accorded "most courteous attention" by Senior Grullon accompanied by Minister Sullivan and were subsequently received by the Dominican president, Bordas Valdes. Upon completion of the mission, they reported the president and his cabinet admitted the commissioners had shown themselves to be "true friends both to the Government and to the opposition." Behind the diplomatic niceties lay the fact that Grullon was a supporter of Banco Nacional, as was Bordas Valdes, the bank whose president was so influential in obtaining Sullivan's appointment as ambassador. Thus, there is the distinct impression the commissioners were given "a guided tour," which may have sheltered them from the unpleasant truths of numerous electoral irregularities. This observation is reinforced by the fact Knight reported Bordas Valdes supporters broke up peaceful meetings of opposition parties. The government used force on several occasions, resulting in the loss of life and serious destruction of property, incurring an additional debt of over $500,000 as a result of the violence of the preceding months.[71] The remarks of the commissioners served Sullivan well initially, but rumors of his alleged misconduct continued to surface.

The opposition elected seventeen of twenty-four delegates to the Constitutional Convention, making Bordas Valdes a leader without much of a following. This was taken at face value the election results were fair and unbiased despite evidence to the contrary. Nonetheless, monies were advanced to the government by Walker Vick under orders from Secretary Bryan at the urging of Minister Sullivan.[72] In return, the Dominican government pledged not to imprison its opponents without due process, a tacit admission as to electoral irregularities. Most importantly, it pledged to place control of its expenditures under the supervision of the American legation.[73] With Bordas Valdes still serving as president, and the Constitutional Convention in process, these concessions were urged by Sullivan as props to his allies, Bordas Valdes and Grullon, the latter guaranteeing control of Dominican finances to American supervision. Note also, during these crises, the Banco Nacional was still the official receiver of Dominican customs revenue. Sullivan urged the Banco Nacional advance funds to the Dominican government, backed by support from the State Department and the receiver of customs.[74]

All was apparently going to plan, but it was essential that Bordas Valdes consolidate power. Unfortunately, the spoiler was Walker Vick, who continued to relay critical reports to Washington, despite Bryan's belief the two would be able to work harmoniously together. Vick, like Sullivan, was not specially trained for his task and, like Sullivan, was a patronage appointee who replaced a more experienced and specially trained diplomat. Nonetheless, as Vick became more cognizant of the conditions at the embassy and the policies of Sullivan, he began to leak information to his superiors in Washington, but Bryan, Wilson, Tumulty, and House refused to investigate or recall Sullivan for over a year.[75] According to Sutton, Wilson and Bryan were using standard damage control techniques of "denial, suppression and press manipulation," hoping such measures would make the issues "fade from the public consciousness."[76] The fact that Sullivan's efforts were praised by an independent commission of veteran diplomats undoubtedly gave him initial credibility with Bryan and his superiors in the State Department. In their official report, the commissioners noted the following:

> The most pleasant and cordial relations with Mr. Sullivan the American Minister, and we desire to express in the most emphatic terms our admiration for his handling of the critical political situation. Under the most difficult circumstances he has maintained friendly relations with the Dominican officials and with the leading members of the opposition. He has shown great tact, skill and resourcefulness and has accomplished a great deal in a practical way towards securing a fair election, prevailing on both sides to carry out their promises and abide by orderly process. During a time of great excitement and partisan bitterness he succeeded in accomplishing definite results and at the same time admirably avoided giving any pretext for criticism to either side.[77]

Sullivan reciprocated the praise of the American Commissioners in his official reply to Secretary Bryan.[78] This was undoubtedly the reason why Vick's allegations were initially dismissed by his superiors.

Nonetheless, one result of Vick's persistence was the return of customs receipts to the National City Bank by May 1914.

This came about as a result of Vick's continued investigations of Banco Nacional's finances. Suspicious as to its fiscal reliability, Vick demanded a security bond of $100,000, which it could not deliver. Sullivan intervened on behalf of his client, urging an extension, but nothing came of it. Essentially, the Banco Nacional's only working capital were the funds from the customs receipts. The issue was discussed by Bryan, Judge Gray, and Frank McIntyre, the latter an Alabama Democrat, career diplomat, and head of the Bureau of Insular Affairs, after Vick had once more communicated his concerns to his superiors.[79] Despite protests from Minister Sullivan, the Dominican government, and Banco Nacional, the funds were returned to control of National City Bank.[80]

Government Investigations II:
The Phelan Report

Following the reassignment of customs receipts to National City Bank, the State Department sent a special counsel to review the situation.

Sullivan allegedly tried to bribe the investigator with the promise of "more lucrative employment as the bank president's attorney." The Phelan Report later condemned the ambassador's behavior, concluding he was unfit for the post.

> I am not satisfied beyond a reasonable doubt that Mr. Sullivan fully realized the grossness of the impropriety of his position, but I am satisfied because of his proposition that he is not a proper person to hold the position that he does hold.[81]

Vick's leaking of Sullivan's machinations to Bryan, Tumulty, and McCombs had thus far produced only some mild warnings from Secretary of War Lindley Garrison and Secretary of State Bryan and Presidential Secretary Joseph Tumulty. However, by December 1913, other elements of Sullivan's behavior became public. The *New York Times* published reports of his Irish nationalist associate and ardent supporter James K. McGuire being in Santo Domingo to obtain business concessions.[82] This opened the door to other charges leveled against Sullivan during his tenure as minister. According to the Phelan Report, McGuire had written to Sullivan soon after his appointment, inquiring as to contracts and concessions. At that time, McGuire was an agent for the Barber Asphalt Company. The roads of Santo Domingo were virtually nonexistent, and obtaining a paving contract would have been extremely lucrative. McGuire stayed at the legation for a week and made a $600,000 proposal to the Dominican government, but nothing came of it. McGuire admitted that Sullivan's position as ambassador made him "more willing to go to Santo Domingo than otherwise."[83] The fact that McGuire returned empty-handed was probably due to the fact he was under indictment for bribery and extortion in the New York State Asphalt Trust scandals. This was the first crisis as to inappropriate concession rigging that Sullivan had to weather. These charges resulted in a brief investigation by the *New York Times* in December 1913. Not unexpectedly, one of Sullivan's key defenders was James K. McGuire, who reported that everyone from President Bordas Valdes on down had nothing but praise for Sullivan's efforts. The *Times* story noted two discrepancies between this statement and one made a week earlier. For one, McGuire said that Sullivan initiated the correspondence as to public works projects and that he stayed at the legation as there was no fit hotel. Secretary of State Bryan, the discrepancies notwithstanding, used McGuire's second statement to defend his appointment of Sullivan. "The letter just reivd [sic] from Mr. McGuir [sic] show (t)he unfairness and injustice of the criticism which has been directed against Minister Sullivan on account of Mr. McGuire's visit to Santo Domingo."[84] Both McGuire and Bryan, having advocated for the appointment of Sullivan in the first place, were obviously defending their choice as minister. It also suggests there was not only a cozy alliance between some members of the Wilson cabinet but between Sullivan and the Bordas Valdes government as well. Aside from a mild warning from Bryan, "the first whiff of scandal soon dissipated, and no congressional reaction resulted."[85] There is some irony to the situation in that Bryan gave credibility to McGuire's testimony even as he was under indictment for soliciting bribes in the New York State Asphalt Trust paving scandals. In addition, one of the witnesses called to defend Sullivan was Bald Jack Rose, Sullivan's client in the Becker-Rosenthal case. That a convicted felon, perjurer, murderer, and general low-life was used as a character witness by Sullivan in itself should have raised concerns.[86]

Other Sullivan associates were also drawn in. Tim Sullivan, his cousin, was involved in several projects for which he had neither the capital nor the experience.[87] Lee Sisson was head of the Sisson Construction Company, a front company organized by special interests, who obtained Sullivan's appointment as minister for the express purpose of obtaining contracts in Santo Domingo. Further, Lee Sisson testified that

> [James M.] Sullivan brought him [Tim Sullivan] down here to get public works contracts . . . O'Neil, Sullivan's brother-in-law, is coming and we must take him and Timothy J. Sullivan and James M. Sullivan himself onto the company and pay the minster five or ten percent interest in the company, as he can throw contracts at us.[88]

Other businessmen were told in order to obtain contracts, a bribe of $5,000 was a prerequisite. Tim Sullivan said later he and McGuire went to Santo Domingo at James M. Sullivan's "invitation" because "the pickings were good and he wanted to keep it all in the family."[89]

Tim Sullivan was to be rewarded for paying for the ambassador's Yale education by being awarded several construction projects. The ambassador allegedly said, "Tim, I always told you I'd make good. How'd you like to go to Santo Domingo and make a bunch of money? . . . I'm going to be appointed minister down there and you can be the head of a $20 million dollar firm, if you will. It may be last chance to help you, Tim and I've got four years at least to work on. I'm going to clean up all I can."[90] The Phelan Report states James M. Sullivan offered his cousin Tim Sullivan the position of director of Public Works in Santo Domingo if he wanted it.[91] The importance of this position for awarding contracts with its attendant graft and patronage cannot be understated. According to Tim Sullivan, James M. Sullivan, the ambassador, was to receive a percentage of the profits from all contracts awarded to McGuire and that he, Tim Sullivan, was to see that the minister "got his bit." The bank that facilitated the scheme was the Banco Nacional, supposedly "solid" with Secretary of State William J. Bryan. Bryan had in fact removed Russell, allegedly because the experienced Republican diplomat favored National City Bank.[92]

Tim Sullivan allegedly received a loan from Banco Nacional through the influence of his cousin, the American minister, who endorsed the note. Part of the quid pro quo was the note would never have to be repaid as the amount would be part of the Minister's "rake-off." Assuming the scheme went through, James M. Sullivan's cut was to be $100,000. Boston businessman James Byrne, in Santo Domingo to build a power plant, was told by Tim Sullivan that James K. McGuire of New York was the contractor for the job. Any work he obtained would have to share a percentage of the profits with Sullivan.[93] Many of these charges were relayed to Sullivan's superiors as early as December 1913 by the receiver of customs, Walker Vick, but his warnings fell on deaf ears. The Wilson administration was obviously still in denial, but a hint of scandal was in the air.

Senator James Duval Phelan (1861-1930)[*]

[*]   courtesy San Francisco Examiner, 31 December 1899 (public domain)

The situation worsened as time went on. By January 1914, Bryan became apparently more concerned as to events in Santo Domingo. According to Kaplan, he wrote to "his favorite minister on the Caribbean, Sullivan," urging the Bordas Valdes government alter its constitution, allowing greater United States interference in Dominican affairs.[94] Apparently, Wilson and Bryan were blinded by their zealous advocacy of "missionary diplomacy," whereby the blessings of democracy would be imported to Caribbean nations whether they wanted them or not. Bordas Valdes, under financial duress, had little option but to accede to U.S. demands that it have an American overseer as financial adviser.

The temporary truce between Bordas Valdes and political rival, Desiderio Arias, began to unravel over issues of patronage and Arias's belief that an American financial adviser was a violation of Dominican sovereignty.[95] Arias, as noted, was a supporter of Juan Isidro Jimenez, a former president of Santo Domingo at the turn of the century. Jimenez had a history of flirtation with imperial Germany, which was actively trying to acquire territories in the Caribbean.[96] Arias instigated a revolution that was condemned by Minister Sullivan, who urged United States military intervention to assist the beleaguered Bordas Valdes. Bryan, fearful for the security of American lives and property, sent two gunboats.[97] Discussions between the parties failed as Bordas Valdes held fraudulent elections, winning in three-quarters of Santo Domingo's provinces, declaring himself winner and hence de jure president.[98] Sullivan refused any concessions to Arias, and the revolution spread. The American minister was summoned to Washington, where he advocated military intervention, a point neither Bryan nor Wilson were willing to consider yet. The result of the discussions was the creation of the Wilson Plan, the full details of which are documented in *Foreign Relations*.[99] The plan forced Bordas Valdes to resign and free, fair elections be held under an interim president. If fraud was evident, the United States would not accord it diplomatic recognition, and new elections would be called. Sullivan, accompanied by James F. Fort and Charles C. Smith, returned to Santo Domingo in August 1914. Thus, the minister's authority was superseded in August 1914 by a commission of which he was member, but of which someone else was in charge.[100] Bordas Valdes initially refused to resign his position, but the Fort Commission forced his hand, and all parties agreed to hold elections by October 1914. Fort, Smith, and Sullivan declared the results fair, and in December 1914, previous President Juan Isidro Jimenez was installed once again.[101] Bryan, flush with victory, insisted the new government honor prior commitments from Bordas Valdes, especially the powers given to the new American Controller of Finances, Charles Johnston. At this juncture, Jimenez found himself in the same position as Bordas Valdes. He had no option but to recognize Johnston, given the financial imperatives of his government. Also, the elections installed a majority of opposition members, Horacistas, loyal to the current minister of war, Desiderio Arias, who had a history of hostility to American influence in Santo Domingo.[102]

Kaplan reported that Minister Sullivan, who had always distrusted Arias, urged the United States purge him from Jimenez's cabinet. The Dominican Congress, composed mainly of Arias's supporters, threatened to impeach Jimenez, to whom Secretary Bryan pledged U.S. support. Jimenez, strengthened by the scandals associated with Sullivan, resisted Unites States pressure. A compromise whereby the status of Johnston was downgraded to that of adviser left no one satisfied.[103] Shortly after, in June 1915, Bryan resigned over foreign policy differences with President Wilson and the Santo Domingo fiasco.

In the interim, the question of Minister Sullivan's activities came under scrutiny once again. His nemesis, Walker Vick, having obtained no support from his superiors, sent a memo-randum to Bryan, outlining his charges on April 14.[104] Three months later, an exasperated Vick resigned. In September, he apparently sought vindication since one of the duties of the Fort Commission was to investigate Sullivan, but no such review was held. Vick renewed his attack by writing directly to President Wilson in December 1914. Vick also released his charges to the *New York World* in forcing the Wilson administration to take action. Sullivan, as he successfully did previously, demanded an investigation to exonerate himself, denying all charges levied against him by Vick.

Sutton alleged the choice of James Duval Phelan as a committee of one was a masterstroke. As a pro-Wilson Democrat and senator-elect from California, it would obviate a full Congressional investigation, which apparently nobody wanted.[105] As noted previously, he was at that time on good terms with James K. McGuire, one of the key backers of Sullivan. He could thus be seen as impartial to both sides.

There was a suspicion the investigation was hastily orga-nized to vindicate Sullivan and would be used in a campaign to condemn Vick. German observers believed Sullivan would survive this investigation, as he had the others.[106] What was not taken into consideration by the Americans was the outrage felt by the Dominican population at the high-handed behavior of the American government and its ambassador, James M. Sullivan.

By January 1915, the Phelan investigation was initiated. Sullivan knew his diplomatic career was in jeopardy. Radiograms from him to Joseph D. Phelan from Santo Domingo suggest he was doing his best to cooperate with the investigator, in whose hands his diplomatic future lay. Dated February 21, 1915, the first message urged Phelan to hurry as an important witness on his behalf was about to leave the country. The second, dated three minutes later on the same date, promised to obtain the requisite permission for Phelan to enter the country.[107]

Hearings were concluded in May. As noted above, some hearings took place in Santo Domingo as well. Testimony amounted to almost 3,500 pages, almost 400 exhibits, and 93 witnesses were examined.[108] Vick, in an apparent effort to rehabilitate himself with his party, had his charges read into the Congressional Record.[109] It was to no avail. Having committed the unpardonable sin of party disloyalty, his career in public life was over. As a result of the Phelan Report, so too was that of James M. Sullivan. Phelan interviewed Vick and others whose testimony destroyed what was left of Sullivan's reputation. The findings declared Sullivan did not have the qualifications necessary for the position, that he was supported by special interests whose backing he hid from the Wilson administration; there was no evidence Sullivan personally profited from any contracts awarded to his associates; he interfered inappropriately in the internal affairs of the Dominican government. Phelan made some concessions to the disgraced Sullivan in his final remarks. "This opinion has been reached, not without much hesitation, for there has been much in the administration of Minister Sullivan that has been kindly and helpful and generous." He concluded by calling for Sullivan's resignation.[110]

Ironically, two pieces of evidence from his erstwhile supporters were significant in calling for his termination. One was Secretary Bryan's "deserving Democrats" letter to Walker Vick; the other was a letter Sullivan sent to Judge Gray of Delaware, lawyer for Banco Nacional. It was marked Confidential and dated January 31, 1914.

> The trouble with the Dominican Republic
> is that many of the people are immoral.
> Religion . . . [sic] is unable to cope with

the savage brutal tendencies of a semi-civ-
ilization . . . [sic] a constant predisposition
to immorality and despoliation . . . [sic] no
moral fibre or stability, and a gross and crass
ignorance prevails throughout the land . . .
[sic] The men of this generation are hope-
less, the highest aspiration of the best being
to make public office the means of private
plunder.[111]

The irony of his comments was apparent to those aware of
his alleged efforts to enrich himself by private interests through
awarding them beneficial contracts. There were also his ties to
Tammany Hall, an organization not known for its beneficent
philanthropy. Sullivan's remarks when made public destroyed
his diplomatic career.

Since the hearings of the commission were public, the
contents of the Gray letter reached Santo Domingo and brought
a wave of condemnation. By February 20, 1915, editors of
various Dominican papers were calling for Sullivan's resignation.

Sullivan's efforts at explanation, that it was a private letter
released without his knowledge or consent, that it did not
express his true opinion of Dominican character were to no
avail.[112] President Wilson downplayed his minister's machinations in Santo Domingo as merely "foolish."[113]

According to author Mary Rose Callaghan, Sullivan's
granddaughter, the minister was unapologetic for his behavior.
In *Emigrant Dreams*, Sullivan, responding to his critics said,
"I was accused of supporting a corrupt dictator. But I was
merely following instructions. Has the White House not always
supported dictators?" The unstated question, however, was
whose instructions was he following? Further along, Callaghan
has Sullivan admit to "transferring funds of Tammany bankers,"

claiming he gained nothing for himself but was trying to alleviate conditions of the poor "rather than having it in banks." As to the charge of encouraging his relatives and political cronies in the awarding of contracts, Callaghan has the minister rationalize it by asking, "What sort of man does not return a favor?"[114] Callaghan claims the Phelan Report demanded his resignation. Instead, Wilson allowed Sullivan to resign before the Phelan Report was made public, revealing a certain empathy for his former minister. The president reserved his anger for Walker Vick, whose persistence caused embarrassment to the Wilson administration. According to Sutton, Wilson revealed a certain vindictiveness. Not only did Wilson ignore requests by Vick's supporters for employment, he knew Vick was an ally of political rival McCombs, whereas Sullivan, despite his machinations, was a protégé of Tumulty.[115]

Wilson was undoubtedly trying to manipulate the press by putting a good face on an embarrassing situation. Sullivan may have been scapegoated for a variety of reasons, only some of which had anything to do with events in Santo Domingo. In the first place, Sullivan's tenure in the country was twenty-two months, from September 1913 through June 1915. Reviewing the longevity of American diplomats serving in Santo Domingo from 1885 to 1945, each served an average of about twenty-four months, ranging from as few as five months to as many as sixty-six months. The sole exception was William W. Russell, dismissed by Bryan in September 1915 after serving for twenty-eight months, to make way for James M. Sullivan. Russell replaced the disgraced Sullivan in 1915 and served in the Dominican Republic for another ten years.[116] And while the reasons given for their recall are not stated, it reveals that Sullivan's tenure was not significantly different than many of his contemporaries in that troubled country.

In addition, there was the issue of the Gray letter. Why would one of Sullivan's ardent supporters have allowed such a damning article into evidence unless he wanted to disassociate himself from the growing scandal. Bryan was convinced it was the furor over the Gray letter that forced Sullivan's dismissal.[117] But the Phelan Report took excerpts of the Gray letters out of context. As reported in the *New York Times*, Sullivan had written to Gray in January 1914. The damning portions are in the first paragraph, which Phelan and others cite. Subsequent sections continue:

> The United States government should do everything to remedy the wrongs inflicted by the irresponsible governments here and to utilize the Church to reclaim the country and the people. The men of this generation are hopeless, but would have the youth taught the tenets of Christianity and the true meaning of patriotism. It would be mighty good politics, (Gray), as well as a glorious philanthropy.[117]

Sullivan praised the efforts of interim president Archbishop Nouel, condemning the high-handed robbery of church lands by City Bank representative, Santiago Michelena. This formed part of his rationale for awarding the contract of customs receipts to Banco National.[118] On the surface, this could appear blatantly self-serving, but it may also reflect a sincere effort to bring stability to Santo Domingo.

In addition, Sullivan's remarks have to be taken in the context of those made by others. For example, J. Fred Rippy made similar disparaging remarks about peoples of the Caribbean referring to them as "mixed and primitive inhabitants [who] depress the level of culture," the masses of them being "poor, disease-ridden, uneducated and apathetic," "deficient in health and energy," "violently impatient [and] ready material for any pernicious agitator" whose leaders were "corrupt, careless and extravagant." Admiral C. D. Sigsbee expressed little hope for the primitive and mixed races of Hispanic America except through "exterior domination."[119]

Sullivan, possibly hoping for forgiveness, lingered on in Santo Domingo through May and then vacationed for a month in Ireland. Possibly he believed there would be intervention by political allies. The Fort Commission, while not conducting a thorough investigation, had exonerated him from any taint of scandal. Fort had been a Republican reform governor of New Jersey who worked with both Wilson and Tumulty during Wilson's tenure as governor of the Garden State. It was Fort who suggested to Wilson that Tumulty be his personal secretary, in part, because of his Irish Catholic background. According to Blum,[120] it was Fort who was a consistent supporter of Sullivan as the scandal unfolded, but by then the minister's career was no longer salvageable. Returning in July, Sullivan found no succor in Bryan's successor as Secretary of State, Robert Lansing, who echoed Phelan's assessment, calling him unfit but not dishonest.[121]

Some of the other charges levied against Sullivan appear almost petty. Even his ardent supporter, J. Franklin Fort noted his "carelessness of dress."[122] "He used to sit about in his home in a negligee shirt and suspenders in trousers larger than a New York tailor would advise one to wear." When asked whether Sullivan, in contrast to the formal attire of Dominican officials, met other diplomats in his undershirt, Fort replied, "It's a hot country down there and most people wear as little as they can."[123]

Judge Gray dismissed as a distortion a press article describing Sullivan running around barefoot in the rain in Washington, DC. The Phelan Report cleared him of any charges relating to deportment or abuse of liquor.[124]

Even if accurate, deportment was apparently never an issue. Joseph P. Kennedy, ambassador to Britain for thirty-three months (January 17, 1938–October 22, 1940) was also noted for his informality of attire and his intemperate remarks.[125] Kennedy's problems began when he publicly diverged from Franklin Roosevelt's foreign policy. The president moved to more open support for the Allied cause as 1940 approached, whereas Kennedy increasingly identified with Chamberlain's policy of appeasement, endorsing the views of aviator turned isolationist Charles Lindberg.[126]

As will be shown with Sullivan, Kennedy attempted unauthorized contacts with German officials.[127] And like Sullivan, when Kennedy's views became public, he was vilified in the press. John Davis, a British politician, stated: "We have a rich man, untrained in diplomacy, unlearned in history and politics, who is a great publicity seeker and who apparently is ambitious to be the first Catholic president of the U.S."[128]

Kennedy was forced out of his diplomatic post, but it was due to policy differences between himself and the president. Could there have been similar reasons not publicly acknowledged by the Wilson administration, which resulted in the dismissal of James M. Sullivan?

The Irish Nationalist Connection

D irect and circumstantial evidence suggests his ties to Irish nationalists were a major contributing factor to Sullivan's dismissal as ambassador. He was in constant contact with some who were actively involved in Irish independence movement. One such individual, alluded to previously, was James K. McGuire.

McGuire organized the Irish press and news service under the supervision of Dr. Alexander Feuhr, a key figure in the German Information Service, imperial Germany's propaganda bureau. Feuhr supplied articles for McGuire's newspapers and other Irish periodicals. McGuire had also written two books endorsing the German cause, *The King, The Kaiser and Irish Freedom* (1915), and *What Could Germany Do for Ireland* (1916). Each was financed by Dr. Heinrich Albert and circulated as GIS propaganda. After America entered the war, the latter was banned by the government, and McGuire was under surveillance by the Secret Service. McGuire was on such good times terms with Albert he presented him with his own copy of *What Could Germany Do for Ireland?*[129]

McGuire was also instrumental in smuggling Roger Casement out of the United States and into Germany to obtain its support for an Irish insurrection against Great Britain.

In addition, along with Irish nationalists, McGuire sought to initiate strikes among dockworkers in order to disrupt American shipments to the Allies.[130]

McGuire was also on the board of directors of the American Truth Society, formed in 1912 by Jeremiah O'Leary, in order to present an alternative perspective to events in Europe to balance what was perceived as British domination of American newspapers. In conjunction with the Clan na Gael, of whom McGuire was a ranking member, the American Truth Society formed the Friends of Peace, the goal of which was to prevent American entry into the war.[131]

By 1914, the Clan, the Irish Republican Brotherhood, and the Imperial German Government were in negotiations for an Irish uprising. Irish nationalists Bulmer Hobson and Padraic Pearse were in America, speaking at Clan rallies and raising funds.[132] At the time Sullivan was leaving his post in Santo Domingo, news broke about German-Irish nationalist collaboration sponsoring an uprising in India against Great Britain. This was followed by the exposure of Dr. Albert's spy and propaganda ring in the United States, resulting in the expulsion of several German diplomats.[133]

Mary Rose Callaghan, Sullivan's granddaughter, believes her grandfather failed as a diplomat because of his pro-German activities, going so far as forbidding British ships to refuel in Santo Domingo.[134]

Thus Sullivan, even if not an active member of those organizations, was in open sympathy with them and their cause. Evidence will reveal he became more proactive as his tenure in Santo Domingo was under review.

President Wilson, irked by hyphenate opposition to his policies and their subversive activities in America, by dismissing Sullivan, may have been sending a message to militant organizations by discharging any Irish American suspected of cooperating with the Germans. Why, soon after Sullivan was ousted, did Wilson demand the resignation of T. St. John Gaffney, American consul to Munich, for his pro-German, pro-Irish policies?[135] There is also direct evidence of Sullivan's complicity. Documents in the German Foreign Office archives reveal he conspired with German diplomats both in Haiti and the Dominican Republic.[136]

This would have been relatively easy as the German ambassador to both countries was the same individual, Dr. Fritz Perl, a longtime career diplomat who specialized in Latin American affairs. He was stationed in Port-au-Prince, Haiti.[137]

Despite long-term historical and cultural tries to France, after 1900, Germany began to dominate Haitian commerce. The United States considered it to be its main rival in the Caribbean.[138] However, according to Reinhard Doerries, the German government did not consider the Unites States a world power. Since its takeover of Hawaii, Samoa, Guam, and the Philippines, the situation had radically changed. The United States had become a major player in global politics, willing to use war to support its claims. Not realizing this, despite warnings from its ambassador in Washington, DC, was a serious misjudgment on the part of Imperial Germany.[139] Germans married Haitian women and mingled socially with the Haitian ruling elite. This gave them an advantage, given America's contemporary Jim Crow racism. In addition, the United States had earlier sought to use Haiti as a site for colonization for former slaves up to the time of the Lincoln administration. America also made periodic efforts to obtain naval bases in Haiti, visiting it multiple times up to the eve of World War I. There were 210 Germans in Haiti by 1915. Many German merchants were active in funding Haitian revolutions, both to the incumbent government and the insurgents, the latter forming armies in the north along the Dominican border.[140] This fostered the same kind of political instability in Haiti as was typical of the Dominican Republic and represented a potential threat to United States interests, which had increased since 1900,[141] especially after completion of the Panama Canal in 1914.

In one excerpt from a private letter obtained from the German Foreign Office dated January 20, 1915, the German consul, Hohlt, spoke of a conversation he had with Sullivan.

> Mr. Sullivan turned out to be a great advocate for our cause. He made strong accusations against England and talked heatedly of all Ireland having only one desire. That is for Germany instead of England to have invaded Ireland. All of Ireland would stand by us and ask for annexation of Ireland to Germany having the certainty this would lead to [Irish] autonomy . . . Mr. Sullivan was incredibly agitated [and] read several defamatory poems by Irish authors about England to me . . . Sullivan, hoped to come to Santo Domingo in good time to be of some sort of assistance to the German cause there, even if it cost him his position.

Apparently, Sullivan was willing to do this despite the public accusations of Walker Vick, whom Dr. Fritz Perl regarded as a very decent man. Sullivan even suggested they "exploit" the French ambassador's wife, an ethnic German, who hated her adopted country and would not be averse to doing anything that would damage French politics. The German consul, who knew the woman,[142] declined the suggestion.

As late as June 1915, the German ambassador, Dr. Fritz Perl, remarked that Sullivan was willing to put in writing the fact the American government had given Bordas Valdez permission to incur additional debt to suppress the rebellion by his rival, Arias.[143]

These documents are especially damning to Sullivan's conduct as ambassador. It is contrary to Article III, Section 3 of the United States Constitution. Specifically it states, "Treason against the United States shall consist only in levying war against them, or in adhering to their Enemies, giving them Aid and Comfort." Sullivan raised his hand against the flag and government he had sworn to defend, which fulfills the constitutional definition of treason. Technically, however, the United States and Germany were not belligerents, and finding the required two witnesses "to the same overt act" would have been problematic.[144] Nonetheless, it clearly demonstrates how far Sullivan had moved in embracing the nationalist cause. It thus makes his career as a producer for pro-independence films following the termination of his appointment as ambassador to Santo Domingo a logical follow-up to his commitment.

The Germans seemed reluctant to embrace Sullivan, aware of the Phelan investigation, although believing the American ambassador would once again emerge unscathed. In particular, Dr. Perl thought the portion of the Phelan investigation which, in part occurred in the Dominican Republic, was assembled "in great haste." Some officials who refused to testify on Sullivan's behalf were fired; others refused to appear. Those who spoke out against Walker Vick later withdrew their testimony. Sullivan was present throughout the hearings and thanked those who gave depositions on his behalf.[145] Given the circumstances, it gave Sullivan a sense that he could ride out this storm as well. It was possibly the furor caused by the public release of the Gray letter that sealed his fate.

The publication of the Phelan Report on May 9, 1915, was two days after the sinking of the *Lusitania*. With its appalling loss of noncombatants, the incident not only shocked the civilized world but made it imperative the United States lodge a strong protest against Germany. To show leniency to Sullivan under such circumstances would have been politically unacceptable, but Sullivan's treasonable correspondence with the Germans was never made public. Allowing pro-Wilson Democrat James D. Phelan to investigate Sullivan and essentially "whitewash" him by saying he was "unfit" but not corrupt, was a face-saver for both Sullivan and Wilson.

The German archives are dated from January through April 1915, during which the Phelan investigation was in progress. Perhaps sensing his diplomatic career was coming to an end, he may have more overtly embraced the cause of Irish independence. As noted previously, Irish in both Ireland and America were in a conspiracy with Germany to overthrow British rule since the outbreak of World War I. Sullivan had been a participant in various activities, and although he may not have been an enrolled member of the Clan na Gael, his activities in Santo Domingo suggest strong support for its actions. Publicly, Wilson may have scapegoated Sullivan for failure of his Dominican foreign policy. That could be a factor, but the assertion is undermined by subsequent events in Santo Domingo, which reinforce the German-Irish nationalist connection. Given the links between Sullivan, McGuire, and German diplomats and U.S. suspicions of German intentions, is it simply coincidence that within three months, May to July 1915, the *Lusitania* was sunk, President Wilson issued multiple warnings to Germany demanding reparations with the threat that any repetition would be regarded as deliberate and unfriendly. This position Secretary of State Bryan regarded as too severe, which led to his resignation on June 8, 1915, leaving Sullivan with no ally in Wilson's cabinet. The Phelan Report forced the resignation of Sullivan. United States Marines began their occupation of Haiti, establishing a pattern soon replicated in the Dominican

Republic. In addition, the German ambassador, Dr. Fritz Perl, was reassigned to Lima, Peru, in June 1915. Both British and American governments refused to grant him safe conduct.[146] All this reinforces suspicion that more than allegations of Sullivan's "unfitness" were responsible for his dismissal.

Part of the Wilson Plan to create stability in Santo Domingo was to bring what he believed was its most persistent trouble-maker, Desiderio Arias, under control.[147]

Located along the chaotic northern Dominican-Haitian border, Arias had assisted Haitian president Cincinnatus Leconte seize power in 1910, whose warm relations with the Germans were a source of concern for Washington.[148]

Americans perceived Arias as a "bandit" and an "enemy." Caudillos had traditionally been bought off by the central government through patronage and by obtaining a cut of the government customs revenues.[149] This created virtual indepen-dent warlords throughout the country, and it was this which successive American presidents since Theodore Roosevelt sought to control. Wilson essentially had two demands: create a national guard under American control, thereby undercut-ting the power of warlord militias, and having a director of public works functioning as fiscal agent responsible directly to the United States. This would cut off the cash flow to regional Caudillos. Both the Dominican president and Congress refused to comply with Wilson's demands.[150] The problem for Wilson, Sullivan, and Bryan was that Arias was an arms smuggler, a mercenary, and a powerful guerilla leader in the north, where, since 1898, Germany had built up a sphere of influence. In fact, Arias's predecessor as Caudillo in the region had been educated in Germany, further adding to America's suspicions.

Arias further alienated Wilson and his new Germanophobe secretary of state Lansing by supporting the revolutionary efforts of Haitian Rosalvo Bobo, who, like Arias in the Dominican

Republic, was an anti-imperialist who could mirror Arias's pose as a popular patriotic hero.[151]

Arias was an active supporter of Juan Isidro Jimenez, then Dominican president (1899–1902) who preferred dealing with Germany rather than United States. It was these two who became the power brokers in Dominican politics by December 1914.[152] These developments, coupled with Wilson's insecurity over hyphenate intrigues in America and his fears of German influence in the Caribbean, made him insist on no more revolutions in Santo Domingo. Jimenez had by then become simply a puppet of the United States, a position resented by the Dominican people. Arias had become a popular hero willing to defend national honor. His tradition of resistance to American domination and his alleged pro-German bias made him suspect in the eyes of Wilson. Apparently, Arias had widespread support. According to the German ambassador, as late as June 1915, the people of Santo Domingo were "very German friendly."[153] Under such circumstances, it was understandable that within ten months after Sullivan resigned, the United States began a six-year military occupation of Santo Domingo.

But there were other reasons that made it expedient for Wilson to dismiss Sullivan. One of Sullivan's supporters, Bryan, was now out of office, having resigned his post over policy differences stemming from his belief Wilson was no longer neutral in his attitude toward the belligerents in the Great War. The other, as noted above, implicate Sullivan in corrupt politics to which Wilson, as a Progressive, was averse. There was also the German connection. As noted previously, the ties between Germany and Irish nationalists both at home and abroad were deep and at odds with Wilson's professed neutrality. The evidence suggests Wilson had deep concerns as to the activities of hyphenates in America at the time. Sullivan, like St. John Gaffney and others, may have been sacrificed by Wilson in order to maintain the legitimacy of his policy of neutrality. According to Sean McConville, St. John Gaffney's difficulties were, like Sullivan's, personal and political. Like Sullivan, Gaffney was a native of Ireland. A lifelong supporter of the nationalist cause, Gaffney was dismissed as United States consul to Munich for holding a dinner for Roger Casement at which anti-British comments were made. There was also the claim that in August 1915, Gaffney had requested passage for Casement aboard a neutral ship from the German government to America to obtain support for the Irish cause.[154] Both efforts would have been in violation of then current U.S. neutrality laws, something that Sullivan could also be perceived of as having violated. For Sullivan, it brought him even closer to embracing the goal of independence for Ireland.

Having vacationed in Ireland for a month while the Phelan Report was finalized, Sullivan returned once again for a longer stay in his homeland. It was to be his finest hour. Having weathered scandal for both his involvement in the Becker-Rosenthal case and as ambassador to Santo Domingo, he went on to establish the Film Company of Ireland, its films, actors, themes, and places encouraging the cause of Irish independence both in America and in Ireland.

End Notes

1 Arthur S. Link, *Woodrow Wilson and the Progressive Era, 1910–1917* (New York: Harper Brothers, 1954), 94; 97; Arthur S. Link, *Wilson: The New Freedom* (Princeton: Princeton University Press, 1956), 106–107; Arthur S. Link, *Wilson: The Struggle for Neutrality, 1914–1915* (Princeton: Princeton University Press, 1960), 497–499.

2 James Watson Gerard, *National Cyclopedia of American Biography*, vol. XLIX (New York: James T. White and Company, 1966), 124–125; Link, *Wilson: New Freedom*, op. cit., 100, 101.

3 Arthur Link, *The New Freedom*, op. cit., 104–106.

4 John Blum, *Joe Tumulty and the Wilson Era* (Boston: Houghton-Mifflin, 1951), 33.

5 Arthur Link, *New Freedom*, op. cit., 108; Link, *Neutrality*, op. cit., 499.

6 "Dan F. Platt, 65, Archaeologist," *New York Times* (7 May 1938); Platt was a Princeton alumnus and faculty member. He was reportedly a campaign supporter and adviser to President Wilson.

7 "Davies, Joseph Edward," John Garraty, ed., *Dictionary of American Biography*: Supplement Six, 1956–1960 (New York: Charles Scribner's Sons, 1980), 146–147; *National Cyclopedia of American Biography*, vol. C (New York: James T. White and Company, 1930), 456–457.

8   James D. Phelan, *Santo Domingo Investigation: Copy of the Report. Findings and Opinions.* (Washington, DC: Gibbon Brothers, 1916), 7, 10; "Phelan Reported Sullivan Unfit," *New York Times* (27 July 1915): 5; "Hurries to Santo Domingo," *New York Times* (9 September 1913); "Dominican Tangle Under Inquiry," *New York Times* (10 December 1913); According to this article, one of the major reasons for Sullivan's appointment to the ministerial post in Santo Domingo was because he "stumped the state of Maine for Mr. Bryan in one of his several campaigns and thereby created a political obligation which Mr. Bryan, with characteristic generosity, promptly recognized."

9   Phelan Report, op. cit., 7, 8.

10   Andy Logan, *Against the Evidence: The Becker-Rosenthal Affair* (New York: McCall Publishing Company, 1970), 282; Mary Rose Callaghan, in the biographical novel about her grandfather, James M. Sullivan, cites Whitman's letter and Sullivan's reply extensively. In *Emigrant Dreams* (Dublin: Poolbeg Press, 1996), 208–209.

11   Blum, op. cit., 111; Alfred Connable and Edward Silberfarb, *Tigers of Tammany: Nine Men Who Ran New York* (New York: Holt, Rhinehart, and Winston, 1967), 249–250; "The Santo Domingo Scandal," *New York Times* (26 January 1915); his connection to the Banco Nacional is noted in "Bryan to Sullivan," *Foreign Relations* (12 January 1914): 197–198.

12   James A. O'Gorman was a second-generation Irish American lawyer closely allied to Tammany Hall. He was a state supreme court justice. He later became a senator as the result of a compromise between Democrat reformist versus Tammany candidates. His Irish nationalist leanings were evident in his efforts to repeal the Panama Canal Tolls Act, which favored Great Britain; "O'Gorman,

James A," *National Cyclopedia of American Biography* (New York: James T. White and Company, 1945), vol. XXXII, 114–115.

13   Baldwin was a Yale graduate, class of 1891. His careers included those of lawyer, judge, and member of the law faculty at his alma mater. A former Republican, he was the successful Democratic nominee for governor of Connecticut in 1910; "Baldwin, Simeon Eben (1840–1927)," Allen Johnson, ed., *Dictionary of American Biography*, vol. I (New York: Charles Scribner's, 1928), 544–547.

14   Homer Stiles Cummings, Yale Law Class of 1893, was a mayor of Stanford, Connecticut, and state attorney for Fairfield County. As director of the Democratic Speakers Bureau in 1912, he probably came into contact with Sullivan. He was vice chairman of the Democratic National Committee, 1913–19, and a United States senator at the time of Sullivan's appointment as minister. "Cummings, Homer Stiles," John Garraty, ed., *Dictionary of American Biography*: Supplement Six, 1956–1960 (New York: Charles Scribner's Sons, 1980), 136–38; "Cummings, Homer Stiles," *Cyclopedia of American Biography*, vol. D (1934), 13.

15   Blum, op. cit., 11–14, 57, 71, 11.

16   Link, *The New Freedom*, op. cit., 109.

17   Ibid., 108.

18   Blum, op. cit., 27.

19   Letter from James K. McGuire to James D. Phelan, 15 October 1912; letter from James K. McGuire to James D. Phelan, 22 October 1912; letter marked "Confidential" from James K. McGuire to James D. Phelan, 16 November 1912; Bancroft Library, University of California–Berkeley, Box 47, Folder 12.

20 "Catholics Chosen," *Catholic Sun* (21 February 1913): 2; "President Wilson's Excellent Appointments," *Catholic Sun* (1 August 1913): 1.

21 "Only $6000 in Bank Sullivan Favored," *New York Times* (27 January 1915); Callaghan has her grandfather's nomination condemned by a bishop of the Catholic Church; Ibid, 209. The accusation was confirmed in "Tumulty's Caution for Sullivan Told," *New York Times* (14 January 1915); the plaintiff was Archbishop Bonaventure Broderick. The archbishop had won a judgment in August 1913 against his own brother, who had been involved in sewer bidding contracts while Broderick was in Havana. This was about the time Sullivan was being considered for the post of ambassador to Santo Domingo. Allegedly, Sullivan was paid for services never rendered. During the confirmation hearings, Sullivan repaid the $1,500 fee; "Broderick Wins; Is Sued," *New York Times* (27 August 1913); this obviously would raise a red flag as to Sullivan's character if it became common knowledge. It also begs the question as to where the money came to repay the fee.

22 Walter A. Sutton, "The Wilson Administration and a Scandal in Santo Domingo," *Presidential Studies Quarterly* 12, no. 4 (Fall 1982): 553. [552–60] Phelan Report, 7–8.

23 "Testifies Sullivan Called Beer Chief," *New York Times* (20 January 1915); for Cortelyou, see "Cortelyou, George Bruce, 1862–1940," Robert Livingston Schuyler and Edward T. James, *Dictionary of American Biography*, vol. XI: Supplement Two (New York: Charles Scribner's Sons, 1935), 122–123. For details on his premature vice-presidential bid, see "Cortelyou Angers the White House," *New York Times* (16 June 1908). Sutton, op. cit., 559, fn. 4, states there were numerous letters from creditors in

Sullivan's personnel file in the State Department attesting to him as a poor credit risk.

24   Sumner Welles, *Naboth's Vineyard: The Dominican Republic, 1844–1924*, vol. 2 (Payson and Clarke, 1928), 718–719.

25   George Harvey, "Diplomats of Democracy," *North American Review* (February 1914, CXIX): 171–172. Most of the negative criticism came after Sullivan's activities in Santo Domingo became public; Sumner Welles, *Naboth's Vineyard: The Dominical Republic, 1844–1924* (Savile Books, 1966), 718–719; Rodman Selden, *Quisqueya: A History of the Dominican Republic* (Seattle: University of Washington Press, 1964), 19; Rippy J. Fred, *The Caribbean Danger Zone* (New York: G. P. Putnam's Sons, 1940), 195; Henry Merritt Wriston, *Executive Agents in American Foreign Relations* (Baltimore: John Hopkins University Press, 1929), 182.

26   Hughes, William (1872–1918). Biographical Directory of the United States Congress, 177–-Present. http://bioguide.congress.gov/scripts/biodisplay.pl?index=h000929. Retrieved 21 March 2012; Blum, op. cit., 109.

27   "Bremner, Robert G. (1874–1914)," Biographical Dictionary of US Congress, 1774–present. Retrieved 20 March 2012.

28   "Two Booms in New Jersey," *New York Times* (17 July 1910).

29   "Ministers Came Here to Thank McGuire," *Syracuse Herald* (28 July 1913): 5; the second minister McGuire supported was former Tennessee governor Benton McMillen (1845–1933), another "deserving Democrat." McMillen was a well-educated lawyer and judge. He served as a congressman from 1878 to 1899, resigning to become governor. He was a reputed expert on monetary affairs and was, like McGuire, a Bryan (pro-Silver) Democrat. He failed to be reelected

to Congress in 1912. Similar to McGuire, he was active in the insurance business. McMillen was appointed to Peru in 1913, a country also noted for political instability and at the time undergoing modernization. It suggests perhaps fortuitous business opportunities, through the intervention of grateful ambassadors, was an item for discussion. This is made more plausible by the fact that after McGuire was exonerated in the wake of the John Doe asphalt investigation, he planned a trip to South America upon his return from a visit to Europe. James K. McGuire hosted a dinner honoring his "good friend Benton McMillen" in August 1913, prior to his departure for Peru. There was no mention of James M. Sullivan; "Brewster or Dillon Will Get Place, says M'Guire," *Syracuse Herald* (24 July 1914); Robison Daniel, "McMillen, Benton," Robert Livingston Schuyler, ed., *Dictionary of American Biography*, vol. XI, Supplement One (New York: Charles Scribner's Sons, 1988), 533–34. "Benton McMillen," The Tennessee Encyclopedia of History and Culture, http://tenesseeencyclopedia.net/imagegallory.php? Entry ID=h054. McMillen was appointed ambassador to Guatemala, 1919–1922 at a time when the United Fruit company dominated the country; "J. K. M'Guire out Of Local Politics," *Syracuse Herald* (16 August 1913): 6. "Tennessee Democrats Nominate Candidates," *New York Times* (30 May 1902).

[30] "Jarvis, Samuel Miller (1853–1913)," *National Cyclopedia of American Biography* (New York: James White and Company, 1914–1916, vol. XV), 345–346; Melvin Knight, *The Americans in Santo Domingo* (New York: Vanguard Press, 1928), 50.

[31] Ibid; Selig Adler, "Bryan and Wilson Caribbean Penetration," *Hispanic American Historical Review* xx, 1940, 199–224.

32 Phelan Report, op. cit., 19.

33 Arthur S. Link, *Neutrality*, op. cit., 499.

34 Adler, op. cit., 203; "Long, Boas," *Cyclopedia of American Biography*, vol. 50. (Ann Arbor, Mich: University Microfilms, 1971), 613–616.

35 "Grace, William Russell (1832–1904)", Allen Johnson and Dumas Malone, eds., *Dictionary of American Biography*, vol. IX (New York: Charles Scribner's Sons, 1932), 463.

36 "McIlheny Company," http://www.fundinguniverse.com/com pany-histories/McIlheny-Com. Retrieved 27 January 2012.

37 James Weldon Johnson, "Self-Determining Haiti: Government of, by, and for the National City Bank," *Nation 111* (211 September 1920); Damu, J. "How The U.S. Impoverished Haiti," http://www.haitiaction.net/NEWS/JD/9_28_3.html. Retrieved 23 January 2012.

38 Melvyn Knight, *The Americans in Santo Domingo* (New York: Vanguard Press, 1928): 50.

39 "Russell, William Worthington," *National Cyclopedia of American Biography*, vol. XV (Ann Arbor, Michigan: University Microfilms, 1967), 58.

40 "Drop Sullivan Charges," *New York Times* (1 October 1914): 6.

41 Quoted in Link, *The New Freedom*, op. cit., 104–105 and Welles, op. cit., 118.

42 Perl to Bethman–Hollweg. German Foreign Ministry Archives, 6 March 1915.

43 Knight, op. cit., 22, 28, 29; "Moore, John Bassett," *Dictionary of American Biography*: Supplement Four. (New York: Charles Scribner's Sons, 1946–1950), 597–600.

44 John Edwin Fagg, *Cuba, Haiti and the Dominican Republic* (Englewood Cliffs, New Jersey: Prentice-Hall, 1965), 152; Rayford Logan, *Haiti and the Dominican Republic* (New

York: Oxford University Press, 1968), 48–55; "British Bondholders," *New York Times* (19 January 1915).

45 Knight, op. cit., 47–48.

46 Rayford Logan, op. cit., 52.

47 Otto Schoenreich, *Santo Domingo: A Country with a Future* (New York: MacMillan, 1918), 239–40; Knight, op. cit., 50.

48 Welles, vol. II. op. cit., 627; Link, *Freedom*, op. cit., 108; Russell to Knox, *Foreign Relations* (27 September 1912).

49 Phelan Report, op. cit., 13.

50 McIntyre to Knox, *Foreign Relations* (13 January 1913); Knight, op. cit., 56.

51 Knox to Russell, *Foreign Relations* (30 January 1913); Jarvis to Knox, *Foreign Relations* (7 February 1913); Knox to Jarvis, *Foreign Relations* (12 February 1913); Knox to Russell, *Foreign Relations* (19 February 1913).

52 Knight, op. cit., 52.

53 Colton, George C. *National Cyclopedia of American Biography*, vol. XXV (New York: James T. White and Company, 1936), 179; *Dictionary of American Biography*, vol. 4. (New York: Charles Scribner's Sons, 1930), 322–323.

54 "Says Bryan Feared Money Trust Bank," *New York Times* (15 January 1915): 5; "Says Bryan Ignored Sullivan Scandal," *New York Times* (17 January 1915): 2.

55 "Tumulty's Caution for Sullivan Told," *New York Times* (14 January 1915).

56 Sutton, op. cit., 553.

57 *Phelan Report*, op. cit., 20; Knight, op. cit., 50.

58 Knox to Russell, *Foreign Relations* (18 February 1913).

59 Knox to Russell, *Foreign Relations* (26 February 1913).

60 Bryan to Sullivan, *Foreign Relations* (31 December 1913); Sullivan to Bryan, *Foreign Relations* (7 January 1914);

Moore to Sullivan, *Foreign Relations* (7 January 1914); Moore to Sullivan, *Foreign Relations* (10 January 1914).

61 Grullon to Sullivan, *Foreign Relations* (12 January 1914).

62 Link, *Progressive Era*, op. cit., 98.

63 Bryan to Sullivan, *Foreign Relations* (12 January 1914).

64 Bryan to Sullivan, *Foreign Relations* (18 January 1914).

65 Sullivan to Bryan, *Foreign Relations* (22 January 1914).

66 Sullivan to Bryan, *Foreign Relations* (2 December 1913); Rayford Logan, op. cit., 58; Bryan to Sullivan, *Foreign Relations* (24 November 1913).

67 Bryan to Sullivan, *Foreign Relations* (2 December 1913); Sullivan to Bryan, *Foreign Relations* (5 December 1913); Sullivan to Bryan, *Foreign Relations* (6 December 1913); Peynado to Bryan, *Foreign Relations* (8 December 1913); Dr. Don Francisco J. Peynado was Dominican minister to the United States, 1912–1913.

68 Sullivan to Bryan, *Foreign Relations* (9 December 1913); Sullivan to Bryan, *Foreign Relations* (17 December 1913); Sullivan to Bryan, *Foreign Relations* (18 December 1913); Representatives of the State Department to Bryan (20 December 1913). The members of the election commission were all veterans of the diplomatic service. Jordan H. Stabler (1885–1938) served in Europe and in numerous stations in Latin America, ultimately heading the Division of Latin American Affairs, 1917–1919, and again 1926–1927. He authored two biographies of Latin American statesmen. "Stabler, Jordan Herbert," *Who Was Who in America*, vol. I (1897–1942). *Chicago: Marquis Who's Who* (1943), 1168–1169. Hugh Gibson (1883–1954) also served in Europe and in Latin America and wrote several books on the problems of European diplomacy and foreign policy. "Gibson, Hugh," *Who Was Who in America*, vol. 3. *Chicago: Marquis Who's Who* (1960), 322. Frederick A. Sterling (1876–1957)

was a cattle rancher and merchant, who later served at posts in Europe, China, and Latin America, serving as chief of the Division of Western European Affairs, 1916–1918; "Sterling, Frederick Augustine," *Who Was Who in America*, vol. 3; *Chicago: Marquis Who's Who* (1960), 818. Sullivan's efforts to bring stability were praised earlier by Secretary of State Bryan. Bryan to Sullivan, *Foreign Relations* (4 October 1913). See also "Ends Revolution in Santo Domingo," *New York Times* (9 October 1913).

69 Report of Walter M. St. Elmo, chief of Bureau of Information, Police Department, Porto [sic] Rico. *Foreign Relations* (20 December 1913). St. Elmo had supervised the activities of twenty-nine American observers of the December elections.

70 Sullivan to Bryan, *Foreign Relations* (28 December 1913).

71 Knight, op. cit., 58.

72 Bryan to Sullivan, *Foreign Relations* (31 December 1915); Sullivan to Bryan, *Foreign Relations* (7 January 1914); Moore to Sullivan, *Foreign Relations* (7 January 1914); Sullivan to Bryan, *Foreign Relations* (9 January 1914); Sullivan to Bryan, *Foreign Relations* (11 January 1914); Sullivan to Bryan, *Foreign Relations* (12 January 1914).

73 Sullivan to Bryan. *Foreign Relations* (12 January 1914); Grullon to Sullivan, Foreign Affairs (12 January 1914); Sullivan to Bryan, Foreign Affairs (12 January 1914); Grullon to Sullivan, *Foreign Relations* (12 January 1914).

74 Sullivan to Bryan, *Foreign Relations* (28 January 1914).

75 Arthur Link, ed., Vick to Bryan, Papers of Woodrow Wilson, vol. 29, 2 December 1913–5 May 1914. (Princeton, New Jersey: Princeton University Press, 1979). Vick to Bryan, Ibid. (14 April 1914).

76 Sutton, op. cit., 552.

77 "Report to the Secretary of State made by the representatives of the Department of State Appointed To Observe the Dominican Elections," *Foreign Relations* (20 December 1913). The election commissioners included Hugh S. Gibson, Frederick A. Sterling, Jordan Herbert Stabler. A total of thirty-three observers were sent; Bryan to Sullivan, *Foreign Relations* (10 December 1913); according to Sullivan, they were accorded a "courteous unofficial audience" with the president; Sullivan to Bryan, *Foreign Relations* (16 December 1913); Gibson (1883–1954) was a former secretary to the legation in Honduras and later in London. In 1910–1911, he served as private secretary to the assistant secretary of state, later serving in Cuba. Ironically, he was one of the early proponents of efforts to professionalize the Foreign Service. Following his involvement in Santo Domingo, his foreign posts included Poland, Belgium, Luxemburg, and Brazil. Gibson authored several books based on his diplomatic experience. Hugh Simons Gibson, http://history.state.gov/departmenthistory/people/gibson-hugh-simons). Retrieved 23 January 2012. Jordan Herbert Stabler (1885–) was born in Maryland and graduated from John Hopkins University. His diplomatic experience prior to the Sullivan commission was assignments in Brussels, Guatemala, Ecuador, Berlin, Sweden. In 1916, he became head of the Division of Latin American Affairs in the State Department. "Jordan Herbert Stabler," *Bulletin of the Pan American Union,* vol. 45, 248. Frederick Augustine Sterling (1876–). Sterling's family had a business background whose wealth enabled him to attend private schools and Harvard University, after which he studied law. He owned and managed a cattle ranch in Texas, later becoming involved in manufacturing woolens. He entered the diplomatic service in 1911. His post prior to the Santo

Domingo Commission was in Russia. Later career assignments were in China, Peru, and England. Sterling was the first <u>USA EE and MP</u> to the Irish Free State in 1927. Subsequent posts were in several eastern European countries and Sweden. "Sterling, Frederick Augustine," *National Cyclopedia of American Biography*, vol. F, 1939–1942 (New York: James T. White and Company 1942), 148–149.

78 Sullivan to Bryan, *Foreign Relations* (23 December 1913).

79 "McIntyre, Frank" (1865–1944), *National Cyclopedia of American Biography*, vol. XXX 11 (New York: James T. White and Co., 1945), 333–334; "Minister Sullivan Omnivorous [sic] Reader," *New York Times* (28 January 1915): 5; "Tumulty's Caution for Sullivan Told," *New York Times* (14 January 1915). The Bureau of Insular Affairs was an arm of the War Department of the United States, which administered overseas islands from 1896 to 1939. It administered customs receivership in both Haiti and the Dominican Republic in addition to similar duties on other United States island possessions. "Records of Bureau of Insular Affairs," http://www.archives.gov/research/tguide-fed-records/groups/350.html. Retrieved 16 March 2012.

80 *Phelan Report*, op. cit., 12–13.

81 Link, *New Freedom*, op. cit., 108, fn. 48; Phelan Report, op. cit., 13.

82 "McGuire Defends Sullivan to Bryan," *New York Times* (14 December 1913).

83 *Phelan Report*, op. cit., 15–16.

84 "McGuire Defends Sullivan to Bryan," op. cit. For a glowing report, see Sullivan to Bryan, *Foreign Relations* (17 April 1914), 225–227.

85 Sutton, op. cit., 554.

86 "Sullivan is Ok'd By Bald Jack Rose," *New York Times* (23 January 1915).

[87] Arthur Link, *Woodrow Wilson and the Progressive Era, 1910–1917*, op. cit., 98; "Says Bryan Ignored Sullivan Scandal," *New York Times* (17 January 1915).

[88] *Phelan Report*, op. cit., 14, 16, 17.

[89] "Says Bryan Ignored Sullivan Scandal," op. cit., "Says Sullivan Got Bryan White Wash," *New York Times* (13 January 1915); "Tumulty's Caution on Sullivan Told," *op. cit.*

[90] "Says Bryan Ignored," *op. cit.* Tim Sullivan allegedly paid for James M. Sullivan's Yale law degree. This was the latter's chance to reimburse him.

[91] *Phelan Report*, op. cit., 16.

[92] Edward S. Kaplan, *U.S. Imperialism in Latin America: Bryan's Challenges and Contributions, 1900–1920* (Westport, Connecticut: Greenwood Press, 1998), 79.

[93] "Bryan's Name Used in Rake-Off Talk," *New York Times* (21 January 1915); "Contracts Controlled by Former Mayor," *Syracuse Herald* (17 June 1915): 1, 2.

[94] Kaplan, op. cit., 73; "Bryan to Sullivan," *Foreign Relations* (18 January 1914).

[95] Kaplan, op. cit., 73; "Sullivan to Bryan," *Foreign Relations* (12 February 1914).

[96] Link, *Wilson: The Struggle for Neutrality*, op. cit., 542–544; Welles, op. cit., vol. II, 751–770.

[97] "Bryan to Sullivan," *Foreign Relations* (30 April 1914).

[98] Link, *Wilson: The Struggle for Neutrality*, op. cit., 510–511.

[99] "Wilson Plan," *Foreign Relations* (1 August 1914): 247–268.

[100] Henry M. Wriston, *Executive Agents in American Foreign Relations* (Baltimore: John Hopkins University Press, 1929), 802.

[101] Kaplan, op. cit., 76. The Phelan Report states that Governor Fort did not have confidence in Sullivan as ambassador to

Santo Domingo and that he was widely unpopular with the Dominican people (27).

[102] Welles, op. cit., vol. II, 748.

[103] Kaplan, op. cit., 77–78; Ray Logan, op. cit., 60; Knight, op. cit., 64.

[104] "Vick to Bryan" (14 April 1914), Wilson Papers.

[105] Sutton, op. cit., 556.

[106] Dr. Fritz Perl. Handwritten Note. German Foreign Ministry Archives (28 April 1915).

[107] "Letters of James D. Phelan," BANSMSSCB800, Radiograms from James M. Sullivan to Senator Phelan (21 February 1915, 6:58 p.m.); Radiogram from James M. Sullivan to Senator Phelan (21 February 15, 7:01 p.m. [sic]). Bancroft Library, University of California. Box 73, Folder 21. 22.

[108] *Phelan Report*, op. cit., 1.

[109] *Congressional Record* (26 February 1915), 4766.

[110] *Phelan Report*, op. cit., 30–32.

[111] *Phelan Report*, op. cit., 28.

[112] Ibid., 29.

[113] Link, *Wilson: The New Freedom*, op. cit., 112.

[114] R.Callaghan, *Emigrant Dreams*, op. cit., 244–245.

[115] Sutton, op. cit., 559.

[116] "United States Ambassadors to the Dominican Republic," Wikipedia.org/wilsi/United_States_Ambassadors_to_the_Dominican_Republic. Retrieved. 2 May 2012, 1-6.

[117] Knight, op. cit., 66; Sutton, op. cit., 558.

[118] "Religion Bryan Aid in Affairs of State," *New York Times* (22 January 1915).

[119] J. Fred Rippy, *Caribbean Danger Zone* (New York: G. P. Putnam's Sons, 1940); 277; Rippy, "The Initiation of the Customs Receivership in the Dominican Republic,"

Hispanic American Historic Review 17 (November 1934): 426–27. [419–517]

120 Blum, *op. cit.*, 27.

121 Sutton, *op. cit.*, 558.

122 "Drop Sullivan Charges," *New York Times* (1 October 1914): 6.

123 "Religion Bryan Aid in Affairs of State," op. cit.

124 *Phelan Report*, op. cit., 20.

125 "Is Democracy Finished?" http://www.pbs.org/wgbh/americanexperience/features/primary-resource..Kennedys-democracy-finished. Retrieved 22 May 2012; 1. Interestingly, Callaghan states that Sullivan wanted to be an old Joe Kennedy but hadn't made it; Callaghan op. cit., 46.

126 "Lindberg Isn't Crazy, You Know," http://www.pbs.org/wgbh/americanexperience/features/primary-resource. Retrieved 22 May 2012: p. 23.

127 Seymour Hersh, *The Dark Side of Camelot* (Back Bay Books, 1998), 28–29.

128 John Davis, *The Kennedys: Dynasty and Disaster* (SPI Books, 1993), 94.

129 *Brewing and Liquor Interests and German and Bolshevik Propaganda: Report and Hearings of the Sub Committee on the Judiciary.* United States Senate, vol. I (Washington, DC, Government Printing Office), 1396–1397, 1307.

130 Reinhart Doerries, *Imperial Challenge: Ambassador Count Bernstorff and German-American Relations, 1908–1917* (Chapel Hill University of North Carolina Press, 1989), 74, 281 (h.205); 340 (n.266).

131 John Price James and Paul H.Hollister, *The German Secret Service in America* (Boston: Small, Maynand and Company, 1918), 248.

132   Harme Hay, *Bulmer Hobson and the Nationalist Movement in Twentieth Century Ireland* (Manchester: Manchester University Press, 2009); Ruth Edward, *Patrick Pearce: The Triumph of Failure* (Gollancz, 1977).

133   Ernest Wittenberg, "The Thrifty Spy on the Sixth Avenue El," *American Heritage Magazine* 17:1 (February 1060), 110–111.

134   Callaghan e-mail to author (14 January 2003).

135   Maryanne Felter and Daniel Schultz, "James Mark Sullivan and the Film Company of Ireland," *New Hibernia Review* 8.2 (Summer 2004): 24–40.

136   Arthur S. Link, *Wilson: The Struggle for Neutrality 1914–1915* (Princeton, NJ: Princeton University Press, 1960), p. 23 fn. 58.

137   Resume of Dr. Fritz Perl. Personal communication to the author by Gerhand Keiper of the German Foreign Ministry Archives (29 April 2015).

138   Hans Schmidt, *The United States Occupation of Haiti, 1915–1934* (New Brunswick, New Jersey: Rutgers University Press, 1971), 34.

139   Doerries, R. op. cit., 4–5.

140   Schmidt, op. cit., 34.

141   Ibid., 37.

142   Hohlt to Perl, German Foreign Ministry Archives (20 January 1915).

143   Perl to Bethman-Hollweg, German Foreign Ministry Archives (2 June 1915).

144   Wayne Andrews, ed., *Concise Dictionary of America History* (New York: Scribner's and Son's, 1962), 242.

145   Dr. Fritz Perl, handwritten communication, German Foreign Ministry Archives (28 April 1915).

146   Private correspondence of Oliver Juengel, secretary of German Mission in Port-au-Prince, Haiti, to the author

(27 April 2015). See also unsigned letter from Perl, German Foreign Ministry Archives, Lima [Peru] (25 September 1916).

147   Nancie Gonzales, "Desiderio Arias; Caudillo, Bandit and Culture Hero," *Journal of American Folklore* 85, no. 335 (January 1972): 44.

148   Brenda Gayle Plummer, *Haiti and the Great Powers, 1902–1915* (Baton Rouge: Louisiana State University Press, 1988), 168.

149   Frank Maya Pons, *The Dominican Republic: A National History* (Princeton, New Jersey: Marcus Weiner Publishers, 1998), 313.

150   Gonzalez, op. cit., 46–48.

151   Sullivan to Bryan, *Foreign Relations* (28 March 1915), 469–470.

152   Link, *Wilson: The Struggle for Neutrality*, op. cit., 542–544; Welles, op. cit., vol. II, 751–755, 770.

153   Handwritten note from Dr. Fritz Perl, German ambassador to Haiti and Santo Domingo, German Foreign Ministry Archives (28 April 1915).

154   Sean McConville, *Irish Political Prisoners, 1848–1922* (London: Routledge, 2003), 561-2, fn29 citing McGarrrity Papers: NLI, MS 17, 590 (2).

CHAPTER IV

Return of the Native James M. Sullivan and the Film Company of Ireland in Ireland and America

Precedents to the Film Company of Ireland

B y July 1915, in the wake of the Phelan investigation, James M. Sullivan resigned his ministerial post in Santo Domingo. He soon returned to Ireland and, in March 1916 with Henry Fitzgibbon, launched the Film Company of Ireland (FCOI) with offices located at 34 Dame Street, Dublin.[1] According to Downing, Sullivan provided the initial capital for the company.[2] Ostensibly Sullivan had returned to Ireland to live with his "dear old mother for a few months, but then decided to remain longer."[3] Was this a subterfuge, given his pro-nationalist sentiment and the fact the British were censoring Irish films they considered controversial? With his credentials as an Irish nationalist, he would have already been considered suspect by the authorities, a fact confirmed by Sullivan's granddaughter, Irish novelist Mary Rose Callaghan.[4]

Rocket el al. state it was the debut of D. W. Griffith's *Birth of Nation* in March 1915 that inspired Sullivan to initiate the Film Company of Ireland the following year.[5] However, there may have been other influences in Sullivan's life that contributed to his founding of the FCOI. For example, when Sullivan found his position as ambassador imperiled by the investigation of the Phelan Commission, one of the men he called to testify on his behalf was Bald Jack Rose, his controversial client in the Becker-Rosenthal case of 1912. At the time of his testimony, in

January 1915, Rose was listed as president of the Humanology Film Producing Company. One of its films was entitled *Are They Born or Made?*, a five-reeler ostensibly based on his life and criminal career. The alleged biopic questioned whether criminals were born into the life or if it was the result of social environment.[6] Rose later reinvented himself, assumed his given name of Jacob Rosenzweig, ironically becoming a popular lecturer on criminality and the evils of gambling. His motion picture company was dissolved in 1917.[7] Because of their close association, it would be logical to assume Sullivan was aware of Rose's business, which may have piqued his interest in motion pictures.

Another possible influence may have been Big Tim Sullivan, whose involvement in a variety of entertainment venues also provided a tantalizing link to Tammany lawyer turned diplomat and later film producer James M. Sullivan. Welch notes Big Tim's support for entertainment, including vaudeville, amusement parks, and motion pictures. His investments in movies were helpful in popularizing them as mass entertainment. Big Tim helped expand existing stage entertainment while promoting the revolutionary new cinematic form.[8] It seemed fitting that Big Tim Sullivan posthumously made his way to the screen. Within seven months of his death, in April 1914, a four-reeler, "*The Life of Big Tim Sullivan or From Newsboy to Senator*," was produced by the Gotham Film Company. The biopic portrayed Sullivan as a Horatio Alger success story. The conclusion of the film had his constituents praying for his soul at his funeral.[9] James M. Sullivan, tied to Tammany Hall, was no doubt aware of Big Tim's involvement in the infant film industry. This too may have been on important influence in James M. Sullivan's founding of the Film Company of Ireland, as New York City was a major center of film production in the first decades of the twentieth century.

There was also a growing market for ethnic cinema in the United States. Both African Americans and the immigrant Jewish community had found their respective audiences.[10] The growing Irish diaspora community was also a population in the United States with significant market potential.

Given Sullivan's ties to James K. McGuire, who was a paid propagandist for the Imperial German Information Service, there may be connection to his film career as well. McGuire, as noted earlier, was familiar with the potential for film in promoting his nationalist agenda. The head of the German Information Service was Dr. Bernhard Dernburg, a former colonial service officer who came to the United States under cover as a representative of the German Red Cross.[11] This agency used monies collected from members of the German-American Alliance, headquartered at the German embassy, for propaganda purposes.[12] One of Dernburg's key assistants was Alexander Fuehr, a major stockholder in the American Correspondent Film Company, the purpose of which was to correct American misperceptions of Germany's war effort.[13] McGuire as a member of the GIS, often met with Dernburg and others.[14] At that time, McGuire and Sullivan were in close contact given their mutual interests in Tammany politics and, later, Sullivan's diplomatic appointment. According to one source, "the notorious Herr Dernburg" was a film producer.[15] That is probably an overstatement. Dernburg, with little experience in cinema, hired others to do the actual work. His choices would lead to charges of subversion and scandal which led to the company's demise. Dernburg's first choice of employees was Matthew Claussen, a Director of the Hamburg-America Shipping Line (HAPAG). Claussen, in turn, hired Albert Dawson, an American photographer for its publicity work. Dawson began his efforts on behalf of the GIS in December 1914, making several well-received films for the German government[16] His efforts were rewarded with the creation of the American Correspondent Film Company in April 1915. Unfortunately, two of other employees, Felix Marlitz and Albert Sander, set up front companies which used the ACFC to supply Germany with scarce war material. They were ultimately charged, tried, convicted and imprisoned[17]. However, the ensuing scandal destroyed Dawson. He was surveilled by agents of the Justice Department and lost his contract with the ACFC in May 1916[18]. These activities occurred at the same time that Sullivan's associate, James K. McGuire was working for the GIS and Sullivan was involved in treasonable correspondence with German diplomats on Santo Domingo. Ironically, Dawson lost his position with the ACFC about the same time Sullivan was launching the Film Company of Ireland. Could this nexus have provided the impetus—and possible the cash—for Sullivan's formation of the pro-nationalist FCOI in March of 1916? The war was still raging, its outcome in doubt. Sullivan's actions in Santo Domingo had shown him to be in sympathy with German designs, and Ireland was perceived as ripe for subversion.

Further, when hostilities commenced in 1914, some Irish film production companies increased their activities. For example, Norman Whitten of General Film Supply, produced a number of pro-war films for the domestic consumption. The English-born Whitten married May Clark in 1908. She had experience working in short films as an actress, as well as in numerous activities behind the camera—as projectionist, carpenter, set decorator and costume designer—all of which facilitated the establishment of their Stanford Film Cleaning Company, a firm which cleaned and repaired damaged films. The couple moved to Dublin in 1913, where Whitten established what became known as The General Film Supply Company.[19] Whitten had a contract to produce recruitment films for the British government. Apparently a supporter of the

British establishment, Whitten nonetheless gave tacit support to the IRB in filming the three-day commemoration of the death of Fenian activist Jeremiah O'Donovan Rossa in 1915. Rossa was a longtime militant who was released from prison in 1870 on condition he leave Ireland. With other Fenians, including John Devoy, he immigrated to the United States. He continued to advocate violence.[20] Upon his death, Tom Clarke, another militant Fenian, seeing the publicity value of Rossa's public funeral, urged John Devoy to send his body home.

Tom Clarke early on perceived cinema as an appropriate vehicle for promoting the nationalist agenda. Clarke was a convicted rebel from the IRB dynamite campaign of the 1880s. After serving a fifteen-year term, he was released in 1898. He worked with John Devoy in the United States, becoming a citizen in 1905. Two years later, he returned to Ireland, helped reorganize the IRB, and was a planner and martyr in the Easter Rebellion. As an active propagandist, Clarke saw the potential of film in promoting the cause of Irish freedom. A letter to John Devoy suggested, "This ring of pictures houses showing our pictures, we will do good business and the Dublin newspapers may go to hell or to Empire."[21]

In the film, mourners were in the thousands, and Whitten's GFS allowed thousands more to witness the ceremony via film. The ritual was made more memorable by the funeral oration of Padraic Pearse, who reiterated the "need for a new generation rebaptised in the Fenian faith to stand together in brotherly union to achieve freedom of Ireland, [not only] free but Gaelic as well, ending with "they have handed us Fenian graves. Ireland unfree will never be at peace while Ireland holds those graves." While inaudible, given the limited technology of the time, pictures of the volley over Rossa's grave by IRB volunteers and the number of people present was elegant testimony to growing Catholic nationalist movement.[22]

After his films showing the destruction created by the Rising of 1916, Whitten specialized in making such "topical" films in a series which became known as "Irish Events". Whitten went on to film such important events as the general amnesty of prisoners from the Easter Rebellion, featuring Irish hero Countess Constance Markievich and the funeral of hunger striker Thomas Asche in September 1917.[23] The latter was considered a major event in the Nationalist cause. The funeral oration was delivered by Michael Collins, with a contingent of IRA volunteers firing a volley over the martyr's casket. Many of the 200,000 mourners later went to see themselves on film. It contributed the popularity of Whitten's "Irish Events" series, helped unify the Nationalist movement and encouraged the use of cinema as a form of Nationalist protest.[24] All these events helped set the stage for the FCOI's long- awaited release of "Knocknagow".

Founder of the Irish Transport and General Workers Union, James Larkin, also early on saw the merit of film as a vehicle to promote their cause, stage-managing his being escorted to and from his trial for sedition during the strike of October 1913.[25] Irish nationalists and Germans saw the importance of the new technology in winning the hearts and minds of the Irish people, but so did the British. Given his periodic trips to Ireland, especially during his final months as ambassador in mid-1915, Sullivan must have been aware of these developments. In addition, there was the growing problem of censorship, both internal, from the Catholic Church, and external, from Great Britain. Rocket traces censorship to the turn of the twentieth century when showing the prizefight film between African American Jack Johnson and James Jeffries was discouraged.[26] There were even attempts to have Olcott's *Manger and the Cross* (1912) banned because of the commercial exploitation of a religious topic.[27] Despite the opposition, the film was a major commercial success. It also established the precedent of censorship, with regulations prohibiting attendance of children at cinemas. Additional purity campaigns were aimed at "evil literature," which received support from the Ancient Order of Hibernians, Sinn Fein and the Gaelic League.[28] Yet in the heady days prior to the Great War, it appeared that Home Rule would be a fact that fueled the aspirations of "an in-creasingly confident Catholic-Nationalist majority."[29] All this changed dramatically when World War I erupted. Thus Irish nationalist film propaganda both preceded and expanded with the formation of the FCOI.

By the time the Sullivan established the FCOI, Britain saw film as "the new national weapon," a vehicle that had three main goals: the inculcation of loyalty to the crown, recruitment, and revenue for its fast-depleting treasury through implementation of an entertainment tax. This was the rationale for DORA, the Defense of the Realm Act (1914–1918), which introduced widespread censorship with accompanying powers of arrest.[30] The Irish were divided about DORA—Redmond's moderate Irish Parliamentary Party supported it, whereas militant trade unionists and nationalists opposed it. Speaking for the opposition, James Connolly, the radical labor leader and head of the Irish Citizen Army, said, "There is no foreign enemy in this country other than Britain. Should a German Army land in Ireland, we should be justified in joining it, if in so doing one could rid this country once and for all from its connection to the Brigand Empire that drags us unwillingly into their war."[31]

By late December, a banner claiming "We serve neither King nor Kaiser" in front of union headquarters had been removed, and the more radical nationalist press "Irish Worker, Sinn Fein, Erie/Ireland, Irish Freedom" had been suppressed.[32]

Apparently, the British weren't the only censors that Sullivan's nascent FCOI had to be aware of. There was also continued surveillance by the Catholic Church, long regarding itself as the bastion of Christian morality in the Emerald Isle. Particularly galling to various vigilance committees were allegations of "body display" and the tempting of youth to antisocial behavior.[33] "The Catholic church went so far as to coordinate sermons warning against "immodest representations [which] should be made to be reprobated by every good man, and every effort should be made to discountenance them", urging a watchfulness to exclude what is objectionable and offensive in a Catholic country.[34] The Church's effort were rewarded in that many young men opposed bringing ladies into picture houses and other seemingly innocuous outings such as picnics and motor drives.[35] Concern was also voiced as to films corrupting the morals of youth, leading some to choose criminal careers. Not only were cinemas closed on Sundays, it also led to the formation of the Irish Vigilance Association (IVA). Dublin appointed four censors, two of each sex, to police cinematic content.[36] In addition, the National Union of Women Workers (NUWW), noting the potential of film for both education and harm, established the Irish Girls Protection Crusade as another weapon in the war against indecency.[37]

One outspoken opponent of "dirty" movies was D. P. Moran, leading spokesman for an Irish-Ireland and editor of the *Leader* who equated Roman Catholicism with true Irishness. In 1915, he castigated popular films "Anglicizing influence which promoted sexual expression at odds with Irish Catholicism."[38]

Apparently Sullivan's FCOI had to deal with the various "culture wars" permeating Ireland-British censors and home-grown vigilance committees, Sinn Fein versus constitutional nationalists and the Irish-Irelanders of D. P. Moran and defenders of the Anglo-Irish establishment. That he came down strongly in favor of the militant nationalist position was obvious in his choice of films, scripts, and personnel. He was also astute enough to take advantage of the democratization of culture via cheap admission prices and rising public interest in contemporary events.

The timing was fortuitous for Sullivan's creation of the FCOI. Ireland and much of the Irish diaspora, had embraced the Gaelic Renaissance, seen in the popularity of such writers as Synge, Yeats, Lady Gregory and in the works of the Abbey Theatre. Yet Barton reminds us there was a countervailing cultural nationalism at work, with a focus on "Irishness" as emphasized by such spokespersons as D. P. Moran and Padraic Pearse. The Gaelic Athletic Association, established in 1884, played Irish as opposed to English sports. It was also a vehicle whereby Sinn Fein could inculcate paramilitary training. The Gaelic League sought to restore the Irish language and encouraged writing in Irish. An offshoot of this was the effort to destroy the stereotype personified by the stage Irishman, generally successful in the diasporic community in America by 1910.[39]

In America, there was also increased interest about Ireland in popular culture, such as plays, vaudeville, and songs, especially those written by Chauncey Olcott and Ernest Ball between 1910 and 1920. They included "My Irish Rose," "Mother Machree," and "Good Bye Emerald Island." They were romanticized tales of Ireland, sentimental ballads of love, and the poignant memories of the "auld sod." They were examples of the diasporic nationalism Julia Wright referred to earlier. Ironically, many ballads were written by Irish Americans or non-Irish. For example, the popular "Danny Boy" was written by an Englishman, Fredrick Weatherly. None of the composers had set foot in Ireland.[40] Nonetheless, their impact on promoting interest in contemporary Irish culture and history in the diaspora community was profound. In addition, Rocket noted the increased market for cinema in Ireland. Between 1909 and 1914, Dublin was issuing twenty-five cinema licenses annually. Nonetheless, until the formation of the FCOI in 1916, the bulk of film production on Irish history and culture was done by foreign companies.[41]

As noted previously, New York City was the site of many early film production companies, including Vitagraph Studios, established in 1906.[42] A year later, the Kalem Company began, the company's title an amalgam of its three founders' names: George Kleine, Samuel Long, and Mark Marion. Originally employed by Biograph Studios, Marion and Long left to establish their own company, obtaining investment capital from George Kleine, whose Chicago optical company had begun manufacturing filmmaking equipment in the 1890s.[43] Not only did the three founders depart from a long association with Biograph, they lured its general manager and film director, Sidney Olcott, to join them.[44] Initially successful, Olcott, with his Irish background, was prescient enough to realize there was a sizeable market for Irish film among Irish Americans. By 1910, he began filming on location in Ireland, the first studio to film outside the United States.[45]

These events connect to James Mark Sullivan, lawyer and Irish nationalist. He was working on the fringes of Tammany at the time, knew Bald Jack Rose and Big Tim Sullivan and James K. McGuire, and he was undoubtedly aware of the potential of film production not only for profit but for patriotic purposes. His earlier ties to Big Tim Sullivan via Tammany Hall and Bald Jack Rose and the popularity of Olcott's work may have also been significant factors encouraging him to establish the FCOI when his diplomatic career was aborted. Big Tim, Bald Jack, and Olcott were involved in movie production. There were also several active studios in New York City at that time. James M. Sullivan might have even seen the movie biography of Big Tim during his periodic "consultations" back in the States or even after his dismissal from the Foreign Service. Nonetheless, it provided a tantalizing possibility that binds James M. Sullivan to his three careers: the seedy underworld of a Tammany politics, as diplomat, and as founder of the Film Company of Ireland, a significant role often overlooked or only briefly noted for its important contributions to Irish freedom.

Prior to the formation of the FCOI, there were several companies in filming Ireland, many of which used Irish themes. The content was accurately considered suspect by British authorities as early as 1904. For example, Martin McLoone notes, "These . . . highly successful feature films in the period 1910–1920 . . . were consciously designed to help the Nationalist cause."[46]

For example, the American Selig Polyscope Company released two films in 1908 that dealt with nationalist themes. In *The Irish Blacksmith*, the hero defends his sister's honor from a rapacious landlord, who, in retaliation, plants weapons in his shop. He informs the authorities who arrest and try and sentence the blacksmith to death. Harboring weapons was a capital offense at that time. His sister, in league with a soldier who is in love with her, helps him escape. Overhearing his plotters boasting of their deeds, the blacksmith convinces a judge to visit the perpetrators' hideaway, where they are caught.[47]

In the same year, Selig also released *Shamus O'Brien*. A leader of rebels during the rising of 1798, he was pursued by British troops, who offered a reward for his capture. An informer alerts soldiers to his hiding place, but he escapes. His followers attack the informer, who is saved by Shamus. Later, Shamus is captured and imprisoned. On the way to the gallows, a friend frees his hands, and he makes his escape, but his mother reproves him, and he returns to his captors. His sweetheart, Mary, obtains a pardon for him, timely returning it to save him from hanging.[48]

In these early Selig efforts, Irish rebellion, the informer, a courageous Irish maid, and a brave, noble, stoic hero and his rescue by loyal friends and/or a timely pardon were constant themes.

In addition to Selig, several films were made by the Kalem Film Company, which sent director Sidney Olcott to Ireland to film at authentic locations.[49] Between 1910 and 1915, Olcott produced nineteen films dealing with Ireland. Olcott knew his audience and made sure in his publicity it was known his films were shot on location and had direct connections to Irish history.[50] These motifs, embodying Wright's blend of romantic and civic nationalism, were reprised by various film companies. Barton states Olcott's films had an overtly nationalistic agenda.[51] Barton's comments would obviously extend to Sullivan's FCOI as well.

Downing noted that Olcott's early films promoted Irish pride in their past and "established the Irishman on the screen as a genuine and natural social being, rather than a red-faced, beer-drinking rustic sterotype."[52]

Kalem's first production, *A Lad from Old Ireland* (1910), was partially filmed in New York. The plot dealt with an Irish youth driven by poverty to escape to America. Achieving success in politics, he returned to a decade later to save his sweetheart and her family from being evicted.[53] This film was among the first to portray not only Irish suffering under British rule but the pain of the emigrant experience. It also noted the increased presence of an Irish ethnic voting block in America and its market potential—things James M. Sullivan with his Tammany connections would have been cognizant of.

Olcott also made several film shorts of Blarney Castle, a historic site of resistance to British rule; Glengariff, a typical Irish village; and the picturesque Lakes of Killarney. Obviously, Olcott was playing to the romantic and cultural notions of the diasporic community, as well as encouraging its perception of the West as the salvation for the Ireland's exploited people. Other films reveal why he was unpopular with British authorities. *Rory O'More*, released in 1911, was loosely based on the life of one of the principle organizers of the Irish rebellion of 1641. Similar to modern directors, Olcott took liberties with history, placing the action instead during the rebellion of 1803. In reality, O'More and other Irish Catholics sought to take advantage of religious infighting, which weakened the hold of Charles I on Ireland. Rory O'More helped establish a Catholic confederation limiting British control to the toeholds of Dublin and Drogheda in the east. An invasion by Cromwell resulted in bloody massacres, famine, the defeat of the Catholic forces, and the confiscation of Irish lands.[54] The long period of Anglicization, transplantation, and ascendancy had begun.

Rory O'More was based on a nineteenth-century novel by Irish writer, artist, and singer Samuel Lover. According to Rocket, this film was the precedent for other historically based films publicizing the rebel cause,[55] a theme later pursued by James M. Sullivan's Film Company of Ireland. Olcott has O'More betrayed by an informer fleeing British troops. He tarries to bid his sweetheart farewell then plunges into a lake to elude his pursuers, one of whom would have drowned had O'More not saved him. A grateful British officer would have granted O'More his freedom had the informer not insisted on his arrest to obtain his reward. O'More is imprisoned and sentenced to death. Olcott has his hero say, "If to fight for Ireland is a crime, then I am guilty,[56] an apparent reference to Emmet's speech from the dock and foreshadowing Casement's final words following the Easter Rebellion. Prior to his execution, his confessor, Fr. O'Brien, cuts O'More's bonds. He leaps across a wall to a waiting horse and, with his sweetheart, leaves for freedom in America. The priest is killed by British troops for his efforts.[57] In this piece, the priest sided with the rebels, a probable reference to the active intervention by the papacy on behalf of O'More's

Catholic confederation. Such was not always the case, however. According to one authority, when filming *The Colleen Bawn* in 1911, the Irish clergy condemned the alleged immorality of the cast[58] and urged the faithful to drive out the "tramp photographers." Such was the cultural climate within which Olcott, Sullivan, and others had to work. There may be some grounds for the clergyman's criticism. Rocket notes that Olcott "played fast and loose with the facts."[59] In Barton's assessment, both British and Irish tenants are portrayed sympathetically. Olcott and later other filmmakers, such as Sullivan, saved their ire for informers and land agents.[60]

According to Rocket et al., Olcott and Kalem came under increased scrutiny and were threatened with expulsion by British officials after filming *Rory O'More* and, in the following year, *Ireland, the Oppressed*.[61] For a brief time, the director avoided controversial themes, only to return to them in *For Ireland's Sake* (1914), *All for Old Ireland*, and *Bold Emmet, Ireland's Martyr*, the latter two filmed in 1915. *For Ireland's Sake*, with its costumed redcoats and pikes, suggests events of the rebellion of 1798. A clever colleen, Eileen Donaghue, tries to hide a blacksmith, Marty O'Sullivan, caught making weapons for the rebels. She is aided by local supporters, who beat the troops and take their weapons. O'Sullivan finds refuge in a lakeside cave. Eileen, bringing him supplies, is followed by soldiers, and after a chase, both are captured. They are visited by Fr. Flannigan, who supplies O'Sullivan with a file that he uses to help him and Eileen escape their cells. As soldiers follow in pursuit, the priest marries the couple, blesses them, and urges them to cast off to the West, "the land of the free." Several themes are visible here—the British are not perceived as nobly as they were in *Rory O'More*, possibly the result of Olcott's increased harassment. The clever colleen and brave rebel receive communal support for their efforts, and as in *O'More*, the priest is supportive of them, and America is once again seen as the land of refuge.[62]

All for Old Ireland also refers to the Rebellion of 1798. Opening scenes show patriots plotting while they await arms and munitions from France. Myles Murphy and Eileen Donaghue are sweethearts, largely unconcerned about the uprising. Fagin, a British informer, wants Eileen and is given a beating for his efforts by Murphy. In revenge, Fagin reports him as a rebel to British authorities. The patriots are warned in advance, and Murphy leads the British on a wild goose chase, allowing his compatriots to unload munitions from the French ship. Murphy is caught hiding in the home of his sweetheart and imprisoned. Eileen and Fr. Flynn visit him, the former concealing a rope under her dress. Murphy makes his escape, again hiding at the Donaghue farm. Concealed under a load of hay, Eileen drives Murphy through British lines. He makes it to the coast, where he escapes to a waiting French ship, promising to send for Eileen when he is settled in France.[63] *All for Old Ireland* employs a similar theme—love, betrayal, a miraculous escape, only this time to France, on a ship loaded with arms for Irish rebels.[64] Catholic France had been a traditional ally of rebellious Ireland in its wars with England. The role of a foreign ship loaded with arms was to prove prophetic because at that time, the IRB and the Clan na Gael were engaged in a similar plan with Imperial Germany for the Easter Rebellion.

Probably the film most galling to British authorities was *Bold Emmet, Ireland's Martyr*. In the film, rebels, including Emmet, are seen making weapons. Evoking memories of the famine and the more recent Land War, British authorities evict a peasant family, inciting a riot. In retaliation, a British officer, Kirke, is ambushed and taken to the cottage of Norah Doyle, sweetheart of Con Daly, a United Irishman. Rebels attempting to seize the wounded soldier are repulsed by Norah and a sympathetic priest. Kirke recovers, returns to Dublin, and resigns his commission. A disguised Emmet is told by Daly the rebels are ready to rise. Fealy, a spy, reports this to the military but is seen by a United Irishman. Insurgents ambush the British troops, who in turn arrest Fealy, suspecting trickery. To win back his credibility, Fealy takes them to the Doyle cottage, where Emmet, in rebel uniform, is hiding. He escapes up the chimney as Norah, Daly, and the widow Doyle stall the soldiers. Daly is arrested and, following testimony by Fealy, condemned to be hanged. Norah is sentenced to seven years in a penal colony. The widow Doyle requests assistance from Kirke, who dispatches a rider with a pardon. Daly's noose is severed by the bullet from a United Irishman under orders from Emmet. Before a new rope can be found, the pardon is delivered, and the spy Fealy is given a sound thrashing by the rebels.[65]

In this film, Emmet and the rebels are portrayed as cunning and brave, the British as oppressive, colonizing foreigners. The potential for violence between the two is a foreshadowing of the Easter Rising only a year away.

The real Emmet was a wealthy Protestant Irish nationalist with profound sympathy for the Irish tenants. In the film, Emmet's friendship with Daly might recall the real hero's ties to fellow rebel and martyr Wolf Tone. The fact the film depicts Emmet in uniform suggests Olcott's assertion of a militant Irish national identity. Emmett was involved in making weapons, but the plot was exposed. Emmet was captured, tried, and condemned to hang. His speech from the dock has been described as a rousing call for continued resistance to British rule. His grave is the site of an annual pilgrimage and celebration as the Father of Irish Republicanism."[66] The film revealed Olcott's growing sympathy for Ireland, its tone reflecting increased tension in Ireland prior to the Easter Rebellion. Soon after its release in Ireland, it was banned by British authorities.[67]

All Olcott's films dealt with glorifying Ireland's rebellious past, featuring brave heroes, noble peasants, and resourceful women. Britain claimed such films interfered with military recruitment efforts in Ireland.[68] Olcott's work not only revived pride in Ireland's past, the films were extremely popular and also helped bury the stage-Irish rustic image. According to Flynn, Ireland was extremely important to Olcott, and he was making "films of an increasingly political and nationalist nature."[69] Olcott also apparently enjoyed "twisting the lion's tail." In 1914, when Irish volunteers were drilling with wooden guns, Olcott supplied a regiment with real rifles and bayonets from the Kalem Company. Flynn suggests this was his revenge for British interference in his film production.[70]

In addition to Kalem's films, there was another which caught the eye of British censors—Walter MacNamara's 1914 production of *Ireland: A Nation* which Barton describes as being pro-nationalist. The Irish-born MacNamara sought to trace the struggle for Irish freedom from the Rising of '98 to the passing of Home Rule in 1914 but focused instead on the period from 1798 to 1803. He made sure to film several scenes on location. MacNamara was arrested for importing arms for the rebels, which later were found to be props for his film. He further alienated British authorities by recruiting for the Nationalist cause.[71] MacNamara's film tells of Ireland's fight for freedom in the years 1798–1803. MacNamara also takes liberties with the truth, but his depiction of Fr. John Murphy,[72] rejecting his clerical superior's demand to refrain from seditious activity, shows him urging his congregation to rebel and, becoming their leader, mirrors actual events. So too is the patriots' forlorn hope of assistance from France, the meeting between Emmet and Michael Dwyer, the successful guerilla leader on the Wicklow Mountains,[73] and the willing sacrifice of Sam McAllister to assure Dwyer's escape during a raid by British troops. Seen only briefly is the portrayal of the soldiers' torture of Ann Devlin. The process was called half-hanging, whereby the victim is hanged until unconscious then revived in the hope of extracting information.[74] Emmet, betrayed by an informer, is captured at his sweetheart Sara Curran's home, and his defiant speech from the dock reveals his stoic bravery to the end. The film was given a limited showing, then proscribed due to the onset of the Great War and later as a result of martial law imposed during the Easter rebellion in 1916. A military observer thought the film would "cause disaffection" and " prejudice the recruitment to His Majesty's forces".[75]

The 1922 edition of the film contains newsreel footage of John Redmond, DeValera's visit to America in 1919–1920, the death of hunger strikers McSwiney and Fitzgerald, and Lloyd George reviewing contingents of Black and Tans about to be deployed to Ireland. Censors removed scenes of soldiers interrupting a hillside mass, the torture of Anne Devlin, the advertisement of a £100 reward for the arrest of any priest, and the scenes of John Redmond and the Irish flag. Both insertions and deletions were an obvious—and belated—effort to reduce tensions during the vicious war of independence. The original movie was like others, seen as an obstacle to recruitment of troops for the Great War. An additional reason was the Irish audiences' positive response to violence against the British.[76]

Hence "Ireland: A Nation" was one of the most important films of the silent film era, appealing both to the Irish Nationalists and the police and military, ironically for the same reason - both saw it as a vehicle for opposition to British rule.

A similar fate befell American Vitagraph-produced film *Whom the Gods Would Destroy*. Loosely based on the life of Roger Casement and the Easter Rising, the plot revolved around two friends, one a British naval officer, the other an Irish patriot, both in love with the same Irish woman. The patriot recently returned from Germany to lead insurgents against England. The English officer, blinded in a naval engagement, was recuperating at the woman's home, where the Irish rebels came to claim their leader. The blinded officer signaled an English warship, and in a bloody encounter, the rebels are killed and scattered. The Irish leader is captured and sentenced to be hanged but is pardoned by the British government. American producers denied any reference to the martyred Casement.[77] Ironically, pro-Irish groups thought it too British; the British believed it too Irish. Its showing sparked protests in the United States by Irish American leaders James K. McGuire, associate of James M. Sullivan and active propagandist for the German cause, and John Goff; leaders of the the Friends of Irish Freedom, a group actively involved in funding the Easter Rising; and Dr. Thomas Addis Emmet, grand-nephew of Robert Emmet and, like the others, an active Irish nationalist. The protestors objected to the portrayal of the Irish rebels as a disorganized rabble, poorly armed with sticks and stones, and its pardoning of the rebel leader by a benevolent British king. Defended by John O'Leary, brother of militant Irish American Jeremiah O'Leary, they were found not guilty by police Court Justice Walsh after they admitted making an orderly protest of the film.[78]

This is important link between militant nationalists in Ireland and America. Dr. Thomas Addis Emmet penned a series of works critical of British policy in Ireland and wrote the introduction to James K. McGuire's *What Could Germany Do for Ireland?*, a propagandist tract elaborating the views of Casement, for the Imperial German Information Service. And while not formally a member of FOIF, Sullivan was defended by the organization's president, John D. Moore, and lawyer Joseph Gavan when interned by British authorities during the Easter Rebellion.[79]

The Film Company of Ireland in Ireland, 1916–1920

With the precedents of Selig, Olcott, and MacNamara and the increased interest in things Irish, the timing was right for the establishment of an indigenous Irish film company. The cloud hanging over it was the oppressive presence of British occupation and the vigilance committees of the Catholic Church with their increased surveillance and censorship. All this was due to a rising tide of unrest among the native Irish and the voracious demands by Britain for manpower to fill the trenches during the Great War. Sullivan had to carefully negotiate between these conflicting demands, which obviously had an impact on his choice of subjects, personnel, and the way they were portrayed in the films made by the Film Company of Ireland in the tumultuous years 1916–1920.

Hence, Sullivan and the FCOI became part of an established movement within the film community to press the case for Irish freedom. Slide suggests this trend preceded the FCOI beginning in 1913 with the debut of *The Life of St. Patrick*, the iconic emblem of the Emerald Isle. Advertisements stressed its Irish cast, director, and authentic costumes.[80] As with the *Life of St. Patrick* the FCOI stressed its all-Irish plots, casts, stars, and directors. According to the Humphy's Family Tree, the FCOI was begun in March 1916 to assist the nationalist cause. It's office was established at 16 Henry Street, close to the General

Post Office, scene of much action during the Easter Rebellion. The FCOI sought authors of photoplays with an Irish background. Looking for a position, actor Felix Hughes saw Joseph Kerrigan, the Abby actor and established film star, ensconced in the main office. Hughes suggested that Kerrigan also was an investor in the FCOI. Apparently the founders knew given their stated goal to produce "challenging" films, they would be surveilled by the British authorities.[81] No fiction Irish films had been shot in Ireland since Olcott left at the beginning of the war. That changed with the establishment of the FCOI. Further, the company's stated goal was to establish films of every description in Ireland and engage in the making of scenic and dramatic motion pictures, engage in the employment of skilled and unskilled labor and of artistes [sic], authors, and performers as the development of the business may require.[82] The FCOI gave hope to the idea that it would produce "challenging films" for growing Irish audiences[83] The FCOI was apparently trying to walk a thin line so that its product would be acceptable to all critical audiences - the Church, the government, and the Nationalists.

The Humphry's Family Tree further states three early films were destroyed in the rising, but the titles are not listed. Those noted began with *O'Neill of the Glens* starting in August 1916. The FCOI then went on a whirlwind of production, making twelve films in eight months, most of which were romantic comedies.

The arrest of cinema owners, the destruction of movie houses and the temporary prohibition of all entertainments suggests the authorities saw them less as vehicles for inculcating loyalty, than as centers of subversion.

James Mark Sullivan was among those listed as "individals with Files in Sinn Fein and Republican suspects, 1899–1921," along with Roger Casement, Michael Collins, Eamon de Valera, and John MacDonough. The list also included fellow Americans Thomas St. John Gaffney and the O'Leary brothers.[84] Hence, Sullivan is once again fused with militant Irish nationalists in the minds of the authorities. So it could not have been the films the FCOI produced prior to the rebellion that lead to British suspicions, but rather it was its stated purpose and personnel, along with the precedents of other Irish films, which brought down the wrath of British authorities. Despite having no direct role in the rising, Sullivan was arrested outside his home on April 28, 1916, and sent to Kilmainham Jail.[85] He was charged with complicity.[86] The fact he was interned with Dick Humphrys confirms British suspicions as to the nature of Sullivan's films. Humphrys' had a long association with Irish Nationalist activity, had been schooled for a while at St. Enda's, was involved in the Howth gun-running episode and fought at the General Post Office until the IRA surrendered.[87] The Film Company of Ireland must have come under the eye of the watchful authorities, not only for its pursuit of loosely nationalist stories focusing on Ireland's past miseries, but also because members of the company were playing a double life as actor and nationalist activist.[88] Sullivan's sisters were openly outraged at the notion of his involvement, but the fact British authorities believed Sullivan was a friend of Michael Collins suggests he and his activities would be under surveillance.[89] Sullivan, in fact, wrote a manuscript about Collins in 1920 that claimed they had a close relationship. Collins was allegedly sheltered by Sullivan, and the two shared stories of the patriotic O'Sullivan's. Sullivan reported Collins confessed his many close escapes, which in Collins' mind affirmed that God was on the side of Ireland. Sullivan also wrote an article for the *Springfield Republican*, emphasizing his closeness to Collins and the importance of Collins' role in the struggle for Irish freedom.[90]

One of the FCOI's major coups was obtaining the services of John MacDonagh, actor, director, Irish nationalist, and brother of martyred Thomas McDonagh, slain during the Rising of 1916. The ties to MacDonagh are significant because it reinforces Sullivan's intimacy with the cause of Irish freedom. Sullivan recruited MacDonagh, ostensibly luring him with promises of financial success.[91] According to McDonagh,

> My next contact with film production was with the Film Company of Ireland. A dynamic Irish-American lawyer named Sullivan had come over to start film making. He had already started, principally with Knocknagow, when we met. He painted rosy pictures of the money to be made, and interested a number of public men, who between them, put up about five thousand pounds.[92]

Given his past financial problems, the source of Sullivan's wealth is open to question.

As noted previously, during Sullivan's confirmation hearings, the State Department's personnel file had numerous letters from creditors indicating he was a poor risk. Was it Fitzgibbons' money and Sullivan's contacts to the Irish nationalist community, or did Sullivan obtain some of the funds promised him by backers of the Banco Nacional in Santo Domingo or some other source, as hinted at by McDonagh? Did Kerrigan contribute? Or was he able to tap into the resources of his wealthy in-laws, the O'Maras?

Recent research suggests such was the case. Not only did the O'Mara family front the money, it funded its productions. In addition, Ellen O'Mara Sullivan was actively involved in production, sales, shipping, distribution and marketing, one goal of which was to establish a branch in the United States. Other family members frequently served in a number of capacities—actors, crew, and workers.[93]

Diog O'Connell also said that such might be the case, stating Ellen O'Mara was much more involved in business operations from 1916 to 1919 than has previously been acknowledged.[94] And it is a matter of fact that she wrote the script for *Knocknagow*, although Casella states it may have been written by others, with Ellen O'Mara Sullivan being given the copyright as the FCOI's director, a point reinforced by Rockett.[95]

Nonetheless, when the Easter Rebellion occurred, Sullivan was arrested and interned. Given the scandals in Santo Domingo, some Irish Americans were reluctant to embrace Sullivan. Joseph Gavan, a lawyer with close ties to the nationalist cause, downplayed Sullivan's involvement.

> Sullivan has never in his whole life been identified with any Irish-American movement looking toward the liberation of Ireland from British misrule. Were Irish-Americans disposed to violate this country's neutrality, which they are not, they would not have selected James Mark Sullivan for any mission that might give the British government an opportunity to complain to the United States.[96]

Muddying the waters as to the nature and extent of his involvement still further, the *New York World* noted Sullivan's friends said he was always interested in events in Ireland.[97] The Humphry's family website asserts that Sullivan fought with the rebels.[98] The *New York World* reported he was held in Dublin

Castle, transferred to Kilmainham Jail, and later removed to an English prison. Patricia Lavelle, an O'Mara and niece to Sullivan, reiterated that point:

> He never made any bones about the opinions he held and when the Rising began, he did not hesitate to with the rebels well. He was promptly taken prisoner . . . They persuaded the authorities that Uncle Jim was a pure-bred American born citizen who had been Plenipotentiary to Santo Domingo, and was a person of some consequence. He was released in time for the christening of his little baby . . . named Ellen Sinn Fein Sullivan . . . Jim Sullivan was the life and soul of the prisoners up at Kilmainham Gaol . . . Uncle Jim came in on them [the prisoners] like a fresh breeze with his hearty laughter and his big voice and his American wise cracks and without tremor of fear; for who could touch an American citizen if all came to all".[99]

So whether he actually took an active part in the rebellion is open to speculation. It is a fact the British interned many suspects, arresting over 3,000, ultimately releasing 1,100 of them.[100]

Sullivan's American citizenship may have been the reason for his release, a claim also used by DeValera. Given the recent embarrassment as to Sullivan's misdeeds in Santo Domingo, President Wilson was unwilling to intervene in the affair should there be evidence of Sullivan's complicity, again implying that links to Irish nationalism was a probable cause for his dismissal as ambassador. Sullivan, however, was also assisted by members of the Friends of Irish Freedom, the organization to which his good friend James K. McGuire was an important figure. John D. Moore, FOIF's national secretary, wrote Wilson concerning Sullivan's detention. That, coupled with pressure from his family and well-placed politicians and the fact that Britain, constrained by its desire to have the United States enter the war on the Allied side, may have led to his release. Wilson may also have been reluctant to become involved given he was under increasing pressure from Irish-Americans to intervene on behalf of Roger Casement. With an eye on the election of 1916, Wilson was consciously trying to avoid alienating the Irish vote. Sullivan, like DeValera, may have been beneficiary of international politics. For whatever reason, the *New York World* on May 9, 1916, reported, "James Mark Sullivan wires that he has been freed."[101] But FCOI, in the minds of the authorities, had strong links to Sinn Fein, which was undoubtedly the cause for his internment.

The FCOI offices, several films, and many documents were destroyed when the rebels occupied the General Post Office. This setback left Sullivan and Fitzgibbon undeterred. They relocated their offices to 34 Dame Street. Fiscal success was imperative, as the FCOI sustained losses of £1,526. It also meant references to Irish nationalism had to be more circumspect to avoid the suspicions of British censors who had become more active in the wake of the Easter Rising. Within months, the three-reel *O'Neil of the Glen* opened with Fred O'Donovan making his screen debut. Its premier was filmed by Sullivan, in the hope people would return a second time to see themselves on film.[102] Often overlooked by film critics, *O'Neil of the Glens* provides a link to later FCOI productions in that its director, J. M. Kerrigan, and several cast members, including Nora Clancy, Brian McGowan, and Fred O'Donovan, starred in its production. While the plot was not overtly nationalistic as in some later FCOI productions, it involves themes of vengeance, love found and lost, a forced marriage rejected by the pure Irish lass, and a reunion with her lost love.

Given the destruction of its facilities during the Rising, it was imperative that "O'Neil of the Glen" be a success. Hence the FCOI emphasized its Irish roots, claiming to be, "the first Irish fiction film produced in Ireland by Irish actors", ignoring others produced in 1912-1913,[103] James Mark Sullivan said that the film took advantage of the imagination, ideals, artistic temperament and beautiful scenery [and] could compete with those [films] made anywhere. The film was considered to be more of a marketing success, than an artistic one. On the positive side, a British distribution deal assured the survival of the FCOI in the short run. "O'Neil" was immensely popular earning praise for FCOI as a "… national, patriotic enterprise that monotonously perfect American films could not match"[104], an apparent slap at earlier efforts by American Selig Polyscope and the works of Olcott for the Kalem Company. This suggests that in Ireland, with the war becoming increasingly unpopular, with Sinn Fein gaining in favor and the IPP in decline, and with growing resistance to conscription, that movies playing theNationalist card would find a sympathetic audience.

The film was shot in Ulster, and the symbolism of star-crossed lovers torn apart by violence and eventually reunited might well represent the hopes of Irish nationalists at a time of political tension and violence in an Ireland threatened with political and sectarian schism. Promoted as a film produced by an Irish company with Irish actors in Ireland, it was well received by critics and the public. Reflecting past British censorship of Irish films and perhaps the nationalist credentials of its cast and producer, the film was labeled as suitable only for adults or children accompanied by adults.

In addition to the implied message of unity in *O'Neil of the Glen*, there is a more direct tie in the title itself. Having been filmed in Ulster, the name O'Neil is significant. O'Neil is considered one of the most illustrious surnames in Ireland. Dating back to prehistory, it embraced kings, warriors, and statesmen of Ulster who fought bravely to protect Ireland from foreign enemies—Northmen in the dark ages, Anglo-Normans of the thirteenth century, and the British in the more recent past.[105] All these nuances would be apparent to an Irish audience, echoing Wright's definitions of romantic and antiquarian nationalism.

The Film Company of Ireland embarked on a busy schedule. Within a year of losing everything in the Easter Rebellion, it produced nine films, both comedies and historical dramas, usually released to critical acclaim.[106] By itself, it is a significant achievement, especially since it had no studio and film production could occur only in the summer months, when there was sufficient light.[107]

At the same time the United States entered the war, April 1917, the FCOI announced it was beginning its second season. "Knocknagow" was in production, but it would be a year later before it reached the public.[108] The FCOI completed two feature films in 1917 - "Rafferty's Rise" and "When Love Came to Gavan Burke" but many of its 1916 films, such as "O'Neil of The Glen" "the Miser's Gift", "Food of Love and "An Unfair Love Affair", " continued to circulate.[109] Unfortunately "Gavin Burke" and "Rafferty's Rise" were not released in late 1917 and fell victim to the focus of FCOI on its epic "Knocknagow". FCOI used its key personnel - Fred O'Donovan, Brian McGowan and Nora Clancy and the romantic drama raised issues of class, gender and generational differences. But despite the stars, the film apparently generated little popular appeal, in part because FCOI's diminishing resources were centered on

"Knocknagow". Appeals to patronize the films because they were "authentic Irish" was an insufficient incentive. The cinema-going Irish public wanted something more. In an effort to avoid British and Church censorship, when the FCOI released "Rafferty's Rise" it stated publicly the Company "seeks keep free from propaganda of every kind in its stories to appeal to all the Irish people ... [I]t sticks steadfast to the idea that its business is to idealize everything Irish that it photographs.[110] In November 1917, "Rafferty's Rise" made its debut. It starred the usual FCOI personnel, including Fred O'Donovan and Brian MacGowan. An "Early Irish Cinema" article noted ominously that "organizational problems within FCOI delayed its exhibition. Early reviews heralded its "improved technique" and its desire to show authentic Irish films. "Rafferty's Rise" won mixed reviews. It received little advanced publicity due in part to the departure of FCOI's chief salesman, Joseph Boland.[111] Another reason might be the subject matter - a "comedy" about the Royal Irish Constabulary which had been long perceived as a force of repression, especially in rural areas where they were usually present to keep the peace during tenant evictions. As rural unrest grew during the Land War and the Depression of the 1870's, they had violent confrontations with militant Fenians. The tensions increased as the RIC became an urban police force during the late 19th century. Such events were fresh in the minds of many Irish and efforts to "idealize them" as part of "everything Irish" may not have had widespread appeal.

Nine films were in production directed by Abbey Theater actor Joseph Kerrigan. He was later joined at the FCOI by such luminaries as Fred O'Donovan, Brian McGowan and others O'Donovan would later replace Kerrigan as actor-director who left to establish a successful film career in the United States.[112] The FCOI's initial success was due in part to its sales staff, one of whom, Joseph Boland, had formerly represented Norman

Whitten's General Film Supply. By late 1916, the FCOI was still focusing on the domestic Irish market. Only later would it move to Britain and the United States.

In 1918, FCOI produced _Knocknagow_, based on the novel by nationalist writer and former chairman of the IRB's Supreme Council, Charles J. Kickham. Given his strong nationalist credentials and the stated goals of the FCOI, Kickham and his novel _Knocknagow_ was an obvious choice. There were other connections as well. Previous mention was made of James M. Sullivan's family ties to Alexander M. and Timothy D. Sullivan, members of the Young Ireland Movement and editors of the _Nation_. T. D. Sullivan was among several prominent nationalists who accompanied Charles Kickham's hearse in 1882. And while Kickham had policy differences with A. M. Sullivan, the latter actively sought publishers for _Knocknagow_, later having it printed by the _Nation_. It is probable that James M. Sullivan was aware of this part of family lore, and it may have served as an additional incentive for his choosing Kickham's novel in what would be FCOI's most significant cinematic triumph.[113]

Kickham was raised during the period of Repeal agitation. His father was involved in the anti-tithe movement during the 1830s. Kickham was a contributor to several nationalist journals, connections that forced him into hiding during the failed uprising of 1848. He was among the organizers of the IRB, becoming editor of its official organ, the _Irish People_. Because of his alleged involvement in the Fenian conspiracy, Kickham was jailed. Released after a few years because of ill health, he

scene from "Knocknagow" in public domain

nonetheless continued his career with the IRB. Prophetically, Kickham believed Ireland's opportunity would come with Britain's involvement in a major war. It would be more than six decades before such an opportunity arose. According to Russell, the 1879 publication of _Knocknagow_

> became the most popular of Irish novels. Its influence derives mainly from its political importance rather than its literary quality, which is about average for a best-seller but not outstanding . . . It attacks the evils of the landlord system in Ireland, and indirectly the English rule that supported that system. For many years Knocknagow was the book-along with a Prayerbook and Old Moore's Almanac—most likely to be found in any Irish home. Most Irish writers born between 1870 and 1950 would have read it as children . . . For all its sentimentality and inept plotting, it gives a very accurate picture of rural Irish life in the nineteenth century. Furthermore, it was written by one of the ordinary people.

Russell noted other sympathetic authors of the rural poor were usually privileged members of the upper class, but _Knocknagow_ was written from the inside.[114]

Even though Kickham's book was Ireland's most popular novel, Donovan suggests it was largely unread by the Irish public.[115] Hence, Sullivan's FCOI could take liberties with the plot, glossing over the complexities of land ownership and reform, catering instead to an imagined collective past.

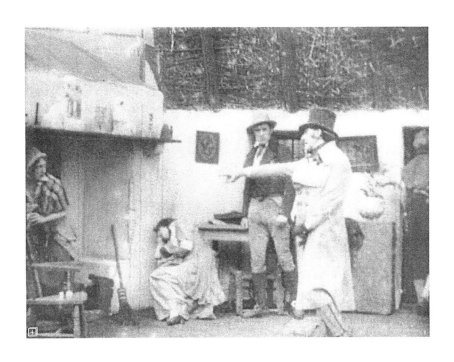

The eviction scene from "Knocknagow" in public domain

In *Knocknagow*, FCOI's nationalist agenda was obvious from the outset. The film version opened with lines from Thomas Davis, a revolutionary writer and poet of the Young Ireland Movement of the mid-nineteenth century. Davis was a Protestant Irish lawyer and poet dedicated to the cause of Irish freedom. He worked tirelessly to eliminate sectarian rivalry and promote Irish unity, even if it meant bloodshed. He advocated cultural nationalism, a revival of the Irish language, and he supported repeal of the Act of Union. Both Padraic Pearse and Arthur Griffith regarded Davis as their mentor.[116] Davis's poetry was first to use the words Sinn Fein (Ourselves Alone). Hence, the film combined memories of resistance to British rule in the nineteenth century, the horrors of the famine, and the recent Easter Rebellion.[117]

As Rocket et al. note, the Kickham novel is set a decade later than the famine years, but the film sentimentalizes the peasant folk of Tipperary of the 1840s, a point noted in the script:

> We ask you to ramble with us through the summer days of Long ago. Come back in spirit to the time when our Great-grandfathers faced a world that had little to offer. We turn back the pages of time to the Ireland of '48' when Irish smiles broke through every cloud of oppression. This story in a series of episodes depicts the joys and sorrows of the simple kindly folk who lived in the homes of Tipperary seventy years ago.[118]

The eviction scenes are especially brutal with the land agent, Prender, watching as the thatched cottage of the O'Brien's is burned to the ground. "Out into the cold roadside in the name of a Christian and benevolent law," the film showed a dispossessed family cowering in a ditch, dependent now on their neighbors for survival.[119]

The sturdy yeoman, Matt the Thrasher, is the central figure, who enshrines the virtue and fortitude of the Irish peasant in contrast to the grasping land agent, Prender. The scene obviously renewed memories for many in the audience of the mass evictions of the 1840s, leaving the Irish the options of either starvation or emigration.[120] Faced with dire circumstances, Matt chose the latter but was prevented from leaving because he was charged with theft. Later cleared, the intertitles declare that through patience and perseverance, the Irish people can rise above adversity.[121] While critical of the absentee landlord, the film glossed over many of the complexities of the landlord-tenant system that emerged in the late nineteenth century. Yet through all, there is the hint of insurgency. Matt the Thrasher, as Prender is preparing to evict his tenants, proclaims, "There will be a stern reckoning for this day, if not in our time, then when other men will know how to deal with their oppression."[122] To an Irish audience, the scene undoubtedly stirred memories of the famine years. The portrayal of the distraught woman against the collapsed wall of her home possibly recalled the mythical icon of Irish resistance to British oppression, Kathleen Ni Houlihan. Generally portrayed as a helpless old woman, she ostensibly summoned young men to rebellion and martyrdom in the rising of 1798. A play of her life was written as a collaborative effort by William B. Yeats and Lady Gregory, first performed in 1902 in Dublin with Maud Gonne playing the lead.[123] Gonne had personally witnessed mass evictions in Donegal in the late nineteenth century and effectively organized protests against them. Obviously, the theme of the play, the actress, and its coauthors reinforced identity with the struggle for Irish freedom.[124]

Also reprising the famine theme, the poem "Dear Old Skibbereen" was republished. Founded in the seventeenth century, the village suffered significant losses during the famine years. It was the home of Jeremiah O'Donovon Rossa and undoubtedly had an impact on him. It became the focus of numerous newspaper accounts detailing the suffering of its inhabitants. The misery was documented by two English visitors, in a narrative of *A Journey from Oxford to Skibbereen during the Year of the Irish Famine.* Initially published in 1880, it was republished in 1915. It related a father answering his son's question as to why he left Ireland to live in America. The poem outlined hardships the Irish people faced in the midnineteenth century and called for vengeance against Britain. The graphic depictions of the Dufferin/Boyle report were echoed in the eviction scene in *Knocknagow.* Allegedly, depictions of Irish rural life made Michael Collins, as a child, weep over the sufferings of the peasantry as described by Kickham.[125]

Sullivan's choice then was logical, and the timing of its release was significant. Initial negative reaction to the Easter Rising had turned in favor of militant Nationalists in the wake of British reprisals, the death of hunger striker Thomas Ashe, the release of the remaining prisoners of the Rebellion, resistance to forced conscription, the election of Eamon DeValera and William Cosgrave to Parliament, and massive defections from John Redmond's Home Rule Party.[126]

The film's director was Fred O'Donovan, long associated with the pro-nationalist theatre.[127] However, the hiring of John MacDonagh was even more significant. Not only was he the brother of the martyred Thomas, like Sullivan, he was interned during the rising and released after several months.[128] In addition, Thomas MacDonagh had, in 1914, along with Joseph Plunkett and Edward Martin, begun the Irish Theatre Company, a short-lived effort formed due to their opposition to the policies of

James K. McGuire (1868-1923)
Irish Nationalist, Associate of James M. Sullivan
The Democratic Party of the State of New York,
United States History Company, 1905[*]

---

[*] no known restrictions, in public domain

Yeats and Lady Gregory.[129] Along with these early stars in Irish theater was a young Cyril Cusack, who portrayed a starving child during the Great Famine in *Knocknagow*. According to Mary Rose Callaghan, Sullivan's granddaughter, Cusack was forced to sit on nettles during the filming. Sullivan and Beffni O'Rorke had a fistfight about Cusack, implying Sullivan was to some degree involved in production more than simply being an absentee producer.[130]

Reaction to the film varied. Bioscope was concerned as to the "vehement Irish point of view of the film about which there is a soupcon of underlying propaganda."[131] The famine theme and British complicity was implicit in intertitles, one stating, "It's a land of plenty and God forgive those who come to starve the Irish." Another read, "What curse is on an Irishman that he cannot ever have poverty's crumb for his dear ones?"[132] Barton, in her assessment, regards the film "the beginning of an overtly politicized cinema: By choosing to adapt Charles J. Kickham's popular novel . . . the Film Company of Ireland invited the audience to locate the revolutionary movement within a historical perspective and, in particular, reminded them of the long history of injustice suffered by the Irish people under colonialism."[133]

A contemporary review of the film praised its content, alleging it was as if Kickham himself would have portrayed it.

"The happy peasantry the prowess of youth at the hurling match, the hammer-throwing contest, the unexpected hunt, the love scenes and the comedy - the life as it was before the agent came like a dark shadow on the scene, and with crowbar and torch laid sweet Knocknagow in ruins - all were depicted by the very perfect actors who made up the cast"[134] "The perfect actors" included FCOI alumni Brian MacGowan, Beffni O'Rourke, Nora Clancy and Fred O'Donovan. James M. Sullivan echoed the comments of the reviewer:

"We desire to show Ireland sympathetically; to get away from the clay pipe and the knee breeches; to show Ireland's rural life with pride in the same; the show Ireland's metropolitan life intelligently depicting men and women of the twentieth century - in short, Ireland at its best in every walk of human endeavor."[135]

So not only was the film striking a blow at the last vestiges of the "stage Irishman", it was immensely popular because it its contemporary political relevance. Typical was the review in Town Hall:

"[The film] pointed to a topical moral at the present time. We saw the evictions, the crowbar brigades, the burnings, the landlord oppression of seventy years ago, the attempt to wipe out a race. Such memories - only of the other day - as it revived scarcely accommodated the mind of the beholder to the nation of conscription."[136]

By reviving the memories of the famine years, the fact that its official opening date was near the anniversary of the Easter Rebellion was probably not lost on the Irish, nor their British authorities. That it occurred during the high water mark of the conscription crisis, opposition to the war and the emergence of Sinn Fein all undoubtedly helped fan the flames of Irish nationalism. Through its official statements, the FCOI was careful not to be too overtly political. It was in financial trouble and its banning by the authorities would spell disaster for its future. For example, Ellen O'Mara Sullivan, the company's creditor, had applied for its "winding up" to allow for reconstruction. She had previously given the FCOI £500 and the company was running at a loss of £1526.[137] This may have been the reason why the company scrimped on the other films to produce "Knocknagow". The surprise popularity of "O'Neill of the Glen" and its successor "Knocknagow" encouraged FCOI to explore the American market. Sullivan's partner, Fitzgibbon had left to explore that potential, but he failed to return to Ireland. It was left to James Mark Sullivan to make that effort.

To buttress its Nationalist underpinnings, its FCOI successor film, *Willy Reilly and His Colleen Bawn*, previewed on the anniversary of the Easter Rebellion.[138] Obviously, the timing was in tune with the FCOI's nationalist agenda. In this context, coupled with the unrest then prevalent in Ireland, it is not surprising the British authorities were suspicious as to the content of *Knocknagow* and its successor, *Willy Reilly and His Colleen Bawn*.

Willy Reilly and His Colleen Bawn continued the nationalist focus of the FCOI. It too was a logical choice. The brainchild of William Carleton, an Irish novelist, who, like Kickham, had strong ties to the Irish peasantry, giving his work a feel of authenticity. Born to Irish-speaking tenant farmers, his family experienced persecution from landlords, later being evicted. Abandoning the idea of the priesthood, Carleton briefly joined the Ribbonmen, a violent secret society. Here the parallels to Kickham end, as Carleton embraced Protestantism and, in turn, was embraced by the ascendancy. His writing was critical of both the Irish peasant and the Catholic Church.[139]

The plot reveals how Willy Reilly, "a Catholic gentleman," rescues the Colleen Bawn, the daughter of a Protestant landlord, from a kidnapper. The two fall in love, but her father, though grateful for his daughter's release, opposes their marriage given their religious differences, preferring instead she marry an anti-Catholic nobleman. The plot twists and turns, but ultimately the evil Protestant landlord and his accomplice are jailed, and the lovers, after a seven-year separation, are reunited.[140]

Despite Carleton's distance from the Irish cause, the script portrays Reilly as an Irish patriot. For example, it has Willy Reilly saying, "I am an O'Reilly—not one of the Queen's O'Reilly's. I am an Irishman." Later, intertitles refer to him as "the bravest-hearted man in Ireland,"[141] "the finest man in County Cavan,"[142] and although "a Papist, a brave man and a gentleman" who, because Britain forbade formal education to Catholic Irish, was educated "by Jesuits on the continent."[143] The Irish audience would probably know that Cavan, located in Ulster, had been ruled by the O'Reilly's, maintaining its independence from British control until the seventeenth century conquest by Oliver Cromwell.[144] Reference to "St. Michins [sic] Church," built in eleventh century, held the graves of "many of Ireland's martyrs."[145] St. Michan's, located in the Four Courts, holds the remains of the Sheare brothers, heroes of the Rising of 1798, and also the body of Robert Emmet, Irish nationalist and Republican rebel, executed during the rebellion of 1803. On the same page of the script is mentioned Gaelic-speaking author John Philpot Curran, eighteenth-century Protestant orator, champion of Catholic emancipation, and critic of the Act of Union. It was this same Curran whose daughter, Sara, had a romantic relationship with the martyred Robert Emmet. A lawyer, Curran defended prominent United Irishmen such as Wolfe Tone and Napper Tandy.[146] Reflecting the arguments of both Roger Casement and James K. McGuire as to British destruction of Irish commerce, the script notes, "The river Shannon, between Clare and Limerick. This river is one of the greatest in Europe and has a channel which permits ships of 35 feet to navigate into the heart of Ireland, namely to the docks in Limerick City. But alas, their [sic] is no navigable river in Europe with such a small amount of shipping disturbing its waters."[147]

A subsequent intertitle reiterates the nascent nationalism in *Willy Reilly*: "The old Parliament House, once the seat of Irish government in Grattan's day, now the Bank of Ireland. It is the hope of the Irish people, that it will be again be converted in to the seat of an Irish Free Government, when self-determination of nationalities is universally established."[148] To Irish and Irish American, this no doubt echoes their endorsement of President Woodrow Wilson's postwar settlement ideal. The allusion to Grattan was also relevant as he was an Anglo-Irish member of the Irish Parliament. Under his leadership, it obtained independence, functioning in that capacity from 1782 until the Act of Union in 1800.[149]

A recurrent theme running through the film is the willingness of the characters to look beyond their sectarian beliefs to achieve a greater good. In *Willy Reilly*, the Catholic hero wins the Protestant maiden. In a dramatic court scene, the Protestant jury believed the notorious Protestant bigot had gone too far in his persecution of Willy Reilly. Instead of convicting him on the charge of robbery—a capital offense for a Catholic—they find him guilty of a lesser charge. The death sentence was instead imposed on the evil Sir Robert and his accomplice.[150] There is, in addition, an underlying theme; that neither Catholics nor Protestants have a monopoly on good or evil. Willy Reilly and Squire Folliard are "good" Irish gentlemen and landowners. Evil is personified in Sir Robert Whitecraft, a Protestant bigot, and Red Rapparee, a Catholic villain. To an Irish audience, the term Rapparee would hold special significance. Rapparee was a designation for Irishmen whose estates had been forfeited during the Cromwellian conquest of the midseventeenth century. Deprived of a livelihood, they allegedly became brigands, rustling cattle, burning homes, committing rape and murder. Their depredations were denounced on several occasions by the Catholic clergy.[151] Given the film was released in 1920, Unionist pressure was forcing the issue of partition. The film's goal, as noted above, to have members of each faith to praise the virtues of the other, was an ultimately unsuccessful effort to prevent sectarian division from bringing greater harm to Ireland. The optimistic message was clear to its Irish audience: all must strive together for an independent, united Ireland.[152]

Sullivan and the FCOI were committed to the cause in other than implied criticism of British misrule. Downing, for example, records the filming of *Willy Reilly*, was interrupted several times when some of the cast members were arrested and jailed by the authorities. Two actors associated with the Abbey Theater, George Nesbitt and Jim Plant, used false names in the credits to avoid identification by the British. The same is suggested for John MacDonagh, who also may have starred in the film.[153]

In addition, in order to subsidize its activities, the Dail Eireann established a Republican Loan Fund in August 1919. John MacDonagh, who directed *Willy Reilly and His Colleen Bawn*, made a film on location encouraging subscriptions from the general public. Featured in it, posed in front of St. Enda's, were Michael Collins, Arthur Griffith, and Diarmuid O'Hegarty selling bonds to Padriac Pearses's mother, Tom Clark's widow, and James Connolly's daughter.[154] Luke Gibbons, perhaps reflecting Wright's antiquarian nationalism, states Pearce specifically moved his school in 1910 to be near the home of Sarah Curran, Robert Emmet's sweetheart.[155] The blending of historic memory with contemporary Irish heroes and victims was undoubtedly successful in obtaining funds from both the native and diasporic Irish community.

The film was exported to America to assist in fund-raising. In Ireland, its showing was of necessity, more coerced. The IRA, over the next year, went into cinemas, forced the projectionist at gunpoint to show the clip, and then disappeared before the police and military could arrive. The brief film brought Collin's name and image before the public as never before and may have been the reason for Sullivan's efforts to identify with him. The extent of Sullivan's involvement in this production is unclear.

He had left Ireland for the United States.[156] But his alleged ties to Collins, the nationalist cause, and the fact it was filmed by FCOI on location at an especially prominent place—St. Enda's—starring significant actors in the cause of Irish freedom hint at his involvement.

St. Enda's was especially relevant to those familiar with the cause of Irish freedom. It was a secondary school for boys established in 1908 by Padraic Pearse. According to one source, the Gaelic version of the school's prospectus urged its students to spend their lives working hard and zealously for their fatherland and, should it be necessary, die for it.[157] Its strong pro-Irish curriculum was influential. Many of its students joined the IRB, with several participating in the Easter Rebellion.[158]

Meanwhile, events in Ireland were proceeding rapidly. By October 1917, a Sinn Fein convention adopted a constitution for an Irish republic, electing Eamon de Valera as president.

In March of the following year, John Redmond passed away, leaving the constitutional Nationalists without an effective leader. The British effort to reinstitute conscription in Ireland resulted in mass protests, which led to the rearrest of DeValera and other Sinn Fein leaders. The public outrage was such that the British government was forced to abandon the unpopular measure. By December 1918, an armistice ended the Great War, and Sinn Fein candidates had won election to the British parliament.

In the United States, many Irish Americans endorsed President Wilson's fourteen points, particularly Articles Five and Fourteen, addressing the issue of self-determination and political independence of colonial peoples. The Irish press, particularly Sullivan ally James K. McGuires's *Catholic Sun*, was extremely outspoken. It urged Irish societies sponsor "Self-Determination for Ireland" demonstrations, publishing a "Petition to the President" to be cut out and signed and sent to the office of the *Catholic Sun*. Articles praised the eight-hundred-year struggle for Irish independence and the sacrifices made by Irish servicemen in the wars of America.[159]

By January of 1919, the Irish nationalists has declared their independence and established their own parliament. DeValera had escaped from prison and began what initially was a popular fund-raising tour of the United States. The net result was twofold: DeValera's activities would shatter the fragile unity of Irish America, and warfare erupted between Sinn Fein and the British. Unfortunately for Ireland, Wilson's idealism on behalf of suppressed nationalities would not prevail in the postwar settlement. The hopes of both Wilson and Irish nationalists were destroyed by the vengeful politics of the victorious Allies, by British intransigence on the Irish problem, and by political schism within the Irish American community.

For the FCOI, however, it generated popular interest in Irish affairs, events the company hoped to capitalize on in marketing its products. Unfortunately, like independence for Ireland at the time, success for the FCOI was elusive.

The Film Company of Ireland in the United States, 1918–1920

S ullivan returned to the United States with the hope of continuing the success the FCOI enjoyed in Ireland. Again the timing seemed propitious.

Letters indicate the family was separated in 1918 with the elder Sullivans in the States and the children left with a nanny in Ireland.[160] Their anticipation of success was not without foundation. Rocket reports when *Knocknagow* was released in the USA, it allegedly grossed more than *Birth of a Nation.*"[161] They possibly sought to capitalize on the publicity surrounding events in Ireland in the wake of British repression following the end of the Great War. The elections of 1918, the beginning of Ireland's War for Independence, and the emergence of Michael Collins undoubtedly were factors. Sullivan identified strongly with Collins, claiming to have been on Collins's staff.[162] According to family correspondence, the American film giant Pathe was interested in marketing their films.[163]

In addition, Sullivan was negotiating with the Shubert organization for showing their films. Beginning in Syracuse, New York, in the late nineteenth century, by 1916 the Shubert Brothers had one thousand theaters nationwide.[164] Had the deal been consummated, it would have augured a successful future for FCOI's American offspring.[165] Nell and James Sullivan separated in December 1918, she returning to Ireland to be with their children and James remaining in the States to attend to FCOI business. Nell's letter reveals the poignant feelings of their parting

> Jim is staying till his business here is more complete . . . We are leaving for Boston Saturday morning . . . There is no news—I hate leaving Jim and and [sic] going 3000 miles away from him.[149] The films [sic] running in Boston he wants to keep near and he's getting more films printed here . . . we are so lonely for our little family that we can't bear to think of Christmas at all.[166]

But financial success was evasive. Nell's letters told of constant moves—Springfield, Boston, Cleveland, New York—living with relatives, in hotels, and of having to pawn jewelry to survive.[167]

Casella states that pawning her jewelry was to get the films out of U.S. Customs and into the film market, pointing to Ellen O'Mara Sullivan's direct economic contribution to the survival of the FCOI.[168]

The return to Ireland was unfortunate. Not only was there continued political unrest, but for the Sullivans, the tragedy was more personal. Nell's letters cited above date from July 1918 to January 1919, when the influenza epidemic was at its height. According to Marsh, the impact of the epidemic was downplayed in both America and the United Kingdom. Emphasis instead was on continental Europe, particularly in Germany, possibly to identify the malady with the now scorned enemy or possibly to minimize panic among the civilian populations.[169] Politics and the war dominated the headlines in Ireland and may have shielded the Sullivans from the true nature and extent of the epidemic. Official statistics record 20,057 deaths in Ireland during the epidemic of 1918–1919. Among them were Nell and Donal Sullivan, possibly succumbing during the last of the three waves of influenza to hit Ireland in early 1919.[170] According to the Humphrys' Family Tree, Donal died in April 1919, and Nell passed away the following month. Both may have died not from the flu but from typhoid, Nell having contracted it from their seven-year-old son.[171] Reinforcing the O'Mara/Sullivan ties to Irish nationalism, both were interred at Glasnevin Cemetery outside Dublin, the repository of the remains of many prominent Irish heroes. Casella states Ellen O'Mara Sullivan received a "full nationalist funeral."[172]

The company ceased production in Ireland in 1920, promising to commence shortly with a new and more up-to-date studio. At the height of Black and Tan repression, British forces ransacked the deserted FCOI offices.[173] Its short but promising career in Ireland had come to an end. If Diog O'Connell is correct, the passing of Sullivan's wife, Ellen O'Mara Sullivan, in May removed her business acumen from FCOI operations, undermining its long-term potential for success in both Ireland and America.[174] According to Colella, some FCOI directors established Irish Photo Plays, making several films from 1920 to 1922. They were directed by John MacDonagh, who continued the FCOI's nationalist agenda.[175]

The Film Company of Ireland in America in Sullivan's Absence, 1920–1922

O bviously distraught and with three small children remaining, Sullivan returned to the United States to try to revive his legal practice. He purchased some real estate in New York City. This may have been the reason for his withdrawal of cash from the FCOI in Ireland. Taylor Downing stated that was a major reason for the demise of FCOI.[176]

Nonetheless, despite its collapse in Ireland, the company struggled on in America for a few years. James M. Sullivan was absent from the company's operations in America after 1920, but there were two individuals whose presence tied the new Irish Film Company of America to its predecessor. They were Henry M. Fitzgibbon, the cofounder of the FCOI with Sullivan in 1916, and later Stephen O'Mara, Sullivan's brother-in-law and other prominent Boston businessmen. O'Mara was an entrepreneur and secretary-treasurer of the K and S Canadian Tire and Rubber Company of Toronto, Canada, in addition to being director of O'Mara Ltd., of Ireland.[177] According to the records of the company in the archives at Cornell University, the new company obtained all rights to films produced by the parent company, the latter simply retaining the right to show films in Great Britain and Ireland. It was assumed, based on the popularity of *Knocknagow* in Ireland, that the FCOI would

185

find a flourishing market niche in England, Ireland, Canada, and the United States, with a special appeal to members of the Irish diaspora communities.

The company was later moved from its previous site in Boston to Madison Avenue, New York City, under the names of Arthur F. Ward and A. V. Feary.[178] Sullivan's name is absent from any correspondence. Although the name Film Company of Ireland was retained, it was controlled by the Wharton Releasing Company of Ithaca, New York. The sale may have been a response to Sullivan's more reduced circumstances or the fact his wife, Nell, who wrote much of the script for *Knocknagow*, was too close to his fond memories of the FCOI.[179] The inventory included some nine or ten films from which the new Film Company of Ireland hoped to profit.

The Wharton Releasing Company of Ithaca, New York was not an unusual choice. The Wharton brothers, Theodore and Leopold, made Ithaca a center for silent film production from 1914 to 1920. They established an elaborate studio in what is now Stewart Park. Theodore Wharton had prior experience as a writer for both Edison and Kalem studios and brought several of their talented technicians with him. In its short career, the Wharton Studio produced over sixty films. Financially underwritten by media magnate William Randolph Hearst, it established the Wharton Releasing Company as an independent distribution service in an unsuccessful effort to compete with Hollywood megastudios. Unfortunately, a contentious relationship with Hearst led to lawsuits and the eventual demise of the Wharton Studio.[180]

The company's two best-known films, *Knocknagow* and *Willy Reilly* initially found a market niche playing in Catholic schools, parish houses, and Knights of Columbus Halls. The films were less successful in being marketed to general theaters, which the emerging Hollywood megastudios would soon dominate.

The marketing methods used by Ward and Feary were already dated. Despite its modern title, the Ward system depended on traveling exhibitions focusing on smaller venues, such as churches, parish halls and Knights of Columbus clubs. Films with larger showings, included live entertainment, typical of the period before large movie theaters were commonplace. Given the Catholic church's concern about amoral films being produced by Hollywood, Ward and Feary specifically targeted parish clergy selling their product as uplifting in contrast to the alleged licentious Jewish-controlled Hollywood films. One priest wrote to Feary:

> The taste of people in general are depraved. They only want off-color pictures for which the Jews are responsible. Why not elevate them? I have been trying to do that for years and (sic) while I have partly succeeded. The results are not gratifying. I was well-pleased with your pictures. They deserve better patronage than they are getting. I have your music here –any time you send for it you may have it.[181]

Despite their limited marketing techniques, the FCOI tried to be competitive. It's files contains lists of numerous pastors, churches, schools, K of C chapters and Irish organizations and their logistical capabilities, such as numbers of seats, membership rolls, and projection facilities, even developing a form letter to tap into this market potential. It reads...

Reverend (sic) Father

We should like very much to bring these pictures to [] but the managers of the theaters are rather skeptical about the support of the church and the Irish people. Our pictures are clean elevating and entertaining. If you would like to see them brought to [] and would go to the trouble of phoning on writing the managers of [] about them, it would undoubtedly create confidence and very likely inspire a booking.

Thank you for your trouble, we are yours sincerely,
FCOI [182]

Irish – American solidarity was emphasized as one vehicle to retail their films. For example, a letter to the Charles J. Kickham Council demonstrated the problem of marketing films to general theaters; -they were often perceived as propaganda by many non-Irish theater owners, a problem they thought could be overcome by focusing on the nostalgia Irish -Americans felt for their homeland.

> As explained to you, the Film Company of Ireland is the only company operating in America presenting to the American public genuine pictures made in Ireland by Irish men and women. Brian Magowan, who is the leading man [in Knocknagow], is a major in the Irish Republican Army and others in the company are actively identified with Irish Republican activities. Seventy percent of all moneys received by the New York office is returned to the parent company. As further explained to you, I have great trouble in booking these pictures, owing to the fact that a great number of theater owners claim they are Irish "propaganda" and will not run them. If every lover of Ireland would get back of us, we could show these pictures in every city, town and village of the United States. [183]

Ward and Feary integrated film exhibition with Irish singers and dancers. They played on what Julia Wright described as romantic and diasporic nationalism, the sentimental attachment of the Irish American community to their native land. They openly marketed their product by inserting nationalist themes in their advertising—flaunting prominent names such as Brian McGowan, showing films on St. Patrick's Day, and urging promoters to Sinn Fein the performances. At least one exhibition featured a speech by Australian archbishop Daniel Mannix. The archbishop often joined DeValera on the latter's fund-raising drive in 1920, mincing no words in his outspoken condemnation of British rule in Ireland.[184] Apparently, Ward and Feary thought such efforts would have the Irish throw their money at the vendors. "What they want is to be excited and to be appealed to upon a patriotic basis with the idea that they are martyrs and bound to win out."[185]

Not only was the name of Brian Magowan openly stated in its marketing, some of its efforts targeted various Irish nationalist groups vying for control of Irish Catholic opinion in America. A response from 1921 found in the Wharton files mentioned the American Association for the Recognition of the Irish Republic. It was formed in 1920 by Eamon DeValera after he found himself in conflict with John Devoy and Daniel Cohalan's Friends of Irish Freedom. An initial warm welcome to DeValera by FOIF became bitter acrimony, as the two groups focused on different agendas for their respective organizations. A second letter also advocated retailing the films to the AARIR.

> The way to handle the pictures is to Sinn
> Fein them. That is to say, appeal to the patri-
> otic side of the Irish people, giving them,
> for instance as a special entertainment at
> the Davidson, some Irish songers [sic],

dancers, and speakers, decorate the theatre with the Sinn Fein color, green, white, and orange and get out your printed matter on these colors. Then get somebody from the American Association for the Recognition of Independent Ireland [sic] to address [sic] the audiences. By pulling this little stunt you can pack the Davison theater for a week as I said before, get back your entire investment and anywhere from two and four thousand dollars to the good.[186]

Ward and Feary also sought to tap the potential in the Friends of Irish Freedom. For example, in an effort to market its products in Chicago, the FCOI urged such a presentation to FOIF as the "right idea." "Unquestionably a special engagement with the Sons [sic] of Irish Freedom would yield a profit to all of us and accelerate a sale." Advertising was also posted in Irish newspapers, including some with a history of support for the Irish cause. They included the *Irish Press*, the *Catholic Standard and Times*, the *Advocate*, and the *Irish World*.[187]

Appeals were also made directly to the Catholic clergy, from ranking members of the church hierarchy down to the parish level openly courting it by appealing to the church's role as guardian of Catholic morality. In a public relations coup, their product obtained an endorsement from Cardinal William H. O'Connell. An American-born conservative head of the Archdiocese of Boston, he condemned Hollywood films as "the scandal of the world."[188] In contrast, his eminence said with reference to the FCOI classic:

Splendid! Splendid! I never enjoyed anything more in life.

The acting of the Irish actors and actresses is typical of the Irish life and being natives of Ireland, they put their very best interest into the work.

"KNOCK-NA-GOW" is a truly wonderful picture and I trust everybody will see it to enjoy it. We should have more of this kind of pictures. They are clean and interesting and serve to elevate the mind.[189]

At the parish level, similar concerns for morally correct pictures were also echoed. A letter to Fr. Coyle of St. Thomas Aquinas in the Bronx stated as follows:

It is no trouble to market and exploit salacious and vicious pictures. It is hard to attract the public to good clean pictures. The church clamors for good clean pictures, and we want to give them, but we must have assistance and co-operation to make them possible of success. Rules and regulations about pulpit announcements should be set aside for the cause. Without aid we fail—and without the fullest cooperation of the church and all rightminded men and women, there is no hope for the clean wholesome picture.[190]

A letter to the FCOI revealed Ward and Feary also tied their appeals to contemporary headlines and religion:

> There is no doubt in my mind that a couple of good Irish films productions depicting the past and present turmoil of the Irish race in trying to represent itself to the nations of the earth will mean a crashing attendance of the Irish and other races that are bound to attend. Of course you will need men who understand the calling upon of the various Irish societies and the churches of Catholicism.[191]

Another letter urges film publicity link itself to the Peace Conference then going on in England.

Apparently, the narrow sectarian nationalism of D.P. Moran was the vehicle whereby the FCOI unsuccessfully sought to financially save itself. Efforts at "packaging" the films with Irish singers and dancers, were in themselves insufficient when there was a dearth of Irish clientele in a specific area. Some locales were openly hostile. For example, an FCOI sales representative complaint to Arthur Warde, that "Harrisburg is a bad Irish town . . . No Irish shows are booked here and even Irish acts is (sic) banned in vaudeville at me.[192] It also reflected the reality of the passage of the Government of Ireland Act of December 1920 and the subsequent failure of negotiations the following year between DeValera, Sir James Craig, and Lloyd George to reach an accommodation. Partition as of December 1921 was a political fact.

Attempts to win support from general theaters, with a more varied ethnic clientele, were not successful, and by the end of 1921, the FCOI was experiencing cash flow problems. The Wharton files show increasing notices of overdue bills and demands for payment. Their prodigious efforts brought limited financial rewards. For example, the records of the Wharton Company from a September 25, 1921, showing of *Knocknagow* earned gross receipts of $467. The company's one-third share was a paltry $164. Subsequent showings yielded even smaller returns.[193] The following month's showing at several parish halls paralleled FCOI's declining revenues in the public theaters.

Some of the past due bills were for as much as $572; others totaled less than $17.[194] Several carried the threat of legal action as in the letter from the attorney for the Plateless Engraving Company for work done on September 20, 1921. Invoices were sent out on October 1, October 18, and November 1.

> Have heard nothing from you since December 17th. Please send check immediately. No further post payment will be granted. Herman Cook, Attorney[195]

Some of the difficulties encountered by the salesmen of FCOI were: they exaggerated the products market potential and had relatively high costs. It also suffered from complaints as to its aging product, then several years old with no new reels in production.[196] In addition, there was resistance from many outside the Irish diasporic community and a reluctance by major theater owners to show FCOI films with its limited potential for profit.

By April 1922, the last effort to market its films was registered. After that, the files are silent. The company fell victim to large Hollywood studios, more sophisticated marketing techniques, and the signing of the treaty accords initially bringing peace to Ireland followed by the horrors of its Civil War, which led to a decline of interest in things Irish.

The FCOI was gone, but its progenitor continued his ties to Ireland in America. That it persisted for six years can be attributed to Ellen O'Mara Sullivan and James M. Sullivan's tenacity, timing, and ties to Irish nationalism. Sullivan would live until 1935, playing cameo roles as diplomat and publicist for the new Ireland. But by 1922, his participation in the cause of Irish freedom was over.

End Notes

1   Flynn, Arthur, *The Story of Irish Film* (Dublin: Curragh Press, 2005), 20. Denis Condon states the offices were located at 16 Henry Street. Condon, Denis, "Early Irish Cinema," "Constant Watchfulness of Irish Cinema," http://earlyirishcinema.wordpress.com/2016/01/31. Retrieved 26 July 2016.

2   Downing, Taylor, "The Film Company of Ireland," *Sight and Sound* 49, no. 1 (Winter 1979–1980): 42–45. There may have been other investors, including the actor J. M. Kerrigan, militant nationalist James J. Walsh, and possibly the O'Mara family.

3   Rockett, Kevin, Gibbons, Luke Hill, John, *Cinema and Ireland* (Syracuse University Press, 1988), 20; "Sister Pleads For Sullivan," *New York Times* (8 May 1916): 6; "James Mark Sullivan Once US Minister Jailed," *New York World* (5 May 1916): 1–2. According to Thom's Dublin Street Directories, he was listed as a resident at 43 Pembroke Road, from 1917 to 1919, moving in 1920 to 4 Palmerstone Park, Rathmines. However, the Sullivans did return to the States between 1918 and 1920, and James was stranded during the war due to his nationalist affiliations.

4   Rocket et al., op. cit., 29; Callaghan e-mail (10 June 2002).

5   Rocket, Kevin, "Knocknagow, The Film Company of Ireland and Other Historical Films, 1911–1920," http://Screening

the Past.com/2012/02/knocknagow-the-film-company-of ireland, p.6. Retrieved 6 June 2012.

6   "Written on the Screen," *New York Times* (17 January 1915).

7   Special Acts of the General Court of Massachusetts, Session Laws 1917, Chapter 157, p. 125; Berger, Meyer. "Baldy Jack Rose Dead at 72. Police Close File on Becker-Rosenthal Case," *New York Times* (9 October 1947): 52.

8   Welch, Richard F., *King of the Bowery: Big Tim Sullivan Tammany Hall and New York City from the Gilded Age to the Progressive Era* (Albany: SUNY Press, 2008), 90–92.

9   Ibid., 192.

10   Bowser, Pearl, Gaines, Jane and Mussor, Charles (eds) *Oscar Micheaux and His Circle* (Bloomington: Indiana University Press, 2001); Hoberman, J., *Bridge of Light Yiddish Film between Two Worlds* (New York: Museum of Modern Art, 1991); Cited in Felter, Maryanne, and Schultz, Daniel, "Selling Memories, Strengthening Nationalism: The Marketing of the Film Company's Silent Films in America," *Canadian Journal of Irish Studies* 32, no. 2 (Fall 2006): 10.

11   Wittke, Carl, *German Americans and the World War* (Columbus: Ohio State Archaeological and Historical Society, 1936), 9; Link, Arthur S., *The Struggle for Neutrality 1914–1915* (Princeton: Princeton University Press, 1960), 31.

12   Jones, John Price, and Hollister, Paul H., *The German Secret Service in America* (Boston: Small, Hayward and Co. 1918), 181–183.

13   Jones and Hollister, op. cit., 238–239; Bernstorff, Count Johan von, *My Three Years in America* (New York: Scribners, 1920), 47; Child, Clifton, *The German-Americans in Politics, 1914–1917* (Madison: University of Wisconsin Press, 1939), 36 fn26.

14   "Former Mayor Asks to Be Judged," Post-Standard (15 December 1918), McGuire File, Onondaga Country Library; Wittke, Carl, *The Irish in America* (Baton Rouge: Louisiana State University Press, 1956), 277.

15   Condon, Denis, "Early Irish Cinema: Irish Cinema and Politics In Autumn 1915," http://earlyirishcinema. Wordpress.com. Retrieved 26 July 2016.

16   von Dopperen, Ron and Graham, Cooper. Shooting the Great War: Albert Dawson and the American Correspondent Film Company, 1914-1918. Charleston, South Carolina. 2013, 45-105.

17   lbid., 33.

18   lbid., 137.

19   Fletcher, Tony. "May Clark". In Jane Gaines, Raide Valsat,and Monica Dell'Astra {eds.), Women Film Pioneers Project. Center For Digital Research and Scholarship, New York City, N.Y. 2013.

20   Martin, Pierce. "O'Donovan Rossa was a terrorist monster." http://irishexaminer.com/viewpoints/your/view/odono-van-rossa-was-a-terrorist-monster346153.html. Retrieved 15 October 2015.

21   "Thomas James Clarke (1857–1916)," http://irishfreedom. net. Fenian Graves/TJ Clarke/TJ Clarke/TJ Clarke htm. Retrieved 6 June 2012; "The 1916 Rising: Personalities and Perspectives: John Devoy, Joseph McGarrity, and the Clan na Gael," National Library of Ireland, http://www. nli.ie/1916/. Retrieved 6 June 2012.

22   Slide, op. cit., 33; Rocket, et al., op.cit, 33.

23   "Early Irish Cinema: Filming The Funeral of Thomas Ashe, September-October, 1917." Retrieved by 3 January 2018.

24   "Peep At Parochial Happenings: Irish Newsreel Begins, June-July 1917. https://early.irishcinema.com/2017/7. retrieved 17 May 2018.

25   ——, "Early Irish Cinematograph: An Unrehearsed Picture," http://earlyirishcinema.wordpress.com/2016/01/31. Retrieved 22 July 2016.

26   "Jack Johnson (1876-1946) was an African-American heavy-weight boxing champion during the Jim Crow era of American history. He is probably best-known for "the fight of the century" in 1910 against former champion Jim Jeffries. His association with white women made him a target of racists at the time. Many Irish-Americans were pugilists. Some, like John L. Sullivan refused to fight him. "Jack Johnson Biography." http://www.biography.com/people/jack-johnson-9355980. Retrieved 7 September 2016. Rocket, Kevin, *Irish Film Censorship: A Cultural Journey from Silent Film to Internet Pornography* (Dublin: Four Courts Press, 2004), 32–33, 39.

27   Rocket, op. cit., 43.

28   Ibid., 37.

29   Condon, Denis, "Early Irish Cinema: in The Grips of Spies," http://earlyirishcinema.wordpress.com/2016/01/31. Retrieved 20 July 2016.

30   Ibid.

31   Ibid.

32   ——, "Early Irish Cinema: Irish Cinema Catches Public Eye in February 1916," http://earlyirish cinema.wordpress.com/2016/01/31. Retrieved 21 July 2016.

33   Condon, op. cit.

34   "The Constant Watchfulness of Irish Cinema In March 1916". https:// early.irish.cinema.com/2016/3. Retrieved 17 April 2018.

35   "Irish Cinema and the Desire For Change In April 1916:. https:// early.irish. cinema.com/2016/04. Retrieved 18 April 2018.

36 "Dublin Vigilance Association" https://early.irish.cinema. com/2015/02. Retrieved 15 May 2018.

37 "Watched By Millions of Eyes: Irish Cinema's Manifest Potentialities in October 1916" https: //early.irish.cinema. com/2016/04. Retrieved 12 April 2018

38 Delaney, Paul. "D.P. Moran And The Leader: Writing An Irish-Ireland Through Partition." Eire-Ireland: Irish-American Culture Institute, vol. 38, November 3, 4, Fall/ Winter 2003, pp. 189-211.

39 For Gaelic Athletic Association, see English, Richard. Irish Freedom: The History of Irish Nationalism in Ireland. Pan Books, 2007, pp. 227-231; For Gaelic League, see "The Gaelic League And The 1916 Rising." https://www.ie/ centuryireland/index.php/articles/the-gaelic-league-and-the-1916-rising. Retrieved 3 November 2013.

40 Marc Gunn Presents "Irish Song Lyrics and Other Celtic Lyrics," www.irish-song-lyrics.com/when_irish_eyes_ are_smiling.shtml. Retrieved 30 November 2014; www. music.folder.com/blog/about-danny-boy. Retrieved 30 November 2014.

41 Rocket et al., op. cit.

42 "A Short-Cuts History of New York and Film," http:// nymag.com/movies/filmsfestivals/newyork/2007/38002, p. 1. Retrieved 20 June 2012; "George Kleine: American Producer, Distributer, Who's Who in Victorian Cinema," http:// www.vicorian-cinema. Net/kleine.httm. Retrieved 19 June 2012; "Samuel K. Long, Dead," *New York Times* (29 July 1915).

43 Rocket et al., op. cit., 20; Flynn, op. cit, 13.

44 Flynn, op.cit., 10.

45 Slide, Anthony, *The Cinema and Ireland* (North Carolina: McFarland and Company, 1988), 1.

46   McLoone, Martin, *Irish Film: The Emergence of a Contemporary Cinema* (London: British Film Institute, 2000), 6.

47   "Irish Silent Films," http://www.tcd.ie/irishfilm/silent/ me_1916_ film.php. Retrieved 20 June 2012.

48   Donovan, Stephen, "Introduction: Ireland's Own Film in Screening the Past," Com/2012 02/introduction-to-ire-land's-own-film. Retrieved 6 June 2012.

49   Barton, op. cit., 19; Downing, op. cit., 42.

50   "The Bioscope: the O'Kalems," http://thebioscope. net/2011/03/26 the –okalems, 1-2". Retrieved 20 June 2012.

51   Barton, op. cit., 20.

52   Downing, op. cit., 42.

53   "Lad from Old Ireland," Irish Silent Films/Trinity College, Dublin,   http:www.tcd.ie/irishfilm/silent/lad_from_old_ ireland. Retrieved 21 March 2013; Barton, op. cit., 19; Langon, Sheila, Irish America.com/…/Blazing-The-Trail-To-Ireland. Retrieved 21 March 2013.

54   Plant, David, "The Irish Uprising of 1641," BCW project. BCW-Project.org/church-and-state/confederate-ireland/ The Irish Uprising. Retrieved 20 January 2015.

55   Rocket, "Knocknagow," op. cit., 2; www.historyire-land.com/ 20th century-contemporary-history-em-met-on-film/. Retrieved 21 January 2015.

56   Silentbeautiesblogspot.com 2012/2013/rory-omore-1911. Retrie ved 20 January 2015; "Rory O'More: Irish Silent Films," Trintity College, Dublin, http/www.ted/irishfilms/ silent/Mary-O-more.php. Retrieved 20 June 2012.

57   Proinsias O Conluain. "Ireland's First Films," *Sight and Sound* 23, no 2 (October–December 1953): 96. Cited in Rocket, et al., op. cit. 10; see also Barton, op. cit. 19

58   www.historyireland.com/20th-century-contemporary-his-tory-emmet-on-film/. Retrieved 21 January 2015.

59   Rocket et al., op. cit., 9.

60   Silentbeautiesblogspot.com/2012/03 for-irelands-sake.1914 html; silent era.com/PSFL/data F/Forirelandssake-1914 html. Retrieved 25 January 2015.

61   Silentbeautiesblogspot.com/all-for-ireland-1915html. Retrieved 25 January 2015; Rocket, et al, 21.

62   Kramer, Fritz: For Ireland's sake (1914): A Silent Film review".moviessilently.com2015/08/for-irelands-sale-1914/.

63   "All for Old Ireland". Irish Silent Films, Trinity College, Dublin, http://www.tcd/ie/irish/films/showfilm/php. fid=58072, Retrieved 20 June 2012.

64   "All for Old Ireland," Lubin Film Mfg. Co. USA. Sydney Olcott, 1915. http://www/tccd.ie/irishfilm. php?fid=58022. Retrieved 22 May 2011.

65   "Bold Emmet, Ireland's Martyr," Irish Silent Films. Trinity College Dublin, http://www.tcd.ie/irishfilm/showfilm/ php?Fid=58023. Retrieved 20 June 2012;

66   "Robert Emmet, 1778–1803; Irish Patriot and Orator," www. Robertemmet.org. Retrieved 21 January 2015.

67   "Blazing the Trail: The Kalem Film Company," op. cit., 4.

68   Barton, op. cit., 19, 20.

69   "Blazing the Trail: The Kalem Film Company," op. cit., 4.

70   Flynn, op. cit., 13–16. Barton 2004 (19) also cites O'Conluain (1953: 97) on this point. This assertion is debated. Rocket marshals strong evidence, which demonstrates British interference in Kalem's filmmaking in Ireland, should be relegated to "Nationalist myth." Rocket, "Knocknagow," op.cit., fn 9, 19–20.

71   Barton, op. cit., 18–19.

72   Fr. John Murphy (1753–1798) was initially hostile to the rebellion but later became a leader after the massacre of Irish peasants by Loyalist cavalry. Initially successful, he was captured, tried for treason by a military tribunal,

tortured, stripped, flogged, hanged and decapitated, his corpse burned, and his head placed on a spike as a warning to others. Instead he became a folk hero whose memory is celebrated in the song "Boolavogue." Retrieved 23 February 2115. www.hibernianrebels.org/father-murphy.html; www.catholicireland.net-father-murphy-of-bool-avogue. "Fr. Murphy was portrayed in the film reacting to the Act of Union of 1800. The real Fr. Murphy was executed during the Rebellion of 1798.

73 Michael Dwyer (1772–1825) was a successful guerilla leader of the 1798 rebellion in Wicklow, enabling his followers to hold out until 1803. He negotiated terms of surrender and was ultimately sent to Australia. His ability as a guerilla leader supposedly inspired Dan Breen and Michael Collins. Retrieved in 23 February 2013. From "Great Irish Journeys-Michael Dwyer," http://wwwyoutube.com/watchv-csVSXu2G4.

74 For details on half hanging, see Deary, Terry. "Cool For Criminals." Loathsome London. Horrible Histories. London: Scholastic, p.63

75 "Would We Ever Have Seen It In Reality? "Ireland: A Nation For Two days Only in January 1917"https://early.irish.cinema.com/2017/01 Retrieved 27 June 2018. Lawlor, op. cit.

76 "Ireland: A Nation," ingb.com/title/tt0004164/?ref= nmflmg.wr.5. Retrieved 23 January 2015; "Ireland: A Nation," www.tcd.ie/irish film/silent/ireland-a -nation. php/. Retrieved 27 January 2015.

77 http:// www.stanford.edu/~gdegrout/AJ/reveiewers/wtgd. htm-3 3http:// www.ed.ie/irish.film/show.php/?fid t58178. Retrieved 6 June 2012. Critics from Variety, New York Dramatic Mirror and Morning Picture World believed the treatment of the subject was even-handed. The producer, J.

Stuart Blackton, was considered on a par with D. W. Griffith. He formed American Vitagraph in 1897, http://fandango. com/ j.stuartblackton/biographies/p185011. Retrieved 9 June 2012. According to one source, the director, Frank Borzage, made films focusing on the "lives of lovers imperiled by the adversity of socio-political events." His long Hollywood career spanned the transition from silent to sound pictures. He was the first to win an Academy Award for directing. "Frank Borzage: A Biography," www.imdb. com/name/nm0097648.bio. Retrieved 3 March 2015.

78 "Say Irish Friends Cause Movie Rows," *New York Times* (25 January 1917): 7.

79 "James Sullivan Once US Minister, Arrested As Rebel," *New York World* (5 May 1916): 1. Gavan, See / Jeremiah A. O'Leary, My Political Trial and Experiences, New York, Jefferson Publishing CO., Inc., 1919. v-x

80 Slide, op. cit., 5–7.

81 "Idealizing Everything Irish: The Film Company of Ireland Releases "Rafferty's Rise" in Late 1917". https:// early.irish. cinema.com /2017/ 12. Retrieved 17 May 2018.

82 Condon, Denis, "Early Irish Cinema: Constant Watchfulness of Irish Cinema, March 1916," http://early-inshcinema.wordpress.com/2016/01/31. Retrieved 20 July 2016. Others say it was on Sackville Street. See McLoone, op. cit., 28.

83 "Irish Cinema Catches Public Eye In February 1916". https:// early.irish.cinema.com/ 2016/02. Retrieved 17 February 2018.

84 "Jim Sullivan," HumphysFamilyTree.com Retrieved 31 January 2011.

85 "British Seize A. [sic] M. Sullivan On Irish Soil." New York Times, 5 May 1916.

86   Lavelle claims Sullivan was too busy with the FCOI to take part in the Rising

87   Rocket et al., op.cit., 17; "British Seize A [sic] M. Sullivan On Irish Soil," *New York Times* (5 May 1916). Sullivan was among many "Sinn Fein and Republican Suspects," along with such notables as Michael Collins, James Connolly, Eamon DeValera, Arthur Griffith, John Kelly, Thomas Larkin, John MacDonagh, and others. This suggests, at least to British authorities, that Sullivan was a significant player in the fight for Irish freedom.

88   Downing, op. cit., 43.

89   "Sister Pleads for Sullivan," *New York Times* (8 May 1916): 6. The issue is open to debate. There was massive roundup of suspects by British authorities in the wake of the Easter Rising. John O'Connor, in *The 1916 Proclamation* (Minneapolis: Irish Books and Media, 1999), 4, notes over three thousand people seized, with slightly over half of that number being interned. "Michael Collins Rise to The Mystery Man of Ireland," *Springfield Sunday Republican* (10 September 1922), 2A.

90   James M. Sullivan Collins Journal. Unpublished. Quoted with permission of Mary Rose Callaghan. Sullivan allegedly maintained contact with Collins through at least 1922. In Piaris Beasli papers, cited in "Jim Sullivan," Humphrys Family website; "Michael Collins Rise to the Mystery Man of Ireland," *Springfield Sunday Republicans* (10 September 1922), 2A. The article notes under a picture of James M. Sullivan that he was "Formerly in Close Association with Michael Collins on Irish Leader's Staff."

91   Downing, op. cit., 42.

92   Ibid.

93   Casella, Donna, "Ellen O'Mara Sullivan," Jane Gaines Radha Vatsal, and Maria Dall' Asta, eds., <u>Women</u>

Film Pioneers Project, Center for Digital Research and Scholarship (New York, NY: Columbia University Libraries, 2013), http://wfpp.cdrs.columbia.edu/pioneer/ellen-omara-sullivan. Retrieved 29 July 2016.

94   O'Connell, Diog, "Ellen O'Mara Sullivan and the Film Company of Ireland," http://www.tcd.ie.film/news. Retrieved 29 July 2016.

95   Casella, op. cit., 3. Casella suggests that Mrs. N. T. Patton is "widely acknowledged as having scripted the screenplay for "Knocknagow"

96   "British Seize," op. cit.

97   "James M. Sullivan, Once US Minister," op. cit.

98   "Jim Sullivan," Humphrys Family Website. http://Humphrys family tree.com/Humphrys/dick.htm/. Retrieved 13 June 2011. Dick Humphrys was educated at St. Enda's, was an active member of the Irish volunteers who fought at the GPO during the Easter Rebellion. He was first housed at Kilmainham gaol, later in Britain. He was interned three times by the British during the War of Independence. He was business partner in the O'Mara Rubber Company, marrying into the family in 1929; Dowling, "Film Company of Ireland," *Sight and Sound* 49, no. 1 (Winter 1979–1980): 42–45.

99   Lavelle, Patrica, *James O' Mara: Staunch Sinn Feiner, 1973–1948* (Dunmore: Canmore and Reynolds, 1961), 112–113.

100   O'Connor, John, *The 1916 Proclamation* (Minneapolis: Irish Books and Media, 1999).

101   "James M. Sullivan, Once US Minister," op. cit. The New York Times described FOIF as a "respectable organization, conceived by John Devoy and the Clan-na-Gael consisting of politicians, clergy and other Irish-American leaders." Golway further described FOIF as a "seemingly non-revo-

lutionary, reform-minded organizations" controlled by the Clan. See "Four More Irish Chiefs In Revolt Are Put to Death," *New York Times* (9 May 1916): 2; Terry Golway, *Irish Rebel: John Devoy and American Fight for Irish Freedom* (New York: St. Martin's Press. 1998), 219–220.

102 McLoone, op. cit., 28.

103 Slide, op. cit., 12. The three-reeler's premier was in July 1916 and shown at the Bohemian Theater on 7 August 1916. According to the Humphrys Family website, it was listed as FCOI's first film. It is currently presumed lost. Rockett et al., op. cit., 16–17; "O'Neil of the Glen," Irish Film and TV Research Online-Trinity College, Dublin, http:/www.tcdieirishfilm/showfilm.php?fid=56597. The film may also have been censored because the plot involved murder, fraud, and attempted murder as well, themes at odds with British authorities and Irish Catholic sensibilities.

104 "Irish Audiences Watch "O'Neill of the Glen" August 1916". https://early.irish.cinema. com. /2018/07 Retrieved 16 May 2018.

105 "O'Neil, Neale, Neil: O'Neill. Among the Most Illustrations Surnames of Ireland," http://www.shatowe.como_neil. htm. Retrieved 29 August 2011.

106 Most were comedies. The plots are summarized in Rocket et al., op. cit, 17–18.

107 Barton, op. cit., 23.

108 "A New Industry: The Film Company of Ireland's First Season" https://earlyirish cinema.com/category/films/knocknagow-ireland-fcoi-1918/ret'd 1026/20170

109 Ibid p.2

110 Ibid, 3

111 "FCOI Releases "Rafferty's Rise " in 1917". https://early.irish.cinema.com/2017/07. Retrieved 13 June 2018.

112   Golway, op. cit., 94.

113   Comerford, R. E., *Charles M. Kickham: A Study in Irish Nationalism and Literature* (Portmarnuck, Ireland: Wolfhound Press, 1979), 75, 76, 173. The biographical data on Kickham, is from "Charles Kickham" http:// multitextucc.ie/d/Charles Kickham. Retrieved 10 June 2011; "Charles Kickham," http:// Charles-kickham.co.tv/. According to the latter source, Kickham, despite his infirmities, did not limit himself to propaganda. He both manufactured and came armed with a pike during the rebellion of 1848. And like Casement four decades later, when faced with a term of life imprisonment, he made a speech from the dock condemning British rule. A brief biography and a picture of Kickham's grave site appears in the Humphry's website. Also in Rockett et al., op. cit., 18–19.

114   Russell, Mathew, "Knocknagow by Charles Kickham: Introduction," http://exclassics.com/knockingw/kbnintro.htm. Retrieved 6 June 2011.

115   Donovan, "Introduction: Irelands Own," op. cit, 7–8.

116   Downing, op. cit., 43. Also in Barton, op. cit, 25. See "Thomas Davis," http://www.irishdrinkging-songs.info/songunites/thomasadavis.red'11 July 2011 htm://Parker.Elizabeth. "Ourselvesalone: History. NationalAndTheNation.1852-45;1-18. http://jour-nals.chapman.edu/ojs/index.php.vocesNovae/article.view/198/537. Retrieved 11 July 2011.

117   Parker, op. cit. The author refers to Davis's poem "Ourselves Alone" in the *Nation* (3 December 1842). Irish News Archives for 34, 15; "Stand Together," *Nation* (29 July 1843), Irish News Archives, for 35, 15; and the term Sinn Fein (Shinbar Fayne) in "The Devil May Care," *Nation* (23 September 1843). Irish News Archives, 15, 36.

118 Rocket et al., op. cit., 19. Barton, op. cit., 28 makes a similar point. The screenplay copyright belongs to Ellen Sullivan, wife of FCOI founder, James Mark Sullivan; "Film Company of Ireland: Wharton Releasing Company," Film Company of Ireland Archives, Cornell University. Appendix C, Intertitle 3 in "Screening The Past" http://www.screening-the-past.com/2012/03/appendix.c-interti-tles, p.16. This is an abbreviated version of the citation.

119 Downing, op. cit., 43. Intertitle 79, "Screening The Past, op. cit., p.8

120 Downing, op. cit., 43; Rocket et al., op. cit., ch. 19–21; Barton op. cit., 26.

121 "Screening The Past", op. cit. Intertitle 155, p. 14.

122 Ibid., Intertitle 76, p. 8

123 Brown, Terrence, "The Twentieth Century," Kennelly, Brendan, ed., *Ireland: Past and Present* (Dublin: Gill and MacMillian, 1985), 81 (80–105); Hogan, Robert and O'Neill, Michael. *Joseph Halloway's Abbey Theatre: A Selection from His Unpublished Journal, Impressions of an Irish Playgoer* (Carbondale: Southern Illinois University Press, 1967), 17.

124 Maude Gonne also edited a nationalist journal in exile and established a revolutionary Irish women's society. She married John MacBride, who was executed during the Eastern Rebellion. She was jailed twice—once for her involvement in the anticonscription movement during World War I, and later for supporting the Republican cause during the Irish Civil War. "Maude Gonne: Yeats' Cathleen Ni Houlihan, Ireland's Joan of Arc," http://www.thewildgeese.com/pages/gonne/html. Retrieved 24 August 2011.

125 Dufferin, Lord and the Honorable G. G. Boyle, *Narrative of a Journey from Oxford to Skibbereen During a Year of the*

Irish Famine (Oxford: John Henry Parker, 1847), http://www.thewildgeese.com/pages/gonne/html. Retrieved 24 August 2011. "Schull and Skibbereen: The Two Famine-Slain Sisters of the South," http://www.movinghere.org.uk/galleries/histories/irish/orgins/skibbereen. Retrieved 18 June 2012.

126 Rocket, et al., op. cit., 20–22; Barton, op. cit., 26–27.

127 Barton, op. cit., 27.

128 "Thomas MacDonagh," *Dictionary of Irish Literature*, vol. 12 1996 (ed.), 750.

129 "Irish Playography Theater Company: Irish Theater Company 1914–1920," http://www.irishplayography.com/search/company.aspx?g=endcom. MacLiammore was a British-born Irish Protestant actor, Alfred Lee Williams, later learning Irish and changing his name to present himself as a more authentic Irishman. Other stars included Brian McGowan as "Matt the Thrasher," Breffni O'Rourke as Billy Hefferman and a young Cyril Cusack. Born in South Africa, Cusack returned to Ireland in 1910 when his parents divorced. Breffni O'Rourke married Cusack's mother. Cusack, fluent in the Irish language, had a long career with the Abby Theater and then later in the United States. "Cyril Cusack (1910–1993): Biography," http://www.mooncave.comcusack/bio.htm. Retrieved 10 June 2011.

130 Callaghan e-mail to authors (20 June 2002). Cited in Felter, Maryanne, and Schultz, Daniel, "James Mark Sullivan and the Film Company of Ireland," *New Hibernia Review* 8.2 (Summer 2004), 24–40. In addition, according to the Humphry's Family website, Sullivan produced *Rafferty's Rise* in 1917.

131 Knocknagow *Bioscope* (16 October 1919), 58. Cited in Slide, Anthony, Cinema and Ireland (London McFarland, 1988): 13.

132   Those exact words are not found in "Screening The Past", op. cit, but close approximations are. See op. cit, Intertitles, 121, p. 11; 124, p. 12; 166, p. 15

133   Barton, op. cit., 27.

134   "Knocknagow" On Film: A Picture Play That Will Create A Furor In America.". In <u>Anglo-Celt</u> 2 March 1918. Cited in "Seeing "Knocknagow" In Irish National Cinemas, January - April 1918" https://early.irish.cinema.com /2018/13/ Retrieved 14 March 2018.

135   Ibid

136   "A Picture Play of Unique National Interest: Seeing "Knocknagow" January - April 1918". https://early.irish. cinema.com/2018/13/ Retrieved 14 March 2018.

137   "Instructive Images On Irish Cinema Screens In Late Summer, 1917." https:// earlyirishcinema.com/2017/08. Retrieved 9 May 2018.

138   Rocket et al., op. cit., 21; 27.

139   "William Carleton," http://trashface.com/williamcarleton. htmltrashfaace.com.williamcarleton.html. In the article, Carlton explicitly denies any taint of Irish nationalism, stating he is neither a Repealer, a Young Irelander, nor a Republican. Retrieved 14 June 2011; "William Carlton: 1794–169," http://www.micro.net/rx/az-data/authors/c/ Carleton_W/life.htm. Retrieved 14 June 2011.

140   Irish film and TV research online, Trinity College Dublin, *Willy Reilly A\and His Colleen Bawn*, http://www.tcd. ie.irishfilm.php?-56619. Retrieved 15 January 2014. See Humphrys Family Tree, "Willy Reilly And His Colleen Bawn" in "The Films of James Mark Sullivan (1916-1920), for a good summary of the film,

141   Intertitle, *Willy Reilly and His Colleen Bawn*, 10. Preserved by Film Company of Ireland. Rare and Manuscript Collection. Carl A. Krock Library. Cornell University, Ithaca, New York. Box 3924. "Willy Reilly And His Coleen

Bawn", p. 1, reel 1, Courtesy of Rare and Manuscripts Collection, Carl Krock Library, Cornell University, Ithaca, N.Y, 3924, Box 1

142 "*Willy Reilly*", op. cit., p.6, reel 1; p.6, reel 3.

143 Ibid., p.6

144 "County Cavan, Ireland," http://members.tripod.com~ScottRichaud/cavahistory.html.

145 "The Mummies of St. Michan's," http://irelandforvistors.com/articles/mummies of_St.Michans.htm:script;intertitle; Willy Reilly, op. cit., 5.

146 "John Philpot Curran," http://1911.encyclopedia.org/John_Phiphot_Curran. Retrieved 17 February 2014.

147 Intertitle, *Willy Reilly*, op. cit., 3.

148 "*Willy Reilly*", op. cit., 2

149 "Henry Grattan," WNDB http://www.nndl.com/peple/993/000103624. Retrieved June 2011.

150 "Willy Reilly", op. cit, pp. 3-4, reel 6; p. 2, reel 7

151 Walsh, Walter, *The Unknown Power Behind the Irish National Party* (London: Swan, Sonnenschein and Co. 1906), 26–32. "Rapparree" is also an Irish term for the half-pike, a common weapon for Irish rebels. Walsh, 30, citing Gordon, *History of Ireland* (London, 1806), 159, 160.

152 Downing op. cit., 45. Slide, op. cit., 14.

153 Downing op. cit., 43.

154 Slide, op. cit., 14. "Republican Loan Film 1919," YouTube video, web, http://humphyysfamilytrees.com/OMara/republican.loan.html. Retrieved 1 June 2011. All three were prominent nationalists active in the IRA and later endorsed the treaty ending the Anglo-Irish War in 1921. This reinforces Sullivan's ties to the Free State, later representing it briefly in the United States.

155   Gibbons, Luke, *Transformations in Irish Culture* (Indiana: University of Notre Dame Press, 1996), 108.

156   A. T. Q. Stewart, *Michael Collins: The Secret Files* (Belfast: Blackstaff Press, 1997), 29. Also in Slide, op. cit., 14. This was an important public relations coup for Collins, given the internal power struggle between himself, Cathal Brugha, minister of Defense, and provisional president Eamon DeValera. The dates conflict as to Sullivan's time in America. His article, "Michael Collins's Rise to 'Mystery Man' of Ireland," *Sunday Springfield Republican* (10 September 1922), 2A, states he was in Ireland from 1915 to 1921.

157   "Patrick Pearse," http://historylearningsite.co.uk/patrick-pearce.htm,p.l. Retrieved. 7 September 2011.

158   Sisson, Elaine, *Pearce's Patriots: St. Enda's and the Cult of Boyhood* (Cork: University Press, 2004).

159   "Call Issued for Irish Cause," *Catholic Sun* (29 November 1918): 5; "Urgent," *Catholic Sun* (29 November 1918): 5 "Let Us Be Up and Doing for Ireland," *Catholic Sun* (29 November 1918): 5; "Why America Should Insist on Self-Determination for Ireland," *Catholic Sun* (6 December 1918): 1.

160   Callaghan e-mail to author (18 June 2002). Cited in Felter, Maryann, and Schultz, Daniel, "James Mark Sullivan and the Film Company of Ireland," *New Hibernia Review*, 8.2 (Summer 2004), 31.

161   Rocket et al.

162   "Michael Collins' Rise to The Mystery Man of Ireland," *Springfield Sunday Republican* (10 September 1922), 2A. Other than his statement, there is little to corroborate Sullivan's claim.

163   Nell Sullivan to Hazel O'Mara (27 July 1918). Cited in Felter/Schultz, op. cit., 31.

164 "Shubert Organization," http://www.shubertorganization. com/theatres/default.asp. Retrieved 2 August 2012.

165 Nell Sullivan to Hazel O'Mara (4 January 1919). Cited in Felter/Schultz, op. cit., 2004, 31.

166 Nell Sullivan to Hazel O'Mara (4 December 1918). Ibid.

167 Nell Sullivan to Hazel O'Mara (19 December 1918); Nell Sullivan to Hazel O'Mara (27 July 1918). Ibid.

168 Casella, op. cit., 3.

169 Marsh, Patricia, "Mysterious Malady Spreading: Press Coverage of the 1918–1919 Influenza Pandemic in Ireland," Quest Proceedings of QUBAHSS Conference, June 2008. Issue #6 Autumn 2008, ISS 1750-9696.

170 Ibid., 167.

171 "Humphry's Family Tree," op. cit., 3.

172 Casella, op.cit., 3.

173 Donovan, "Introduction: Irelands Own," op. cit fn. 3, 23.

174 O'Connell, op. cit.

175 Colella, op. cit., 4.

176 Downing, op. cit., 45.

177 O'Mara, Stephen, "O'Mara Family Home Page, 3. www.compapp.dcu.ie/~humphrys/Fam/Tree/Omeara/ Stephen.html. Other early members of the board included President Francis Flynn (Boston Globe), Bernard J. Heaney (Hibernian Savings Bank, Boston), Stephen O'Mara as treasurer, and Timothy J. McKeon and Peter J. Nathan as directors (Donavan "Introduction: Ireland's Own Film," op. cit., fn. 10, 23).

178 Wharton Releasing Company Records. Cited in Felter and Schultz, 2004.

179 Ibid., 2004, op. cit., 31.

180 "History of Silent Films Made in Ithaca." http://ithacamademoves.com/history. Retrieved 16 November 2016; Terry Harbin. Ithaca had Movies.

http"//ithacamoves.proboards.com/thread199. Retrieved 19 November 2016.

181 Felter/Schultz, ibid.

182 Felter, Maryann and Schultz, Daniel. "Selling Memories, Strengthening Nationalism: The Marketing of the Film Company of Ireland's Silent Films in America." Canadian Journal of Irish Studies vol.32, no.2, fall 2006, 11.

183 Felter, Maryann and Schultz, Daniel. "James Mark Sullivan and The Film Company of Ireland." New Hibernia Review 8.2, Summer, 2004, 35–36.

184 Broderick, Joe, "DeValera and the Archibishop Daniel Mannix," www.history irleand.com/20th century contemporary-history/de-valera-and the-archbishop-daniel-mannix-by-joe-broderick. Retrieved 7 February 2015.

185 Felter/Schultz, op. cit, 2006, 11.

186 Cited in Felter/Schultz, op. cit, 2004, 38.

187 Cited in Felter, Maryann, and Schultz, Daniel, "Selling Memories, Strengthening Nationalism: the Marketing of the Film Company of Ireland's Silent Films in America, "Canadian Journal of Irish Studies 32:2 (Fall 2006): 15.

188 O'Toole, James M., *Militant and Triumphant: William Henry O'Connell and the Catholic Church in Boston, 1859–1944* (Notre Dame: Indiana University Press, 1992), 243. O'Connell was strongly identified with Ireland, receiving its leaders and advocating its independence at a major Irish convention in December 1918; Carroll, Francis M., "Friends of Irish Freedom," Funchion, Michael F. *Irish Voluntary Organizations* (Westport, Connecticut: Greenwood Press, 1983), 119–126). He had recently weathered personal scandals as to his sexual preferences and his longtime secret protection of a married priest who was his nephew and who had a prominent position in the Boston Church hierarchy. Hence, his desire to maintain a

high moral profile in public. For details, see O'Toole, op. cit., 173–207.

189 Cited in Felter/Schultz, 2006, op. cit., 16.

190 Letter from Elizabeth Shaw 5 October 1921, Wharton Folder 1-2; Cited in Felter and Schultz, "Selling Memories, 16.

191 Cited in Felter/Schultz 2006, op. cit.

192 Letter from Brightly Dayton to FCOI 2 September 1921, Wharton Folder, 1-23. Cited in Felter and Schultz, op. cit., 2006, 14.

193 Wharton Releasing Company Files. Box 3924, Files 1–56.

194 Ibid.

195 Ibid.

196 Ibid.

CHAPTER V

Epilogue
Sullivan's Ghost

J
ames M. Sullivan lived on until 1935 under diminished circumstances. His Film Company of Ireland had moved from Boston to New York City, and his name disappeared from any company records by 1921. Having returned to America in 1920 with his surviving children, he tried to resuscitate his law career. The Humphrys Family Tree website lists Sullivan registered as a lawyer three times: in New Haven, Connecticut, 1903–04; in New York City, 1904–1916; and once again in New York City from 1924 to 1930.[1] His ties to Tammany Hall, which made it possible to obtain some financial stability, undoubtedly disappeared with the deaths of Big Tim Sullivan in 1913 and Boss Charles Murphy a decade later. New leaders of Tammany emerged during Sullivan's second tenure in New York City—George W. Olvany, from 1924 to 1929, and John F. Curry, from 1929 to 1934. Olvany was a graduate of New York University Law School, an alderman, a lawyer, a counsel to Governor Al Smith, and later a judge. Within six months, he resigned from the bench and became sachem of Tammany.[2] It was Olvany, who with other Tammany leaders, urged State Senator James J. Walker to run for mayor.[3] Olvany was forced out as Tammany leader in 1929 after charges of corruption surfaced. A subsequent investigation by the Seabury Commission found that Olvany had obtained over $5 million from clients who did business with the city. One reason given for his ouster: "The other Tammany lawyers wanted him out; he had virtually monopolized the market."[4] This may, in part, explain Sullivan's lack of financial success during his stay in New York City. He may have found himself defending the dregs of society, not a lucrative calling. Being cash-strapped and the

onset of the Depression were undoubtedly factors in his moving to Florida.

Olvany was replaced by John F. Curry, son of a cattle dealer, an athlete, a teetotaler, a former state assemblyman, and according to Connable and Silberfarb, a "political incompetent." Tammany's attention was mostly focused on local politics, racketeering, scandals, and corruption.[5] It is unlikely the machine would bother with a former associate, now in reduced circumstances and himself tarnished with scandal.

An additional reason for his diminished circumstances was his loss of another key ally from his Tammany days—James K. McGuire, part of which was related to postwar politics of Irish America. As noted previously, each had become allied with a rival faction in the struggle for power in independent Ireland.

A factor that may have contributed to the demise of Sullivan's FCOI in America may be related to the schism in Irish America between Devoy and Cohalan's Friends of Irish Freedom and DeValera's American Association for the Recognition of the Irish Republic. It fostered intense competition between the two for loyalty and fiscal support. That competition occurred in films also. One of the AARIR's agents was former Sullivan ally, James K. McGuire, who at the time was trying to broker deal between the two factions to reunite them. According to Joseph Fahey, McGuire was "a keen student" of propaganda who realized motion pictures could further the Irish cause.[6] Undoubtedly much of this background was acquired as the result of his association with the German imperial government as propagandist from 1914 to 1917.

McGuire received the abstract of a movie script in May, 1920 from Padraic Colum, who was seeking financial backing for his project. This was no small matter. Colum was a famous Irish dramatist, author, folklorist, and a leading figure in the Irish literary revival. He was friends with Yeats, Lady Gregory,

James Joyce, and founder of Sinn Fein, Arthur Griffith. Colum was also a leader in the Gaelic League. During the Great War, he immigrated to the United States.[7]

The plot was similar to other pro-nationalist films of the FCOI and its predecessors. An American falls in love with an Irish girl who is also the love interest of a British officer. She involves him in a plot to deliver arms to the Irish Volunteers, something McGuire would have been familiar with, given his ties to an AARIR scheme to smuggle Thompson submachine guns into Ireland in 1921, an issue made public by the *New York Times* and later by John Devoy.[8]

McGuire got some support for the film project, and he forwarded the information to Eamon DeValera's secretary. Nothing came of the proposal,[9] undoubtedly due to the factious infighting, which consumed so much of his time.

What is relevant here is that it reveals McGuire's ties to the DeValera faction; the proposal specifies the production of an Irish propaganda motion picture, and it would have put McGuire in competition with Sullivan's struggling FCOI. By then, Sullivan had aligned himself with Devoy, Cohalan, FOIF, and the Free State.

Sullivan maintained some limited contact with Irish nationalists in the early 1920s, but his activities in America were eclipsed by his in-laws, the O'Maras. His manuscript on Michael Collins remained an unfinished fragment. Sullivan's only publication on Collins was an article in the *Springfield Republican* on September 10, 1922.

The article recalls Sullivan addressing a meeting of Irish nationalists in Cork in 1907. Among the people in attendance was a young Michael Collins. He claimed his address on Republicanism at the grave of Wolfe Tone in 1911 made him known to Irish nationalists upon his return to Ireland in 1915. Three years later, at the height of his career with the

FCOI, Sullivan met Collins, claiming he was willing to assist in any way possible to further the cause of Irish independence. Sullivan allegedly met Collins at his home on several occasions, claiming Collins thanked him for his services. His assessment was that the Irish struggle was at a low ebb in 1916–1917, after the rebellion's brutal repression by Sir John G. Maxwell, under whose orders its leaders were executed. The net effect, however, was an increase in nationalist feeling.

This was precipitated by the release of DeValera in 1917 and other leaders of the rising. The Sinn Fein convention in October of that year adopted a constitution for an Irish Republic. By the spring of 1918, the death of John Redmond destroyed what little support there was for the moderate nationalists. The failed attempt by the British to adopt a constitution for Ireland and the subsequent arrest of DeValera led to a major victory for Sinn Fein in Parliamentary elections of December 1918. It established its own Parliament, the Dail Eireann. British efforts to suppress the Dail culminated in guerilla warfare led by Michael Collins the following year, who lead the Irish Republican Army against the well-armed Royal Irish Constabulary with IRA gunmen focusing on raids on police stations, British agents, and informers. Calling the fight against Britain a Homeric struggle, Sullivan compared Collins' efforts with Richard de Clare, better known as Strongbow, a twelfth-century Anglo-Norman nobleman and warrior who invaded Ireland. Remarking on the success of guerilla tactics in the American Revolution and by the Boers in South Africa, Sullivan resuscitated the theme of Irish military prowess long used by its propagandists, including John Devoy and Sullivan associate James K. McGuire. Collins' familiarity with the country's topography, his stubborn resistance, and a well-functioning intelligence service destroyed the Royal Irish Constabulary by 1920 and unified the country in resistance to British rule. Irish success, however, fostered the

growth of the Black and Tans and the auxiliaries who instituted a terror campaign. Within a year, they too were defeated.
Because of his success, Collins gained the respect of both Irish
and British forces. In the last few paragraphs of the article,
Sullivan praises Collins's successor, Richard Mulcahy, who was
by then minister of Defense in the Provisional Government and
member of the Dail Eireann. This ties Sullivan firmly to the
pro-treaty faction and to his brief tenure as representative of the
provisional government to the United States, to which he was
appointed by Michael Collins. Sullivan indicated Collins's story
will be one of the "most thrilling . . . when it is properly told."[10]
Unfortunately, Sullivan never finished his manuscript; the task
went to Piaras Beasli. After Collins's death, Sullivan fell out of
favor with the new Free State government, being replaced by his
in-laws, the O'Mara brothers.

Nonetheless, he was put in charge of arrangements for
representatives of the Irish Free State who visited America in
1922. An incomplete and undated list of stops with names
of people to meet and hotels apparently in Sullivan's hand-
writing revealed an ambitious schedule. Included were stays
at several towns in Massachusetts, New York, Pennsylvania,
Ohio, Michigan, Illinois, Minnesota, Iowa, and Kansas. One
letter from a supporter urged Sullivan to consider Connecticut
"as a fertile field for missionary work for the Irish Free State
Mission."[11]

The free state government representatives were
Commandant General Piaras Beasli and Councilor Sean
MacCaoilite. A replica of the ticket for their reception is in the
Piaras Beasli papers from the National Library of Ireland. A
telegram to John Buckley of Boston from Sullivan dated April
1, 1922, informed Buckley the two representatives of Irish Free
State would be in Boston to meet informally with their supporters
and assure them the subscribers to the National Loan Fund

would be repaid. Interestingly, the telegram urged no additional funds be subscribed given "the present state of difficulties," an obvious reference to the FOIF-AARIR schism. Sullivan signed it as "Legal Advisor of [the] High Commission."[12] A follow-up draft of a news release from the Boston Reception Committee wished success to Collins and Griffith in "their efforts to build up a free and prosperous nation."[13] Similar comments were made in a resolution passed by the mayor and board of commissioners of Hoboken, New Jersey.[14]

The tone and tenor of the letters and telegrams reveal his complete adherence to the FOIF position and its support, albeit reluctant, for the treaty ending the Anglo-Irish War. In turn, it shows Sullivan's ties to this faction in the struggle for Irish freedom. Further evidence of this position is a letter entitled "Invitations from New York Globe," December 10, 1921. Its contents detail the dinner celebration given by Sir William Wiseman, the British spymaster and diplomatic confidante of Colonel Edward House, Wilson's primary adviser during the war years, in honor of the marriage of Dudley Field Malone, the anti-Tammany Democratic lawyer and Wilson-appointed collector of customs of the Port of New York. Many notables were listed, but "Note II" of the letter reveals that Wiseman was head of the British Secret Service in America. That information was allegedly supplied by Dr. W. Maloney, "an open enemy of the Friends of Irish Freedom and its leader, [who] is the mentor and evil genius of DeValera and McCartan, having been instrumental with McGarrity, Boland, James O'Mara and J. C. Walsh." The letter accuses Maloney of causing the split in the Irish ranks in America.[15] The document reinforces Sullivan's commitment to the provisional government and reveals the divided political allegiances of the O'Mara family.

Sullivan also apparently did some public relations work on behalf of the delegation. In an undated letter, he indicated his intent to write a series of articles for American papers. The letter refers to the rough draft of a news release he purportedly wrote to appear as if it had been written by members of the mission of the provisional government.[16] The Piaras Beasli papers contain the rough draft of one such news release, detailing recent events in Ireland—the ratification of the treaty ending the Irish war for independence, the evacuation of British troops from Irish bases, the pending schism, the threat of continued violence from the DeValera's antitreaty faction, and the possibility that such division had a negative impact on Irish opinion in America. The final paragraph outlines the true purpose of the delegates' mission, to prevent any assistance "to a minority group bent on rebellion,"[17] an obvious reference to DeValera's AARIR. Two Irish delegations were by then present in America.[18] Sullivan's sympathies lay with the Free State, possibly because he perceived them as the winners in the struggle for power with DeValera. His position as American liaison to the provisional government was, like his diplomatic career, short-lived. He was soon replaced by his brother-in-law, James O'Mara, who had also endorsed the Anglo-Irish Treaty. With his ties to Irish nationalist politics cut, his film company in the hands of others, and his presence no longer relevant to the new elites in Tammany Hall, Sullivan struggled on. Probably the onset of the Depression in 1929 was the final straw.

Apparently Sullivan retired in 1930 and moved to St. Petersburg, Florida, returning to his initial career as journalist and sportswriter. He died of a heart attack in 1935. His body was returned to Ireland the following year and interred next to his wife at Glasnevin Cemetery, Dublin.[19] This, however, was not the end of his Irish legacy. There were the films he produced for the Film Company of Ireland, some of which are still in existence. Sullivan also had several children who survived—a son, Stephen, born in 1913, when Sullivan had just been appointed to his diplomatic post in Santo Domingo, and two daughters. Ellen, born in 1916 right after the Easter Rebellion, was baptized as Ellen Sinn Fein Sullivan, and Sheila, who in turn had six children, one of whom, Mary Rose Callaghan, is a prominent Irish novelist. Mary Rose authored numerous books, some of which dealt with the controversies and events surrounding the life of her grandfather, James M. Sullivan. Many of these works, according to Felter, "cross the border from fact to fiction."[20]

Possibly the Callaghan novel that best catches the essence of Sullivan's life is *Emigrant Dreams*. In it, the author is pursued by the ghost of her grandfather, who wants her to write his authorized biography, a sanitized version of his life, a case study of upward mobility in the tradition of Horatio Alger.[21] The effort is a struggle, as the ghost of her grandfather seeks to have her put him in a favorable light, having participated in a number of unsavory activities—illegal prizefights, Tammany politics, the Becker-Rosenthal murder case, the Santo Domingo imbroglio, the Easter Rebellion. One of her characters, with a limited knowledge of Irish history, names her children Jessica Sinn Fein and Jason Ira.[22] Just as contemporary characters in her novel seek to romanticize the realities of Irish history, so too did her protagonist, the fictionalized James M. Sullivan. Similar to the novelist in *Emigrant Dreams* who makes periodic trips from Ireland to America and back, so too did Sullivan. He was interred in the land of his birth. He was tied to both Ireland and America. He sought an Ireland free of British rule. He lived to see that dream come true. Sullivan's role is often overlooked, although his pro-German diplomacy in Santo Domingo, his alleged role in the Easter Rebellion, his ties to the O'Mara family and Michael Collins, and his purported role as propagandist with FCOI strongly link him to Sinn Fein.

The atrocities committed on both sides during the bitter civil war and the outbreak of religious conflict in Northern

Ireland undermined any confidence nativist America may have had in Ireland's ability for self-government. By 1923, the AARIR was in disarray, having experienced multiple changes in leadership over the issue of treaty ratification. The Friends of Irish Freedom was also in decline. From 725 branches registering over one hundred thousand members, in less than a decade, FOIF had slipped to only 13 branches with less than seven hundred members.[23] Not only was 1923 significant in that it saw the death of Sullivan's fellow nationalist James K. McGuire, but the Irish Nationalist organizations were at the twilight of their respective careers as well. In addition, the Irish Civil War ended. DeValera was arrested in August, having emerged from hiding to campaign in the elections of 1923.[24] And as noted previously, much to the disgust of FOIF, the Irish Free State applied for entry into the League of Nations. Soon after, in October 1923, the free state government of William Cosgrave, Griffith's successor, introduced a constitutional amendment aimed at the IRA, abolishing terrorist organizations. Physical force nationalism was, for the time being, over.[25]

The year 1923 may be significant in another way. Ireland was about to set its own course. Most of Sullivan's friends and colleagues of earlier days had predeceased him or would soon follow. Sullivan witnessed and participated in key events and organizations that made Irish freedom possible.

Sullivan remains a complex individual, given the various causes to which he attached himself. When looked at carefully, they seem less a matter of commitment but of opportunism, efforts to obtain financial gain. For example, while he was linked to the Democratic Party as a spokesman in the early 1900s, that loyalty comes into question with his involvement in 1908 to George Cortelyou, Republican president Theodore Roosevelt's postmaster general, who, with support from William C. Beer and Sullivan, was trying to obtain the Republican nomination for vice president. Failing that, Sullivan reattached himself to the Democratic Party actively campaigning for it in the election of 1912. Beer, remember, encouraged Sullivan's appointment as ambassador.

In addition, Sullivan's machinations during the Becker-Rosenthal case, where he actively suborned perjury, reveals a casual attitude toward legal ethics designed primarily to curry favor with Tammany Hall insiders. Nonetheless, his involvement in these events led to his appointment as ambassador to Santo Domingo, where he imported the Tammany model of corruption into an already unprincipled Caribbean republic. Was he used by his allies, or was he an active player seeking his own advantage? In the case of Sullivan, despite his professed concern for the people of Santo Domingo, as noted in the latter portion of the Gray letter, his own words and actions incriminate him. His apparent motive was personal financial gain. And his treasonable correspondence with German diplomats, coming as it did toward the end of his tenure as diplomat, suggests he may have been fishing for an alternative career as activist for the German cause, as had his fellow conspirator James K. McGuire. Recall the Clan na Gael and the Sinn Fein were by then actively involved in a plot with Germany to overthrow British rule in Ireland.

His role as Irish nationalist is also suspect. Despite family members proclaiming his adherence to the cause of Irish independence, there is the statement by his lawyer after his arrest during the rising, that Sullivan had never been identified as a member of any group endorsing such aspirations. A legal stratagem? Perhaps, but again it raises the issue of Sullivan's commitment.

Accordingly then, throughout the periods of Sullivan's life—as newsboy, campaign speaker for the Democrats, a Tammy-linked lawyer, diplomat, and as founder of the

FCOI—the picture of Sullivan that emerges is one of a self-serving, politically ambitious figure obtaining modest success by hanging on the margins of Tammany Hall. His commitment to Irish freedom was vague, largely drawn from his own and his wife's family members and communal ties to the Irish diaspora community in New York City. His bonds to revolutionary nationalism were apparently a byproduct of his friendship with former Democratic mayor of Syracuse, prominent Clan na Gael member James K. McGuire, who was active in the campaign to elect Woodrow Wilson president in 1912. The two figures who defined his life in New York, Bald Jack Rose and James K. McGuire, reveal Sullivan used and was in turn used by those he thought would advance his career. Rose was a gambler and murderer, a central figure in the Becker-Rosenthal case, who turned to Sullivan because of their prior acquaintance in Connecticut. Rose could leverage his knowledge of Sullivan's gambling past to pressure him to cut a deal. Sullivan suborned perjury from two witnesses to convict Becker in his first trial, despite having doubts as to his guilt. The fact that he reported first to Tammany Boss Charles Murphy suggests Sullivan was looking for payback for his services. McGuire also had a checkered past. As mayor, he was indicted twice for malfeasance in office, was castigated in the local press for his lavish use of patronage, and was also surrounded by charges of corruption. After a failed effort for a fourth consecutive term, McGuire moved to New York City, becoming the chief lobbyist for the Asphalt Trust, a group whose monopolistic practices he previously condemned as mayor. McGuire was the focus of an investigation by politically ambitious New York City district attorney Charles Whitman, who was investigating charges of bid-rigging and bribery on paving contracts in New York. Whitman, interestingly, was also the chief prosecutor in the Becker-Rosenthal case. He successfully used the publicity to win the governorship in 1914. Whitman was pivotal in garnering support for Sullivan's appointment as ambassador to Santo Domingo. McGuire retreated there to temporarily escape a subpoena from Whitman, using Sullivan's close ties to the Bordes Valdes government in an unsuccessful effort to win paving contracts. Had McGuire been successful, Sullivan would have been amply rewarded. Following Sullivan's dismissal, there is no record of contact between the two. The one bond was their support for Germany as the means by which Ireland could obtain independence. Like Sullivan, McGuire was also the object of a federal investigation; both were fortunate to escape federal prosecution.

McGuire had, since 1914, been an active propagandist for the German cause, authoring two books, numerous articles in his newspapers, and being an active speaker on its behalf. Sullivan's treasonable correspondence with German diplomats on Hispaniola stated that one reason for his coming to Santo Domingo was to assist the German cause. That effort collapsed in the wake of the Phelan Report and Sullivan's resignation.

His prior connections with Bald Jack Rose and Big Tim Sullivan, who were involved in motion pictures, may have influenced James M. Sullivan's interest in filmmaking. There was, as noted, a decade of established tradition of filmmaking in Ireland, but by expatriates, often aimed at assisting the nationalist cause. Once again, the evidence questions Sullivan's commitment to Irish freedom, raising the issue that is was simply another move to try and recoup his career. The same could be said of his work on behalf of the free state government and his exaggerated claims of "close" ties to Michael Collins.

In *Emigrant Dreams*, Mary Rose Callaghan has her grandfather's ghost, on several occasions, demand a biography. Elsewhere she says, "He died poor, an utter failure."[26]

This manuscript is probably not the biography Sullivan would have wanted, a festschrift celebrating his achievements.

Yet it does reveal the struggles of a man, using all means at his disposal, to achieve material prosperity yet overcome by personal deficiencies and by situations beyond his control. He was not a major player in the struggle for Irish independence, but his efforts to obtain it, as questionable as some were, should not be overlooked. Probably his most important contribution, as fleeting as it was, was the establishment of the Film Company of Ireland.

In 1924, the United States extended diplomatic recognition to the Free State. FOIF disbanded by 1935, the year James M. Sullivan passed. Sullivan's contributions are perpetuated not only in the writings of his granddaughter and in the few remaining films produced by the Film Company of Ireland, some of which continue to be shown and celebrated, not so much by Irish nationalists as in the past, but by students and scholars of Irish film. With time, the scandals, his controversial role in the infamous Becker-Rosenthal trial and the Santo Domingo fiasco have faded. His most enduring contribution, as Irish Nationalist is the film he and his wife Ellen produced in the short-lived FCOI. They are both now receiving the rightful recognition which is long overdue.

End Notes

1   "Jim Sullivan," http://humphrysfamilytree.com/Omara/jimsullivan.html. Retrieved 28 January 2011.

2   Connable, Alfred and Silberfarb, Edward, *Tigers of Tammany: Nine Men Who Ran New York* (New York: Holt, Rhinehart and Winston, 1967), 273.

3   Ibid., 274, 275.

4   Ibid., 277.

5   Ibid

6   Fahey, Joseph E., *James K. McGuire: Boy Mayor and Irish Nationalist* (Syracuse, NY: Syracuse University Press, 2014), 223.

7   "Padraic Colum: Analysis. "https://www.enotes/topic/padraic colum/in-depth. retrieved 17 November 2016."

8   Fitzpatrick, David, *Harry Boland's Irish Revolution,* Cork: (Ireland: Cork University Press, 2003), 57, 98–99; "Fenian Chief's Estimate of James K. McGuire," *Catholic Sun* (19 July 1923); "Seized Irish Guns Provide Mysteries within Mysteries," *New York Times* (17 July 1921).

9   Fahey, op. cit., 225.

10 "Michael Collins Rise to the Mystery Man of Ireland," *Springfield Sunday Republican* (10 September 1922): 24.

11 Undated, unsigned letter, Kansas City, National Library of Ireland, Piaras Beasli Papers, Letter, "J. H. McGodell to Hon. James Mark Sullivan" (20 March 1922). Box 44, File 16.

12 Telegram from James M. Sullivan to John Buckley (1 April 1922). National Library of Ireland. Piaras Beasli Papers. Box 44, File 16.

13 "Reception Committee," n.d. National Library of Ireland. Piaras Beasli Papers. Box 44, File 16.

14 Undated letter, from "P.R. Griffin, Mayor to the Heads of the Provisional Government of the Free State of Ireland," National Library of Ireland, Piaras Beasli Papers. Box 44, File 16.

15 Letter, "Invitations from New York Globe" (10 December 1921), National Library of Ireland. Piaras Beasli Papers. Box 44, File 16.

16 Letter, "Dean Sean from James M. Sullivan," undated, National Library of Ireland, Piaras Beasli Papers. Box 44, File 16.

17 Untitled, undated news release. National Library of Ireland. Piaras Beasli Papers. Box 44, File 16.

18 "Rival Irish Envoys Here on Aquitania," *New York Times* (18 March 1922).

19 "James M. Sullivan, Ex-Diplomat, Dead," *New York Times* (17 August 1935), 13: 4.

20 Felter, Maryanne, *Crossing Borders: A Critical Introduction to the Works of Mary Rose Callaghan* (Newark: University of Delaware Press, 2010), 91.

21 Ibid., 93. Callaghan dedicates a chapter to a "biography" of Sullivan, which closely parallel the known facts in his life. See *Emigrant Dreams* (Dublin: Poolberg Press, 1996), ch. 19, 233–250. Felter gives a brief overview of the real Sullivan in *Crossing Borders*, op. cit., fn. 2, 136–138.

22 Felter, op. cit., 99.

23 Doorley, op. cit., 150, 151, 154; Cronin, Sean, *The McGarrity Papers: Revelations of the Irish Revolutionary*

Movement in Ireland and America, 1900–1940 (Dublin: Anvil Press, 1972).

[24] Carroll, op. cit., 186.

[25] Cronin, op. cit., 150, 170.

[26] Callaghan, op. cit 46, 52, 119.

WORKS CITED

"A Picture Play Of Unique National Interest : Seeing Knocknagow in Irish National Cinemas, January - April 1918" https://early.irish.cinema/2018/05.

"A New Industry: The Film Company of Ireland's First Season." https://earlyirishcinema.com/category/irish/knocknagow-ireland.fcoi. 1918

"A Description of County Kerry from Guy's Postal Directory of Munster 1886." http//homepage.eirecom.net/~dingle-maps/genoki.KER/Guy 1886.htm. Retrieved 2 December 2013.

Adler, Selig. "Bryan and Wilson Caribbean Penetration." *Hispanic American Historical Review*, xx, 1940, 199–124.

"All For Old Ireland." Irish Silent Films. Trinity College, Dublin. http://www.tcd/ie/irishfilm/phpfid=58072. Retrieved 4 November 2012.

"A Short Cuts History of New York and Film." http://nymag.com/movies/filmsfestivals/newyork 2007/38002. Retrieved 9 November 2012.

"Ancient Order of Hibernians". *Catholic Encyclopedia*. http://www.newadvent.org/cathen/07320a.htm. Retrieved 6 August 2014.

Asbury, Herbert. *Gangs of New York*. New York: Thunder's Mouth Press, 1927.

"Baldwin, Simeon Eben." Johnson Allen (ed). *Dictionary of American Biography*, vol. I, New York: Charles Scribners, 1928, 544–547.

"Baldy Jack Rose, Dead at 72: Police Close File on Becker-Rosenthal Case." *New York*

Times. 9 October 1947, 52.

Barton, Ruth. *Irish National Cinema*. New York: Routledge, 2004.

Piaras Beasley Papers. National Library of Ireland. Box 44 File 16.

Beatty, Jack. *The Rascal King: The Life and Times of James Michael Curley, 1874–1958*. New York: MacMillan, 1992.

"Bioscope: The O'Kalems." http://thebioscope.net/2011/03/26 the-okalems 1-2. Retrieved 13 June 2013.

Blum, John. *Joe Tumulty and the Wilson Era*. Boston: Houghton-Mifflin, 1951.

"Bold Emmet, Ireland's Martyr." Irish Silent Films. Trinity College. Dublin. http://www.tcd.ie/irishfilms/showfilm/php? Fid=58023. Retrieved 15 June 2013.

Bouser, Pearl and Mussor, Charles. *Oscar Micheaux and His Circle*. Bloomington: Indiana University Press, 2001.

"Bremner, Robert G." *Biographical Dictionary of the US Congress, 1774–Present*. US Government Printing Office, 2005. Retrieved 17 May 2014.

Brewing and Liquor Interests and German and Bolshevik Propaganda: Report and Hearings of the Sub-Committee on the Judiciary. United States Senate, vol. I. Washington, DC, Government Printing Office, 1307; 1396–1397.

"Brewster or Dillon Will Get Place, Says McGuire." *Syracuse Herald*. 24 July 1914.

"British Seize A. M. Sullivan on Irish Soil." *New York Times*. 5 May 1916.

Broderick, Joe. "DeValera and the Archbishop Daniel Mannix." www.historireland.com/20th Century contemporary-history/devalera-and-the-archbishop-daniel-mannix-by-joe-broderick.

"Broderick Wins, Is Sued." *New York Times*. 27 August 1913.

Brown, Terrence. "The Twentieth Century." Kennelly, Brendan (ed.). *Ireland: Past and Present*. Dublin: Gill and MacMillan, 1985.

Brown, Thomas. *Irish-American Nationalism, 1870–1890*. New York: Lippincott, 1966.

"Bryan to Sullivan." *Foreign Relations*. 12 January 1914. 197–198.

"Bryans' Name Used In Rake-off Talk." *New York Times*. 21 January 1915.

Bryk, William. "Mayor William Gaynor Primitive American." Http://wordpress.com/tag/policecommissioner-rhinelander-waldo. Retrieved 13 May 2014.

Callaghan, Mary Rose. *Emigrant Dreams*. Dublin: Poolbeg Press, 1966.

——. E-mail to author. 9 October 2002.

——. E-mail to author. 18 June 2002.

——. E-mail to author. 20 June 2002.

——. Sullivan letter. Nell Sullivan to Hazel O'Mara. 27 July 1918.

——. Sullivan letter. Nell Sullivan to Hazel O'Mara. 4 December 1918.

——. Sullivan letter. Nell Sullivan to Hazel O'Mara. 4 January 1919.

"Call Issued For Irish Cause." *Catholic Sun*. 29 November 1918: 5.

"William Carleton." http//trashface.com/williamcarlton. html. trashface.comwilliamcarleton.html. Retrieved 3 June 2014.

"William Carleton: 1794–1869." http:// www.micro.net/rx/ az-data/authors/c/carleton_w/life.h.

Carroll, Francis M. "The Friends of Irish Freedom." In Funchion, Michael F. *Irish Voluntary Organizations*. Westport, Connecticut: Greenwood Press, 1983.

Casella, Donna. "Ellen O'Mara Sullivan." Jane Gaines, Rhadda Vatsa and Monica DallAsta, eds. *Women Film Pioneers Project*. Center for Digital Research and Scholarship. New York, NY: Columbia University Libraries 2013. http:/ wfpp.cdrs.colubia.edu/pioneer/ellen-omara-sullivan/>Retrieved 26 July 2016.

"Catholics Chosen." *Catholic Sun* 21 February 1913:2.

"Thomas James Clark (1857–1916)." http://www.irishfreedom. net/Fenian Graves/T.J.Clark/T.J. Clark/htm. Retrieved 3 February 2014.

"Cochran, William Bourke (1854–1923)." Johnson, Allen and Malone, Dumas (eds). "Colum, Padraic. Analysis." https:// www.enotes/topic.padraic-colum/in-depth. Retrieved November 16, 2016.

Comerford, R. E. *Charles M. Kickham: A Study in Irish Nationalism and Literature*. Portmarrick, Ireland: Wolfhound Press, 1979.

"Commissioner Rhinelander Waldo: Joe Bruno on the Mob." http:// wordpress.com/tag/police commission-rhinelander-waldo. Ret rieved 3 March 2015.

Condon, Dennis. "Early Irish Cinema: Irish Cinema and Politics in Autumn 1915." http://earlyirishcinema.wordpress.com. Retrieved 26 May 2016.

——. Early Irish Cinema: Sceen-Stunning Views of Cripples. The First Irish National Pilgrimage to Lands." http://early-irishcinema.wordpress.com. Retrieved 19 July 2016.

———. "Early Irish Cinema." Procession, Protest and Perfect Women in Picture Houses, Later Summer 1915": http:// earlyirishcinema.wordpress. Retrieved 19 July 2016.

———. "Early Irish Cinema: An Unrehearsed Picture." http:// earlyirishcinma.wordpress.com. Retrieved 22 July 2016.

———. "Early Irish Cinema: In the Grip of Spies." http://earlyirishcinema.wordpress.com. Retrieved 20 July 2016.

———. "Early Irish Cinema: Irish Cinema Catches Public Eye In February 1916." http://earlyirishcimena.wordpresscom. Retrieved 21 July 2016.

———. "Early Irish Cinema: Experiments against Public Taste in Irish Picture Houses, August 1915." http://earlyirishcinema.wordpress.com Retrieved 19 July 2016.

Congressional Record. 26 February 1915, 4766.

Connable, Alfred and Silberfarb, Edward. *Tigers of Tammany: Nine Men Who Ran New York,* New York: Holt, Rhinehart, Winston, 1967.

"Cortelyou Angers White House." *New York Times* 16 June 1908.

"The Constant Watchfulness of Irish Cinema in March 1916." https://earlyirishcinema.com/2016/03. Retrieved 17 October 2017.

"Cortelyou, George Bruce (1862–1940)." Schuyler, Rober L., and James Edward. *Dictionary of American Biography vol xI. Supplement Two.* New York: Charles Scribner's Sons, 1935, 122–123.

"Contracts Controlled by Former Mayor." *Syracuse Herald* 17 June 1915, 1; 2.

"Country Cavan, Ireland." http:// members.tripod.com" Scott Richard/cavahistroy.html. Retrieved 6 June 2011.

Cronin, Sean. *The McGarrity Papers: Revelations of the Irish Revolutionary Movement in Ireland and America, 1900–1940. New York Anvil Books, 1972.*

"Cummings Homer Stiles." Garrity, John (ed). *Dictionary of American Biography Supplement Six, 1956–1966.* New York: Scribners sons, 1980, 136–138.

"Cummings, Homer Stiles." *Cyclopedia of America Biography* vol. D, 1934, 13.

"Cyril Cusack (1910–1993) Biography." http://www.moon-cave.com.cusack/bio.htm. Retrieved 4 January 2011.

"John Philpot Curran." http://1911.encyclopedia.org/ John_ Philpot_ Curran. Retrieved 2 February 2011.

Damu, J. "How the US Impoverished Haiti." http://www.haiti-action.net/NEWS/JD/9_28_3.html. Retrieved 7 May 2013.

Davis, John. *The Kennedy's: Dynasty and Disaster.* SPI Books, 1993.

"Thomas Davis." http://irishdrinkingsongs.info/songunites/ thomasdavis. Retrieved 3 February 2011.

"Davies, Joseph Edward." Garraty, John (ed). *Dictionary of American Biography, Supplement Six, 1956–1960.* New York: Charles Scribner's Sons, 1980, 146–147.

"Davies, Joseph Edward." *National Cyclopedia of American Biography,* vol. D, New York: James T. White and Company, 1930, 456–457.

"Death of Prominent Limerick Citizen". *Limerick Leader,* n.d. Accessed on "Stephen O'Mara". http:// en.wikipedia.ord/ wiki/Stephen NO%27 Mara. Retrieved 4 March 2012.

"Dominican Tangle Under Inquiry". *New York Times.* 10 December 1913.

Doerries, Reinhard. *Imperial Challenge: Ambassader Count Bernstorff And German –American Relations, 1908–1917.* Chapel Hill: University of North Carolina Press, 1989.

Doorley, Michael. *Irish-American Diaspora Nationalism: The Friends of Irish Freedom.* Four Courts Press, 2005.

Donovan Stephen. "Introduction to Ireland's Own Film." In "Screening the Past." com/2012/02/introduction-to ireland's own-film. Retrieved 14 March 2012.

Downing, Taylor. "The Film Company of Ireland." *Sight and Sound* 49, 1 (Winter 1979–80). 42–45.

"Drop Sullivan Charges." *New York Times*. 1 October 1914:6.

"Dublin Vigilance Association". http://early.irish.cinema.com /2015/12.

"Dublin Wreckage Films, Martial Law and Daylight Saving Time in May, 1916." http://earlyirishcinema.com/2016/. Retrieved 13 November 2017.

Dufferin, Lord and The Honorable G.G. Boyle. *Narrative of a Journey from Oxford to Skibbereen during a Year of the Irish Famine*. Oxford: John Henry Parker, 1847.

"Robert Emmet." www.historyireland.com 20th Century_ contemporary.history-on-film/. Retrieved 2 May 2011.

"Robert Emmet, 1778–1803; Irish Patriot And Orator." www. RobertEmmet.org. Retrieved 4 May 2011.

"Ends Revolution in Santo Domingo". *New York Times*. 9 October 1913.

Fagg, John Edwin. *Cuba, Haiti and The Dominican Republic*. Englewood Cliffs, New Jersey: Prentice-Hall, 1965.

Fahey, Joseph E. *James K. McGuire: Boy Mayor and Irish Nationalist*. Syracuse, New York. Syracuse University Press 2014.

"Father John Murphy". www.hibberrianrebels.org/father-murphy.html. Retrieved 3 March 2011.

"Father John Murphy. www.catholicireland.net-father-mur-phy-of-bollavogue. Retrieved 3 May 2011.

"FCOI Releases" Rafferty's Rise In 1917". https://early.irish. cinema.com /2017/07/.

Feeley, Pat. "Whiteboys and Ribbonmen: Early Agrarian Secret Societies." Limerick: City of Limerick Public Library, n.d. 23–27.

Felter, Maryanne and Schultz, Daniel. "The Making of an Irish Nationalist: James Mark Sullivan and the Film Company of Ireland in Ireland and America." *In Screening the Past.* http://screeningthepast.com/2012/02/themaking —of an-irish-nationalist. Spring 2012. Retrieved 11 April 2013.

——. "James Mark Sullivan and the Film Company of Ireland." *New Hibernia Review* 8.2. Summer, 2004.

——. "Selling Memories, Strengthing Nationalism: The Marketing of the Film Company of Irelands Silent Films In America." *Canadian Journal of Irish Studies.* vol.32, no. 2. Fall 2006.

Felter, Maryanne. *Crossing Borders: A Critical Introduction to the Works of Mary Rose Callaghan.* Newark: University of Delaware Press, 2010.

Fletcher, Tony. "May Clark". In Jane Gaines, Radha Vatsal and Monica Dell'Astra (eds.) Women Film Pioneers Project. Center For Digital Research and Scholarship. New York, N.Y. Columbia University Libraries, 2013. https// wfpp. cdrs.columbia.edu/pionreer/ccp-may-clark/>

"Film Company of Ireland: Wharton Releasing Company." Film Company of Ireland Archives. Cornell University.

"Fitzgerald Getting Well." *New York Times* 16 September 1913.

Flynn, Arthur. *The Story of Irish Film.* Dublin: Curragh Press, 2005.

"Four More Irish Chiefs In Revolt Put To Death." *New York Times* 9 May 1916: 2.

Fulwider, Chad. "Film Propaganda and Culture:The German Dilemma, 1914-1917". Film and Industry: An Interdisciplinary Journal, 45, No. 2 Winter, 2015, 4-12.

"George Klein: American Producer." *In Who's Who in Victorian Cinema*. http;//www. victoriancinema.net/Kleine httm. Retrieved 13 May 2011.

"Gerard, James Watson." *National Cyclopedia of American Biography*. vol. XLIX. New York: James T. White and Company, 1966, 124–125.

German Foreign Ministry Archives. Volumes R20180 (Der Weltkrieg, secr, vol. II); R17004 (All gemeine Angeiengenheiten Santo Domingo, vol. 9)

Resume of Dr. Fritz Perl. Personal Communications to the Author by Gerhard Keiper of the German Foreign Ministry Archives, 29 April 2015.

Personal Communication from Oliver Juengel, Secretary of the German Mission in Port-au-Prince, Haiti to the author, 27 April 2015.

Gibbons, Luke. *Transformations in Irish Culture*. Indiana: University of Notre Dame Press, 1996.

———. *Gaelic Gothic: Race, Colonization and Irish Culture*. Galway, Ireland: Arlen Horse, 2004.

"Gibson, Hugh". *Who Was Who In America, vol. 3*. Chicago. Marquis Who's Who, 1960, 332; http://history.state. govdepartmetnhistory/people/gibson-hugh-simon. Retrieved 14 June 2010.

"Goff, John William." Johnson, Allen, and Malone, Dumas (eds). *Dictionary of American Biography,* vol. IV New York. Charles Scribners and Sons, 1932, 359–360.

"Goff, John William." *National Cyclopedia of America Biography* vol. xv. Ann Arbor: University Microfilms, 1967, 254.

Golway, Terry. *Irish Rebel: John Devoy and the American Fight For Irish Freedom*. New York: St. Martin's Press, 1998.

"Maude Gonne: Yeat's Kathleen Ni Houliham, Ireland's Joan of Arc" http;//www._the_wild_geese.com/pages/gorne/html. Retrieved 11 May 2011.

Gonzales, Nancie. "Desiderio Arras: Caudillo, Bandit or Culture Hero? *Journal of American Folkore*, vol. 85, no. 335. January 1972.

"Grace William Russell" (1832–1904). Johnson, Allen and Malone, Dumas (eds). *Dictionary of American Biography* vol.IX. New York: Charles Scribmer's Sons, 1932, 463.

"Henry Grattan." http;//www.nndl.com/People/993/000103624. Retrieved 6 April 2011.

"Great Irish Journeys. Michael Dwyer." http://www.youtube. com/watchv-csVSXu2G4. Retrieved 7 June 2012.

Halton, Timothy and Williamson, Jeffrey. "After the Famine: Emigration From Ireland, 1851–1913." *Journal of Economic History*, vol. 53, no. 3 (September 1993), 576–600 Table I, 577.

Harvey, George. "Diplomats of Democracy." *North American Review*. February 1914, cxix.

Hay, Harme. *Bulmer Hobson and the Nationalist Movement in Twentieth Century Ireland.* Manchester: Manchester University Press, 2009.

Hersh, Seymore. *The Dark Side of Camelot.* Back Bay Books, 1998.

"History Without Tears in Irish Cinema, June 1916: https://earlyirishcinema.com/2016. Retrieved 3 January 2017.

"The History and People of Connecticut." http://kindertrails. com/Connecticut-History-2html. Retrieved 6 May 2010.

Hoberman, J. *Bridge of Light: Yiddish Film Between Two Worlds.* New York: Museum of Modern Art, 1991.Hogan, Robert and O'Neil, Michael J. *Joseph Halloway's Abbey Theater: A Selection from His Unpublished Journal. Impressions of an Irish Playgoer.* Carbondale: Southern Illinois University Press, 1967.

"Hughes, William (1872–1918)." *Biographical Dictionary of the United States Congress, 1774–Present.* http://bioguide.

congress.gov/scripts/biodisplay.pl?index=h000929. Retrieved 3 February 2010.

"Honor Levy at Dinner." *New York Times* 4 December 1913.

"Humphreys, Mark." Humphreys. Family Tree. http:// humphreyfamilytree.com

"Hurries to Santo Domingo." *New York Times* 9 September 1913.

"Idealizing Everything Irish: The Film Company of Ireland Releases "Rafferty's Rise" in Late 1917". https://early. irish. cinema.com/2017/12/.

"Instructive Images On Irish Cinema Screens in Late Summer 1917." http://earlyirishcinema.c/2017/08. Retrieved 5 January 2018

"Ireland: A Nation." ingb.com/title/h0004164/?ref+nmflmg. nr.5. Retrieved 7 May 2010.

"Ireland: A Nation." www.tcd.ie/irishfilm/silent /ireland-a-na-tion.php. Retrieved 9 May 2010.

"Ireland: King, Church, Dublin, Time and Called." http:// www.libraryindex.com/encyclopedia./pages/cpxlgeny/2b/ irelan. Retrieved 13 May 2010.

"Irish Silent Films". http;//tcd.ie/irishfilm/silent/me_1916_film/ php.

"Irish Blood on the Streets: The Easter Rising of 1916." http://www.suite101.com/content/irishbloodinthestreet/. Retrieved 13 May 2010.

"Irish Audiences Watch "O'Neill of the Glen", August 1916". https://early.irish.cinema.com/2016/08/.

"Irish Cinema and the Desire For Change in April 1916." https:// early.irish.cinema.com/2016/04/.

"Irish Cinema Catches Public Eye in February 1916". https:// early.irish.cinema.com/2016/02/.

"Irish Regiments Meet". *New York Times* 11 August 1912.

"Is Democracy Finished?" http://www.pbs.org/wghb/american-experience/features/primary_resource. Retrieved 17 May 2012.

"Jack Johnson Biography." http://www.biography.com/people/jack-johnson-9355980. Retrieved 7 September 2012

"J.K. M'Guire Out of Local Politics." *Syracuse Herald* 16 August 1913:6.

"Jarvis, Samuel Miller (1853–1913). *National Cyclopedia of American Biography*. New York: James White And Company, 1914-1916, vol. XV, 345–346.

Johnson, James Weldon. "Self-Determining Haiti: Government of, By and For National City Bank." *Nation* III (September 1920).

Jones, John Price and Hollister, Paul H. *The German Secret Service in America*. Boston: Small, Maynard and Company, 1918.

Juengel, Oliver, Secretary to the German Mission in Port-au-Prince, haiti. Letter to the author, 22 April, 2015.

Kramer, Fritz. "For Ireland's Sake (1914)" moviessilently.com2015/08/for-irelands-sake-1914/. Retrieved 7 November 2017.

Kaplan, Edward. S. *US Imperialism In Latin America: Byran's Challenges and Contributions*. Westport, Connecticut Greenwood Press, 1998.

"Charles Kickham." http://chalres-kickham.co.t.v./. Retrieved 6 January 2010.

"Charles Kickham." http://multitextucc.ie/d Charles Kickham. Retrieved 10 January 2010.

Keiper, Gerhard, German Foreign Ministry Archives, "Resume of Dr. Fritz Perl". Letter to the author 29 April 2015.

Knight, Melvin. *Americans in Santo Domingo*. New York: Vanguard Press, 1928.

"Knocknagow" on Film: A Picture Play That Will Create A Furor In America". Anglo-Celt. 2 March 1918.

Lad From Old Ireland." Irish Silent Films/Trinity College Dublin http://www.tcd.ie/irishfilms/silent/lad_from_old_ireland. Retrieved 7 May 2011.

Langdon, Sheila. "Blazing the Trail to Ireland: The Kalem Film Company." Irish America.com/archive. December/January 2012. Retrieved 22 January 2014.

Lavalle, Patricia. *James O'Mara: Staunch Sinn Feiner, 1873–1948.* Dunmore: Canmore and Reynolds, 1961.

"Let Us All Be Up and Doing for Ireland." *Catholic Sun* 29 November 1918: 5.

"Lindberg Isn't Crazy You Know." http:// pbs.org/wgbh/american experience/features/primary-resource

Link, Arthur (ed.). *The Papers of Woodrow Wilson,* vol. 29. Princeton University Press, 1979.

———. *Woodrow Wilson And The Progressive Era*, 1910–1917. New York: Harper, 1954.

———. *Wilson. The New Freedom.* New Jersey: Princeton University Press, 1956.

———. *Wilson: The Struggle for Neutrality.* New Jersey: Princeton University Press, 1960.

Logan, Andy. *Against The Evidence: The Becker-Rosenthal Affair.* New York: McCall Publishing, 1970.

"Long, Boas." *Cyclopedia of American Biography*, vol.50, Ann Arbor, Michigan: University Microfilms, 1971, 613–616.

"Marc Gunn Presents Irish Song Lyrics and Other Celtic Lyrics." www.irish_song_lyrics.com/when-irish-eyes-are-smiling.html. Retrieved 14 June 2013.

Marsh, Patricia. "Mysterious Malady Spreading: Press Coverage of the 1918–1919 Influenza Pandemic in Ireland." Quest Proceedings of QUBAHSS Conference June 2008. Issue no. 6., Autumn 2008.

"May Be Sammy Schepps." *New York Times*. 22 July 1912.

"Bat Masterson." http://www.history net.com.html. Retrieved 7 May 2015.

"Mayor William J. Gaynor, Primitive American." http:// nypress.com/mayor_william-j-gaynor-primitive-american. Retrieved 10 May 2015.

McCaffrey, Lawrence. "Forging Forward and Looking Back." Bayor, Ronald, and Meaghan, Timothy (eds). *The New York Irish*. Baltimore: John Hopkins University Press, 1962.

McCloone, Martin, *Irish Film: The Emergence of a Contemporary Cinema*. London: British Film Institute, 2000.

McConville, Sean. Irish Political *Prisoners*, 1848–1942. London: Routledge, 2003.

"McGuire, James K." *National Cyclopedia of American Biography*. 1897, 16.

"McGuire Defends Sullivan to Bryan." *New York Times* 14 December 1913.

Letter from James K. McGuire to James D. Phelan, 22 October 1912. Bancroft Library. University of California, Berkley. Box 47. Folder 12.

Letter marked "Confidential" From James K. McGuire to James D. Phelan. 16 November 1912. Bancroft Library. University of California, Berkley. Box 47, Folder 12.

"McIntyre Company." http://fundinguniverse.com/company_ histories/McInery_com. Retrieved 7 February 2014.

"McIntyre, Frank (1865–1944)". *National Cyclopedia of American Biography*, vol. XXXII, New York: James T. White and Company, 1945, 333–334.

McNickle, Chris. "When New York Was Irish And After." Baylor, Ronald, and Meagher,

Timothy (eds.). *The New York Irish*. Baltimore: Johns Hopkins University Press, 1962.

Miller, Kerby. *Emigrants and Exiles: Ireland and the Irish Exodus to North America*. New York: Oxford University Press, 1985.

"Minister Sullivan Onivorous (sic) Reader." *New York Times*. 28 January 1915, 5.

"Ministers Come Here To Thank McGuire." *Syracuse Herald* 28 July 1913: 5.

"Moore, John Bassett." *Dictionary of American Biography. Supplement Four*. New York: Charles Scribner's Sons, 1946-50, 597–600.

"D.P. Moran (1869-1936) Life, Works, Criticism, Commentary, Quotations, References, Notes." http://www.ricorso.net/rx/az-data/authors/m/Moran_DP/life.htm. Retrieved 5 October 2015.

"The Mummies of St. Michan's." http://irelandforvisitors.com/articles/mummies_of_St>Michans.htm. Retrieved 3 February 2012.

Myers, Gustavus. *History of Tammany Hall*. New York, 1917.

"Ocean Travelers." *New York Times*. 12 January 1907.

O Conluain, Proinsias. "Irelands First Films." In *Sight and Sound* vol. 23, no.2, October–December 1953.

O'Connell, Diog. "Ellen O'Mara Sullivan and the Film Company of Ireland." http://www.ted/ie/films/news. Retrieved 30 July 2016.

"O' Gorman, James A" *National Cyclopedia of American Biography*. New York: James T. White and Company, 1945, 114–115.

"O' Mara, Stephen". www.company.dcu.ie~humphreysFarm/Tree/Omeara/Stephen.html. Retrieved 14 June 2011.

"Rory O'More: Irish Silent Films. Trinity College Dublin. http://www.tcd/irishfilms/silent/Rory-O"more.php. Retrieved 15 May 2011.

"On this Day: February 28, 1880." http://nytimes.com/ Learning/General/onthisday/harp/0228.html. Retrieved 17 May 2011.

"O'Neil of the Glen." Irish Film and TV research OnLine. Trinity College Dublin. http://www.tcd.ie.irishfilm/show. php? Fid=56597.

"O'Neil, Neale, Neil: O'Neil: Among the Most Illustrious Surnames of Ireland. http://shatowe.como-neil.htm. Retrieved 16 July 2011.

"Only $6000 in Bank Sullivan Favored." *New York Times* 27 January 1915.

O'Toole, James. *Militant and Triumphant: William Henry O'Connell and the Catholic Church In Boston, 1859–1944*. Norte Dame: Indiana University Press, 1992.

Papers Relating to the Foreign Relations of the United States 1904–1917. Washington, DC: Government Printing Office, 1905–1931.

Parillo, Vincent. *Strangers to These Shore*. 4th edition. Boston; Allyn and Bacon, 1995.

Parker, Elizabeth. Ourselvesalone History. National and the Nation 1852, 1–18. http://journals.chapman.edu/ojs/ index.php.vocesNovae/article.view/198/537. Retrieved 14 February 2014.

"Patrick Pearce." http://historylearningsite.co.uk/partickpearce. htm.

"Peep At Parochial Happenings: Irish Events Newsreel Begins, June - July 1917". https://early.irish.cinema.com/2017/7 /.

Phelan, James Duval. *Santo Domingo Investigations: Copy of Report of Findings and Opinions*. Washington: Gibson Brothers, 1915.

"Phelan Reported Sullivan Unfit." *New York Times* 27 July 1915, 107.

Letters of James Duval Phelan. Bancroft Library. University of California. Box 73, Folders, 21; 22.

Plant, David "The Irish Uprising of 1641." BCW Project BCW Project.org/church-and-state/confederate-Ireland/The Irish Uprising. Retrieved 14 June 2013.

"Dan Platt, Archaeologist". *New York Times* 7 May 1938.

Plummer, Brenda Gail. *Haiti and the Great Powers, 1902–1915.* Baton Rouge: Louisiana State University Press, 1988.

Pons, Frank Maya. *The Dominican Republic: A National History.* Princeton, New Jersey: Marcus Weiner Publishers, 1998.

"President Wilson's Excellent Appointment." *Catholic Sun* 1 August 1913.

"Records of the Bureau of Insular Affairs." http://archives.gov/research/guide-fed records/groups/350.html. Retrieved 6 May 2010. Retrieved 7 June 2011.

"James Redpath" http://american abolitionist Liberal arts. iupui.edu/redpath/htm.

"Religion Bryan Aid in Affairs of State." *New York Times* 22 January 1915.

"Republican Loan Film, 1919." You tube video.

"Rival Irish Envoys Here on Aquitania." *New York Times* 18 March 1922.

Rippy, Fred. *The Caribbean Danger Zone.* New York: G.P. Putnam's Sons, 1940.

———. "The Initiation of the Customs Receivership in the Dominican Republic." *Hispanic American Historic Review.* 17 November 1934, 419–517.

Robison, Daniel "McMillen, Benton." *The Tennessee Encyclopedia of History and Culture.* http://tenneseencyclopedia.net/imagegallery.php? Entry ID=h054. Retrieved 14 April 2012.

Rockett, Kevin, Gibbons, Luke, Hill John. *Cinema and Ireland.* Syracuse University Press, 1988.

Rocket, Kevin. "Knocknagow, the Film Company of Ireland and Other Historical Films, 1911–1920." http://ScreeningThe Past.com/2012/02/knocknagow-the-film-company-of-ireland. Retrieved 7 June 2010.

———. *Irish Film Censorship: A Cultural Journey from Silent Film to Internet Pornography*. Dublin; Four Courts Press, 2004.

Russell, Mathew. "Knocknagow by Charles Kickham: An Introduction." http://exclassics.com/knockingw/kbinko.htm. Retrieved 14 June 2010.

"Russell, William Worthington." *National Cyclopedia of American Biography*. vol xv. Ann Arbor, Michigan: University. Microfilms, 1967, 68.

Ruth, Edward. *Patrick Pearce: The Triumph of Failure* Gollanz, 1977.

"Samuel K. Long, Dead." *New York Times* 29 July 1915.

"The Santo Domingo Scandal." *New York Times* 26 January 1915.

Sante, Luc. *Low Life: Lures and Snares of Old New York*. New York: Random House, 1992.

"Says Irish Friends Cause Movie Rows." *New York Times* 25 January 1917 7.

"Says Bryan Ignored Sullivan Scandal." *New York Times* 17 January 1915.

"Says Sullivan Got Bryan Whitewash." *New York Times* 13 January 1915.

Schmidt, Hans. *The United States Occupation of Haiti, 1915–1934*. New Brunswick, New Jersey: Rutgers University Press, 1971.

Schonreich, Otto. *Santo Domingo: A Country with a Future* New York: MacMillan, 1918.

"Schull and Skibbereen: The Two Famine-Slain Sisters of the South." http://morninghere.org.uk/galleries/histories/irish/orgins/skibbereen. Retrieved 14 April 2011.

"Screening the Funeral Of Thomas Asche, September, 1917". https://early.irish.cinema.com/film-directors/ norman-whitten/2017/9/.

Sedgewick, Hulbert. "Sullivan Had Rapid Rise to Success." *Hartford Courant* 18 August 1935.

"Seeing "Knocknagow" in Irish National Cinemas, January - April 1918" https://earlyirishcinema.com/ 2018/133/. Retrieved 4 February 2018.

"Seeks Terms for Becker." *New York Times* 13 July 1914.

Selden, Rodman. *Quisqueya: A History of the Dominican Republic*. Seattle: University of Washington Press, 1964.

"Shadows of Revolution in Irish Cinemas, March 1917." https://earlyirishcinema.com/2017/03. Retrieved 17 October 2017.

"Shapiro Clears Up a Point". *New York Times*. 7 August 1912.

"Sheehan, Winfield R." Artist Direct.com/mad/store/movies/ principal/O, 1988 484co.html. Retrieved 6 May 2010.

"Shubert Organizations." http://shubertorganization.com/ theaters/default.asp. Retrieved 8 May 2011.

"Silentbeautiesblogspot.com 2012/2013 rory-o-more-1911. Retrieved 9 May 2010.

"Silentbeautiesblogspot.com for-irelands-sake-1914." html. Retrieved 7 April 2012.

"Silentbeautiesblogspot.com/2012/2013 emmet-irelands- martyr-1915". html Retrieved 8 May 2013.

"Silent era.com/PSFL/dataForiresake-1914." html.

Sisson, Elaine. *Pearce's Patriots: St. Enda's and the Cult of Boyhood*. Cork: University Press, 2004.

"Sister Pleads for Sullivan." *New York Times* 8 May 1916, 6.

"6000 Years of History on the Dingle Peninsula." http://www. celticnative.com/history.html. Retrieved 17 March 2010.

Slide, Anthony. *The Cinema and Ireland*. North Carolina: McFarland and Company, 1988.

"Some Seabury Bias." *New York Times* 7 May 1958.

Special Acts of the General Court of Massachusetts, Session Laws 1917, Chapter 157, 125.

"Stabler, Jordan Herbert." *Who Was Who in America, vol. I 1897–1942*. Chicago: Marquis Who's Who, 1168–1160, 1943; *Bulletin of Pan American Union*, vol. 45, 248.

"Sterling Fredrick Augustine." *Who Was Who in America, vol.3*. Chicago: Marquis Who's Who, 1960, 818; *National Cyclopedia of American Biography, vol. F, 1939–1942*. New York: James T. White and Company 1942, 148–49.

"State to Call Becker's Aids." *New York Times* 18 May 1914.

Stewart, A. T. Q. *Michael Collins: The Secret Files*. Belfast: Blackstaff Press, 1997.

"Summon Levy to Court." *New York Times*. 4 November 1913, 4.

"Sullivan." http://www.ireland101.com/tri. Retrieved 6 February 2009.

"Alexander Martin Sullivan (1830–1884)." worldheritage. org/articles/Alexander-Martin-Sullivan (Irish Politician). Retrieved 7 March 2009.

"Sullivan, James Mark." *National Cyclopedia of American Biography*, vol. xixx. New York: James T. White and Company 1941, 362–363. Retrieved 7 March 2009.

"James Mark Sullivan, Once US Minister, Arrested as Rebel." *New York World*. 5 May 1916, 1–2.

"James M. Sullivan, Ex-Diplomat Dead." *New York Times*. 24 August 1920.

Sullivan, James M. "Michael Collins Rise to the Mystery Man of Ireland." *Springfield Sunday Republican*. 10 September 1922, 2A.

"Sullivan Is Ok'd By Bald Jack Rose." *New York Times*. 23 January 1915.

"Jim Sullivan." Humphreys Family Website. http://Humphreys familytree.com/Humphreys/dick.htm. Retrieved 18 April 2010.

"Timothy Daniel Sullivan: Biography." www.farmpeople.com/cat-timothy-daniel-sullivan. Retrieved 7 March 2009.

Sutton, Walter A. "The Wilson Administration and a Scandal in Santo Domingo." *Presidential Studies Quarterly*, vol.12, no. 4, Fall 1982, 552–560.

"Testifies Sullivan Called Beer Chief." *New York Times*. 30 January 1915.

"The Constant Watchfulness of Irish Cinema in March 1916". https://early.irish.cinema.com/2016/04/.

"The 1916 Rising-Personalities and Perspectives: John Devoy, Joseph McGarrity and the Clan Na Gael." National Library of Ireland. http://www.nli.ie/1916/. Retrieved 18 May 2009.

The History of the Democratic Party in New York State. James K. McGurie(ed) vol. II, 445 New York American Hisory Book Company in public Domain.

"Tennessee Democrats Nominate Candidates." *New York Times*. 30 May 1902.

"Though Not An Irishman: Henry George and the American-Irish-Special Issue: Commemorating the Hundredth Anniversary of the Death of Henry George." http://find-articles/mi_n0254/is_n4_v56ai_20381866. Retrieved 23 June 2014.

"Tumulty's Caution for Sullivan Told." *New York Times*. 14 January 1915.

"Two Booms in New Jersey." *New York Times*. 17 July 1910.

"United States Ambassadors to the Dominican Republic." Wikipedia.org/urlsi/United_States_Ambassadors_To_The Dominican_Republic. Retrieved 17 June 2012.

"Urgent." *Catholic Sun*. 29 November 1918: 5.

Von Dopperen, Ron and Graham, Cooper. Shooting the Great Was: Albert Dawson and the American Correspondent Film Company, 1914-1918. Createsaoce: Charleston, South Carolina, 2013

Walsh, Walter. *The Unknown Power Behind the Irish National Party: Its Present Work, Its Criminal History*. London: Swan, Sonnenschein and Company, Ltd., 1904.

Warn, Alex. "Charles Francis Murphy: Human Being." *New York Times*. 22 February 1914.

"Watched By Millions of Eyes: Irish Cinema's Manifest Potentialities in October 1916." https://early.irish.cinema. com/201510/.

"What Was Dublin Like in 1911?" http:// www.cansors.national archives.ie/exhibition/dublin/main.html. Retrieved 14 March 2011.

Welch, Richard F. *King of the Bowery: Big Tim Sullivan, Tammany Hall and New York City from the Gilded Age to the Progressive Era*. Albany: State University Press, 2008.

Welles, Sumner. *Naboth's Vineyard: The Dominican Republic 1844–1924*, vol. II. Payson and Clarke, 1928.

Werner, Morris Robert. *Tammany Hall*. New York: Doubleday, Doran and Company, 1928.

"When Did Love Come To Gavin Burke? An Irish Film Finds an Audience in Early Summer 1918." https://early.irish. cinema.com/2018/07/.

"Whom The Gods Would Destroy." http://www.stanford. edu/~gdegrout/AJ/reviewers/wtgd.htm-3. Retrieved 18 April 2010.

"Whom The Gods Would Destroy." http://www.ed.ie/irish. film/show.php?fidt58178. Retrieved 18 April 2010.

"Why America Should Insist on Self-Determination For Ireland." *Catholic Sun*. 6 December 1918: 1.

Willie Reilly and His Colleen Bawn. http://www.tcd.ie.irishfilm. php?-56619. Retrieved 16 May 2010.

Willy Reilly and His Colleen Bawn. Rare and Manuscript Collection. Carl A. Krock Library. Cornell University Ithaca, New York.

Wittenberg, Ernest. "The Thrifty Spy on the Sixth Avenue El." *American Heritage Magazine* 17. 1 February, 1960.

"Work of Strong Arm Squad." *New York Times.* 2 September 1911.

"Would We Ever See It In Reality "lreland: A Nation" For Two days Only In January 1917" https://early.irish.cinema. com/2017/11/.

Wright, Julia N. *Representing the National Landscape in Irish Romanticism.* Syracuse University Press, 2014.

Wriston, Henry Merritt. *Executive Agents in American Foreign Relations.* Baltimore: Johns Hopkins University Press, 1929.

"Written on the Screen." *New York Times.* 17 January 1915.

INDEX

Royal Irish Constabulary (RIC): 165
Russell, Walter W.: 70; 104

S

Sander, Albert: 140
Sante, Luc: 21
Santo Domingo: 10; 25; 31;
    32; 61; 70; 80
St. Enda's: 30; 180
Schepps, Sammy: 50; 52; 53; 54
Seabury, Samuel: 58; 60; 62
Sedgewick, Hulbert: 25; 26; 29
"Shamus O'Brien" (film): 147
Shubert Theaters: 182
Sigisbee, Admiral C.D.: 106
Sinn Fein ("Ourselves
    Alone"): 170; 180
Sisson, Lee: 96
Smith, Al: 58
Smith, Charles: 100
Society of the Friendly Sons of St.
    Patrick (SOFSOSP): 23; 29
Springfield Republican (news-
    paper): 219
"stage Irishman": 29; 145
Steuer, Max: 52; 54; 62
Sullivan, Alexander, Martin: 28; 166
Sullivan, Donal: 184
Sullivan, James Mark: 9; 13; 15; 16;
    17; 18; 19; 23; 24; 25; 26;
    27; 29; 30; 31; 32; 43; 44;
    46; 48; 54; 56; 57; 61; 62;

72; 75; 76-77; 78; 80; 81;
82; 83; 84; 85; 89; 90; 92;
03; 94; 96; 97; 99; 100; 101;
102; 103; 104; 105; 106; 11;
112; 137; 138; 142; 143; 146;
157-158; 161; 166; 174-175;
182; 185; 194; 217; 229
Sullivan, Timothy Daniel: 28; 166
Sullivan, "Big Tim": 20; 22; 47; 48;
    52; 57; 59; 62; 138; 217
Sullivan, "Little Tim": 26; 96; 97
Sulzer, William (Governor of
    New York): 48; 58
Sutton, Walter: 101

T

Taft, William Howard (USA
    President): 75; 76
Tammany Hall: 10; 19; 20;
    26; 32; 43; 44; 61
Thaw, Evelyn Nesbitt: 44
Thaw, Harry: 27; 44
Tone, Wolfe: 31
Tumulty, Joseph P.: 70; 72;
    73; 74; 80; 104

U

"Unfair Love Affair" (film): 164

V

Vick, Walker: 70; 72; 80; 90; 91;
92; 93; 94; 97; 100 101;
102; 104; 111; 112
Victoria, Queen: 29

W

Wagner, Robert: 58
Waldo, Rhinelander: 48
Walker, James: 217
Ward, Arthur F.: 186
Weatherly, Frederick: 145
Webber, Bridgey: 52
Welles, Sumner: 76
Wharton Brothers: 186
Wharton Releasing Company:
186; 193
"When Love Came to Gavan
Burke" (film): 164

Whitman, Charles: 47; 49; 53; 57;
58; 59; 60; 61; 62; 73; 229
Whitten, Norman/General
Film Supply Company:
140-142; 165-166
"Whom The Gods Would
Destroy"(film): 154-155
"Willy Reilly and His Colleen
Bawn" (film): 176-179; 186
Wilson Plan: 99
Wilson Woodrow: 25; 32; 69; 70;
101; 103; 104; 109; 115
Wiseman, Sir William: 224
World War I: 9
Wright, Julia: 17; 145

Y

Yale University: 9; 24; 26; 31
Yeats, William Butler: 29; 171

ABOUT THE AUTHOR

D r. Daniel Schultz is professor emeritus at Cayuga Community College in Auburn, New York. He has been honored with the prestigious Chancellor's Award for Excellence in both teaching and scholarship. His publications have appeared in *Crossroads*, *New Hibernia Review*, the *Canadian Journal of Irish History*, *New York History*, *Teaching in the Community College*, *The ECCSSA Journal* and *New Directions for the Community College*. He has presented papers at American Council on Irish Studies, the Northeast Modern Language Association, the New York State Political Science Association, and the East Coast College Social Science Association.

CPSIA information can be obtained
at www.ICGtesting.com
Printed in the USA
FSHW021604300519
58556FS

9 781641 380904